The Other Side: Melinda's Story

by

Starr Gardinier

The Other Side Series

The Other Side: Melinda's Story

Cover Art by *Angela Anderson*

The Wild Rose Press, Inc.
PO Box 708
Adams Basin, NY 14410-0708
Visit us at www.thewildrosepress.com

Publishing History
First Black Rose Edition, 2015
Print ISBN 978-1-5092-0312-3
Digital ISBN 978-1-5092-0313-0

The Other Side Series
Published in the United States of America

"Your mother said you were in shock. I can see you still are," Dad said as he steered me to a chair.

"I sat down, well I sort of fell into the chair. My legs were wobbly. Anxiety? I think it was shock like they said.

"Beth's accident was unexpected. Drowning in the Mosamic River…" Dad was saying.

"He trailed off. I felt as though I'd awakened in someone else's family. It was Dad that drowned in that river, not Beth. Maybe I was dreaming or having a horrible nightmare, deep in sleep where nothing made sense. I shook my head as though to get rid of the cobwebs. I tried to tell myself to wake up. I even screamed inside my head, 'Wake up, Melinda!' Still I sat in the kitchen looking at my family. Or were these people really my family?

"I looked at my father and asked, "What are you talking about? I spoke to Beth this morning."

"My mom sat down in the chair next to me and took my hand. "We'll help you get through this, honey."

"I snatched my hand out of my mother's and looked at her. She must be an alien or something. She wasn't my mother. And Dad…well, I couldn't deal with any of it anymore. I ran from the room, my head full of thoughts. I tried the nightmare route and that didn't work, so something must be seriously wrong with me. Do I have some weird medical problem that was making me see and hear things? Either that or I was living in someone else's world.

Praise for Starr Gardinier's
THE OTHER SIDE: MELINDA'S STORY

Dedication

A special thank you to my husband,
Robert Smith,
for his unselfish acts of allowing me to neglect him
while I penned this story for my readers.

Prologue

I tried to tell them it was going to happen, but nobody would listen. They all said I was just having bad dreams, or that I was crazy.

It started at my father's funeral. It's been so long since it first began, about eight years ago. Sometimes though, it seems like yesterday. My father was there. No, I don't mean just in the casket. He was *there*. He talked to me, begged me to tell Mom that we all needed to run and hide. He said we were all in danger.

I asked him why he didn't tell Mom himself. He said he tried, but she wasn't listening. I heard him fine. But I didn't believe him. Why would we be in danger? We can't just up and leave. My friends are all here in Beaumont. When I told him that, he said it was important, that it was a matter of life and death. He seemed so worried, but I was so confused, I blew him off.

I guess when it first happened I didn't pay any heed to his warning. We went on with our lives. Mom was grief stricken, my brother Kyle was in his own world playing videos and I was trying to shut my father out of my mind. Was I going crazy? What was wrong with me? Dad was dead, but I could still see and hear him.

If I tell you the story, will you believe me?

Chapter One

I'm sitting in the garden. The sun is shining down on my face. I'm with my family. Mom, Dad, and Kyle and Beth, my best friend, just got here. I'm smiling. I'm so happy at this moment. An ordinary moment in a life that has too few precious normal days. I can see all of us sitting here and just being together. It's glorious.

Then a shadow falls across my face.

"Melinda, it's time. Dr. Leever is expecting you."

It's nurse Hamilton and she's waken me from my dream. The normalcy just flew away along with the chirping birds.

"Okay."

"I'll take you to his office," she tells me.

She escorts me upstairs and to a door.

"I'll see you soon, Melinda. Have a good session."

And with that she leaves me standing there. I tap on the door and it's quickly opened.

"Melinda, my name is Dr. Alex Leever. Why don't you come in and sit down."

I follow him into the room and he shuts the door so softly that I can barely hear the click of the latch.

I sit down in the chair in front of his desk. The chair is padded leather and seems comfortable enough. It dwarfs me. I'm petite, but not too short. And I'm kind of thin. I try to put weight on, but it never works. The caretakers here tell me it's from having fast metabolism.

My first thought when entering Dr. Leever's office is here I go again. For so long, I've been subjected to one doctor after another. Not to mention all of the group therapy sessions and various medications.

For the first few months, they had me on drugs that made me feel comatose. I was withdrawn and depressed. I was hardly able to have a coherent thought for myself. I felt like I was just drifting along on an endless sea of horrible memories and the ever-present ache of being an orphan.

I've been committed to Skyview Haven, judged to be suffering from a mental disorder. My aunt and uncle put me here when they didn't know what else to do. They refused to take in a mentally unbalanced child. I heard them say those exact words to the health service executive—what they call HSE. They agreed with my only remaining family that this is where I need to be because of mental issues. There was no argument from my aunt and uncle…no surprise there.

Don't let the name of this disturbing place fool you. It's far from a haven. Many—well, most—of the patients here are between five and ten years old mentally, but they treat all of us like little kids. They monitor what we watch, what we say, how we act, who we talk to, and what we read. Before I came here, I watched more horror movies and cussed more than I do now at the ripe old age of twenty-two. Okay, I have to be honest, I rarely swore even then.

After years of being monitored in every facet of my life, it's been difficult to remember I'm not a child. I also have to constantly remind myself that I'm not incapacitated like ninety-five percent of the other patients here.

The director and many of the doctors explained to me over the years that when I reached the age of eighteen and wanted to be released, a consultant psychiatrist must either discharge me or arrange for an examination by another consultant psychiatrist. The second consultant must then issue a certificate stating that I should either be detained because of a mental disorder or discharged. That was back when I began the process of meeting with psychiatrists and ended up seeing one after the other.

Doctors would come and go, moving on to other patients and I would be assigned a new doctor time after time. I'd have to start all over again and it was so frustrating to begin with a new doctor every few months. It's one of the reasons they did not really listen to me. Finally, I stopped trying to tell my story because none of them stuck around long enough to hear it and besides, it was obvious that what little they did hear was enough to make them think I was loony.

The more frustrated I got, the angrier I got. I began to act out. When I first got here, I refused to eat and was pretty much a petulant, angry child. That's when they medicated me for a while to calm me down. I couldn't come to terms with the fact that I was abandoned here by my own aunt and uncle without so much as an afterthought.

Then group therapy started. That was certainly enlightening, but not for my recovery. That only served to show me that I was the least crazy of everyone in here. There were those who suffered from bulimia and other eating disorders, suicidal patients, and some just incapable of caring for themselves. The latter were the worst. It's like their minds were there, but their bodies didn't recognize any of the signals their brains sent out.

Sitting there in a room full of other patients and listening to horror stories of how one sat in a tub with a razor blade at the ready while candles flickered trying to find the courage to kill herself, how one stood in front of her mirror and saw rolls of fat when all I saw were bones, and how another vowed to either kill himself or if he was thwarted, to kill the person closest to him, was surreal. Actually, maddening. If I'd stayed in that group one day longer, *I'd* be homicidal.

It took a while, but I finally realized I had become my own worst enemy and finally resigned myself to the fact that I wasn't going anywhere. At least for a while. Don't get me wrong, I was never happy to be here and never will be. I started eating and stopped using derogatory names for the staff members. Then I became quiet, hardly spoke with anyone unless I had to. I guess it's like a grieving process. I mourned the family I lost and the life I lost—my own.

After about four years and more doctors than anyone should see in a lifetime, I loosened up and even smiled every now and then. But having to subject my psyche to all of those doctors and tests was more than maddening. However, I was powerless to do anything about my situation. That was then. This is now. I'm not as helpless and weak as I was.

Before each new doctor, I was reevaluated. Have I made any progress? If not, do they think I ever would? Am I capable of making solid decisions? Did my prior doctor think I was fit to live in a normal society? Apparently not as I'm still here. I was constantly put through tests. I think I have memorized all the ink blots and what the doctors think I should see in them. They explained to me that I needed to have the ability to understand information about my treatment and how it should apply to my situation, and that I need to be able to make choices and express them. That was how I'd be able to live individually without assistance in the world. I think I was able to do all that before I even got here. It was how I stayed alive when my family was killed.

I'm bitter from all that I've been put through, both before and after my arrival at Skyview Haven. And now it's time to start with another doctor. Dr. Alex Leever. The medical director said that he is pretty much my last chance. He's supposedly different from the other doctors I've seen. But the fact remains that if he says I'm crazy, I may never get out of here.

I don't anticipate any extraordinary breakthrough now any more than I did with any of the other doctors. He's just one more doctor with another round of tests, trying to pry into my brain to see if I'm stable.

But oddly enough, the minute I sit down in Dr. Leever's office, I feel a sense of calm. It's the first time I've felt like this since before my father died. I look across the wide, mahogany desk at Dr. Leever. He looks like a big teddy bear with his full, round face, dark brown eyes, and large stomach. But unlike a stuffed bear, his brown beard and mustache are turning gray. When I look into his eyes, I feel like I can tell him anything. This is so odd. I've never felt like this. I cling to the hope that maybe this time, it'll be different.

So I guess it's time I try telling my sad saga again. And it's the story I'm going to share with you—piece by weird piece.

"It's James, correct? Melinda James?"

"Yes,"

"So, what brings you here today?"

"I thought you already knew that," I say as I brush my long brown bangs away from my left eye.

Usually, I wear my hair short, kind of like a bob. I'm trying to grow it out. I need a different look. But the bangs have been driving me crazy lately.

Even though I'm more cooperative and less confrontational than I used to be, I'm still a bit sarcastic. Nurse Hamilton once told me it was my tough exterior. Really though, I've had enough of doctors and don't like any of them.

"I know what the other doctors' files say and what the medical director told me. I've even read all about your group therapy sessions. I want *you* to tell me."

"They say I'm crazy."

"What do you think?"

"I'm not crazy, Dr. I know what I know."

"First, let's start out by you calling me Alex."

Despite myself, I begin to like him. He is soft spoken and seems kind. But time will tell. After I begin my story, I'll know if he is going to be like the other doctors who tried to get me to talk.

"I should tell you all the other doctors before you didn't believe me and tried to medicate me, thinking I had a split personality or some other mental disease."

"Is that right?"

"Yes. I even heard a few doctors talking one day and they said I had dissociative identity disorder, which I now know used to be called multiple personality disorder."

At the time, I didn't know what any of that meant. Now, I can roll those words off my tongue easily, I hear

7

them so much.

"You haven't spoken to me yet," Alex says.

"True, but you should know that a few doctors and the police even thought I did it all and was trying to dig up a get-out-of-jail-free pass by claiming my father told me."

"Told you what?"

"I'll get to that. Anyway, I wasn't arrested. There was no evidence. I didn't go off to prison, at least not the ones with a small cell and an hour in the courtyard for exercise. Instead, I was thrown into a different kind of jail, with a room not much bigger, where the guards—caretakers—think I'm just this side of nuts, but at least I have a little more freedom. Still, it's not home, it never will be, and I hate having to be here."

"I can understand that."

"So," I ask, "how long do we have? Is this like all the other times? Fifty minutes and then I get to come back in a few days or a week? Then you leave and I start all over again with someone else?"

"Actually, no. We have as long as it takes. Now of course, we'll have to stop at lunchtime and in the evening. But we can meet every day, if you wish. I'm not going anywhere. You are my top priority right now."

"What about your other patients?"

"I don't work as a normal hour-by-hour psychiatrist. I contract with this facility and many others on a patient-by-patient basis, which means that I work with you until you feel you don't need me anymore."

"Every day?" I blurt, surprised at the loudness of my voice.

"Yes. Then when you feel comfortable, we can talk occasionally. But I'm here for you for as long as you want me to be."

"How do you get paid?"

"From what I understand, your family's estate is paying. Your parents set up a sizable trust fund for you. But you already know that."

"Yes, of course. My lawyers told me."

"So, now that you're done qualifying me, shall we begin?"

"I'm not done. I want to know more about you first."

"Okay, what would you like me to tell you?"

"How long have you been doing this?"

It feels good to be the one asking the questions instead of answering them. I like this. Maybe I can study to become a psychiatrist.

"Since I graduated from college. I started out as a typical counselor who saw about seven to eight patients a day. I soon grew to realize a lot of people needed uninterrupted time to really begin to heal. That's when I got this job. I've been doing it since and find it very rewarding, not only for my patients, but for me as well. I know I'm helping."

"Why are you telling me all this willingly?"

"Because you wanted to know and if you don't feel comfortable, you won't feel safe opening up to me."

I'm beginning to feel more confident about his willingness to help, at least. However, I'm still hesitant. Will he judge me like the others? I begin to come down off my high horse and ease up on him. I just may have hope.

"So, Melinda, why don't we start at the

beginning?"

"The beginning…which one? Before my father died or the start of what everyone labels as my craziness?"

"You decide."

"Okay, but I hope you don't end up being like the rest, thinking I'm nuts and putting me on medications."

"I'll be honest. If that is what I believe, I will tell you. Then you can decide whether to continue to see me. As far as medication is concerned, I only believe in that for the most extreme cases. After reviewing your file, yours does not seem to fit that protocol. But we'll see how it goes. Is that fair?"

It is all I can expect, I guess. I run my hand through my hair and once again, brush aside my bangs. Butterflies flutter in my stomach. After the first few doctors, it became old hat. Now though, it's like I'm seeing a real shrink for the first time. Perhaps it's because I know he's the last doctor I'll see, for better or worse.

I begin my story. *Again.*

Chapter Two

"It started in April of 2004, but first let me tell you about my family so you get an idea about who I am and where I came from.

"My dad's name was Paul James. He was an accountant and investment advisor. We lived very comfortably. Dad mostly kept to himself and didn't like going to fancy functions. He was a simple man who lived a simple life. He went to work every day, came home on time for dinner, and tucked us in every night.

"But I guess Dad got tired of helping clients with his expertise in investing. His insight was making all the money for the bigwigs while Dad lived off the commission. He made money on the side for acting as a 'stock broker,' but his main job was as an accountant. My father dreamed of a better life, one that would allow us to take long vacations to all kinds of places, for as long as we wanted to stay. I know, it sounds like everyone else. Why does the world have to revolve around money? Dad didn't have the same amount of cash to invest as his clients did, but put in what he could afford. It still didn't make him the millions he wanted, but he apparently did pretty well.

"I didn't know all this then. And I didn't know that he rationed spending to put savings away for Kyle and me. He set up that trust that you mentioned. Half for me and half for Kyle. With wise investments, it grew substantially over time. But then all I knew was we were doing okay, so it was a surprise to learn he lived a life of deception. I don't mean to say he had another family or anything, but he lied to us. That lie cost him his life and ultimately, ours. I was so angry with him when I found out. Don't misunderstand me. I love my father very much. He was a great man, good to all of us and was always there when we needed him. That is, until he died."

I pause and walk to the large window that overlooks parts of the garden and parking lot. I look down and see some of the patients sitting outside with the caretakers. It's sunny, but I feel like brooding clouds are hanging low over my head everywhere I go.

"My mom Meredith was a hair stylist, a job she was pretty good at. She said she enjoyed talking to people and coming up with creative hairstyles. But her work always came second to Kyle and me. When I needed a ride to school, or Kyle had a basketball game, she was always available. She was a good mother.

"She, too, liked the simple life. She wasn't glamorous by any means, but she was beautiful. She never asked Dad to go to any event that required a tuxedo. If they went out alone, it was generally to dinner and a movie. Our family vacationed twice a year, but never quite made it to places like the Caribbean or Italy. Instead, we went to see the Grand Canyon, Disneyland, and other amusement parks. They always made sure Kyle and I had fun.

"Kyle was a big pain growing up, but that's nothing out of the ordinary. He was two years older. He was my brother and I loved him, but we didn't always get along. All siblings fight. Back then, all I wished for was for him to go away. I didn't really mean it though. If I was ever in trouble, I knew I could always go to Kyle. Despite everything, he was a good big brother.

"So, I guess I had a pretty good childhood growing up. We were the perfect little family. We lived in the suburbs in a nice-sized house that had four bedrooms and three bathrooms and a big back yard. We knew our neighbors and occasionally would throw barbecues and invite them over.

"Nice. Normal. A happy family of four. At least that's the way it was, until *it* happened."

I pause, stretch, and pace the office for a few minutes trying to find the nerve to continue. I pour a glass of water and sip.

"Are you okay?" Alex asks.

"Yes, I'm fine."

"Do you want to continue?"

"That all depends on whether or not you want to hear it."

"It's what I'm here for. As I said, however long it takes you to tell me is fine. There is no hurry."

I sit back down, set my glass on the small table next to the chair, and resume talking.

"I was young, only thirteen when my father died. It was a difficult age for me. I was barely a teenager. I wasn't rebellious, but I think I did things then I wouldn't think of doing now. Swearing, for instance. It's not permitted here and if I swear now, it seems wrong, foreign even. What I'm trying to say is being raised in a normal family and being thirteen, I wasn't as...prudish I guess you can call it, as I am now. Not to say I was bad, but you know how teenagers can be.

"Anyway, Dad was in a bad accident on the long

bridge near our house. His car went into the Mosamic River. The river is pretty deep, or at least that's what I'm told.

"The cops said that because it was raining hard and visibility was poor he probably lost control of the car and went into the river. He was trapped inside and drowned. No one argued with the theory."

I stop again and close my eyes. I want to erase the image from my head, but I've never been able to do so. I rub my eyes, as if that will help. I sigh and continue without any interruption from Alex.

"We were all devastated. Kyle withdrew into himself, so I never knew how he really felt. He did cry at the funeral, but after that, it was as if he was made of stone with no feelings. It was sad to see my family in shambles like that. Even though I was younger, I knew keeping my pain inside could rip me apart. I tried to talk to him, but he shut me out.

"Mom wasn't much help with him because she was dealing with her own grief. She stayed in her room most of the time. I could hear her crying. When I tried to go in, she would wave me away. My family fell to pieces. That was the beginning. I would like to be able to say that in time, we all healed and got on with our lives—but that's not what happened."

I stop speaking and recall the first time Dad spoke to me after he died at his funeral.

"I guess I should tell you that Dad's funeral was…weird. It's when he first talked to me. I thought I was losing what grip I had. I tried to ignore the voice I knew so well. But it didn't work. He kept trying to tell me that we needed to leave town. That we were in danger. I guess Mom wasn't hearing him when he tried to contact her, so I was the one hearing the dead. *Lucky me*. Thinking I was nuts, I tried to forget about what happened.

"But the day after the funeral, I realized I wasn't crazy, that I did really hear my dead father talking to me. I was in my room when my curtains ruffled. The window wasn't open, neither was my bedroom door."

I look at Alex for a reaction. His expression is open, non-judgmental. "Sounds like a scary movie, but it really happened. Seconds later, Dad was in my head again. It doesn't make any more sense now than it did at his funeral. I didn't understand why my curtain would move but I could hear my father audibly—from physical movement to mental whispers.

"He told me that he knew who killed him. "You died in an accident, Dad," I said out loud.

"I probably didn't need to speak out loud. Since he was in my head, I could probably just have thought the words."

"Tell me about your conversation with your father," Alex says.

I tell him of that first real conversation in my bedroom.

****

"No, I didn't. It wasn't an accident. You must listen to me. You must go to Mom and tell her to take you and Kyle away. They think your Mom has it."

"Has what and who are they?"

"Right now, that doesn't matter."

"Yes, it does. How can we protect ourselves from someone we don't know?"

"You're too young to understand. I need you to convince Mom that this is real, that I'm real."

"You're not real, Dad. You're dead."

"I know I am. But I cannot move on. I think it's because I need to keep all of you safe. Once you are, I might be able to cross over."

"What does that mean? Cross over? Cross over to where?"

"I don't know, honey. Heaven, maybe. They talk a lot about the Other Side."

"What other side? What are you talking about? And who are they?"

"Never mind that right now. Just please talk to your mother."

"You have to go now. I have to check on Mom again and I can't do it if you're in my head."

"Listen to me, please," he begged me. "There isn't much time. I don't know when they'll try to come here."

"I'm pretty mad at you. You died and left us. Mom cries all the time and Kyle hides in his room. No one talks to me."

"I do."

"It's not the same. You're not real. I need real people to talk to. Go away!"

"I was mad. He wasn't getting it. I screamed at him and still he stayed in my head.

"I'm sorry for leaving you. I miss you all very much. I wish it could be different and I could be with you."

"Then why aren't you?"

****

"My question went unanswered. My father simply disappeared from my head. What was he talking about? Think we have what? And what is crossing over?

Where is the other side?

"I was still angry. My father died and left us. I felt so alone. Now he was trying to get into my head. For some weird reason, I never doubted he was talking to me. It never occurred to me that I was making it all up, because I missed him and wanted to talk to him. I simply believed. I guess I had faith that Dad would always take care of us. He was still trying to from his grave."

I sip some water and again look at Alex. I'm trying to judge his reaction about what I've told him so far. His expression is still neutral, not smiling nor frowning and his eyes are looking at me without any apparent judgment. He isn't rolling his eyes and doesn't have them closed, nor is his brow furrowed. I take that as a good sign and keep talking.

"I was simply too young to understand stuff like crossing over and all that. It was not something that was prevalent in my world or something they taught in school, so I never thought about it.

"I was glad when he left me alone that day. But it didn't last long. He was back the next day.

"I was getting ready to go to my mom's room to wake her up. It seemed she slept later and later every day. Kyle didn't care because she wasn't nagging him about something, but I was worried. Apparently, I was now the adult in the house. A thirteen-year-old adult."

I shake my head at the thought and sit back down in the chair.

"Anyway, on my way out of my bedroom, my father stopped me—literally. I crossed the threshold of my doorway and bumped into something soft, but firm. There was nothing in my way. I tried to step forward again, but ran into something I couldn't see. I backed up into my room, frightened."

****

"Don't be scared. It's just me."

"Suddenly, he was there. Standing right in front of me."

"Dad!"

"I hugged him. I missed him and needed to feel his arms wrapped around me. I forgot about being mad at him. He finally pulled away from me.

"I can't go to your mother yet. She needs to believe first. Like you do."

"Believe that you're dead but not dead?"

"Something like that."

"What do you want?"

"I didn't want you to go wake your mother until I spoke with you."

"How did you know where I was going?"

"I'm in your head. I know almost all your thoughts."

"Great. I couldn't have a moment's peace when he was alive and now he was in my head knowing all my thoughts. That's just what a young, teenage girl wanted.

"Leave me the hell alone," I told him as I tried to move around him.

"As much as I missed him, and as much as I knew I wasn't making all of this up, I still wondered if I was imagining it in order to make myself feel better, not so lonely. You can tell my thoughts kept bouncing back and forth. First I believed then I didn't. All that soon changed.

"I can't. I'm sorry to put you through this, but I need you to get through to your mother. She has to open her mind to me. I must warn her."

"About what? Wait. How do I even know you're my father? I'm probably going crazy."

"You're not crazy. I am your father. Ask me anything...ask me something only I would know."

"I thought for a few minutes and remembered a time when I was ten years old at the Grand Canyon. I was afraid to get too close to the edge. Dad, sensing my fear, held me close and whispered in my ear something that took my fear away.

"Fine. What was it you said to me at the Grand Canyon?"

"I whispered in your ear that I had your hand and would never let go, not now, not ever."

"He takes my hand then and my heart aches, wanting him back. Really back. I grabbed my hand away from his. Tears welled in my eyes at the memory of that trip to the Grand Canyon.

"You're in my head. You said so yourself. That's how you know it. I remembered it."

"No. I know it because I said it. I'll tell you something then that happened when you were very small."

"What?" I demanded.

"When you were two, you were running one day in the house. Your mother and I couldn't contain your enthusiasm once you started to walk. You were all over the place. On one particular day, you were scampering down the hallway. You lost your balance for some reason and slid into the small table by the front door. There was a vase sitting on it holding fresh flowers. The vase fell on your forehead and cut you across the left eyebrow. You have a scar. It's barely visible, but it's there."

"I was quiet for a moment. I knew I had a scar there and I knew how I got it. My parents told me the story.

"Go to the mirror and look for the scar."

"I moved to my dresser mirror and stared at my eyebrow. I knew it was there. I didn't need to see it again, but I looked anyway. I ran my finger over it as if to erase it along with my father's voice.

"That's when I blacked out."

Chapter Three

"You blacked out?" Alex asks.

"Yes," I answer with tears streaming down my face.

I get up from the chair again and move once more toward the window. I don't see anything outside, only the past. I run my finger across my brow and still feel that scar. The wounds hidden inside me are worse, that much I can say for certain.

"I need to go to the ladies' room. I'll be right back."

"Take your time."

I leave and go down the hall to the restroom and stand at the sink. I don't look at myself. I never do. I turn the water on and it reminds me of the river. I can't go there. *Not yet.* It's not time. I shake my head to clear the image, use the facility, and return to Alex's office.

Inside, I sit back down and tell him I'm ready to continue.

"Do you know why you blacked out?" he asks me.

"No. All I know is when I came to, my mother was holding my hand, and I was in my bed. Frankly, I was surprised she was even out of her bed."

I hold back my tears and stand up. I'm fidgeting. I sit, I stand, I pace. It's what I've been doing for years.

"Are you okay to continue with your story?"

An overwhelming desire comes over me to let it

out…to let it *all* out.

"Yes," I quickly respond.

Alex stands and refills my glass of water and brings it around his desk to where I'm standing at his window. I look out and scan the area below me; almost as if I am making sure my father isn't there. I feel a little guilty telling a total stranger all about my father and our family. It is almost as if I am unearthing skeletons from our family's closet. But it is way past that. The world heard me admit that a dead man told me that he was murdered, that his death wasn't an accident. They also heard me say that other people—the same people—were responsible for his death and the deaths of Kyle and my mother.

In my opinion, the only one who doesn't think I am crazy is me. It took a long time to come to the realization that I wasn't nuts and that everything actually did happen the way I remembered. It is now a matter of trying to convince someone on a professional level that I am sane so I can leave this wretched asylum. I desperately need to get on with my life. Actually, I've never gotten to start one.

"So," Alex prompts. "Your mother was tending you when you woke up?"

"Yes. I was so glad to see her there. As I said, for the last six days, since my dad's accident, she had been withdrawn, just a shell of herself. She was different then. Let me try to explain. Just keep in mind that things are not always what they seem."

Chapter Four

"My mother was wiping my face with a cool cloth, like she used to do when I was sick. But I wasn't sick, at least not physically. I looked at her and she kept trying to tell me things were going to be okay.

"It's okay, honey. Everything's okay now."

"Mom, Dad was…"

"We'll talk about it later."

"You don't understand."

"I understand that you had a terrible experience. Losing a best friend isn't easy."

"I sat up and slapped the cloth from my mother's hand as she extended it toward my face again.

"What are you talking about?"

"Krissy called me because she knows how upset you are. Even amid the terrible time she's going through after losing her only daughter, she worries about you."

"What *the hell* are you talking about?" I screamed at her.

"Honey, calm down. Here," she fluffed my pillows behind me and pressed me back down into them.

"Lie back down. Your father will be home very soon. I called and told him."

"My *father*?" I asked, sitting back up again.

"I didn't want to lie back down. I wanted to know what was going on. What she was saying was absurd.

23

Completely bizarre.

"He's concerned too, so is Kyle. Krissy will call me with the funeral details. I expect all her friends at school will want to be there. I told her I'd take care of letting them all know."

"School? *Beth's dead?*"

"You're in shock, it's to be expected," she said as she stood up and told me, "I'm going to get you some tea to help calm you. I'll be right back."

"I don't want any tea. Mom! Come back and tell me what you're talking about!"

"My mother kept walking so I sat there and thought about what she said. My mind was reeling. What in the world was going on? Beth wasn't dead, *Dad* was. My first thought was that Mom had definitely lost it. It was the only explanation. I hadn't been to school since my father died and Beth and I spoke that morning on the phone. I was confused and angry because I couldn't grasp what my mother was saying. I needed *answers*, not tea.

"I decided to talk to Kyle. He would tell me what was going on. I ripped off the blankets and walked to Kyle's room only to find it empty. I looked at his bedside clock. It was only two thirty p.m. Where was he? He hasn't been back to school yet either and he usually spends all his time in his room playing the video games. He must be downstairs.

"I descended the stairs and stopped short. I heard Dad's voice coming from the kitchen. Not from my head this time. I frowned. My chest felt heavy, it became difficult to breathe. I couldn't label it then, but now I realize I was experiencing an anxiety attack. Things were more than strange. I closed my eyes and willed myself to calm down, worried I'd pass out at the bottom of the stairs. I finally slowed my breathing.

"I walked into the kitchen and found Dad sitting at the table with my mother and Kyle. My father rushed to me and took me in his arms.

"I'm so sorry about Beth, kitten."

"It was a nickname he gave me long ago, but in my utter confusion of seeing him and being enveloped in his arms again—his real arms—it wasn't something I dwelled on.

"Dad? Is it really you?"

"Of course. I came right home after your mother called."

"Kyle?" I croaked, looking at him with pleading eyes.

"I wanted him to tell me I wasn't losing my mind. I can't explain how mixed up I was. Dad was supposed to be dead, but Mom told me Beth was. Dad was not only standing in the house, he was hugging me. The real Dad. The alive Dad!

"Kyle didn't understand the look in my eyes. He stared at me with a blank expression and I couldn't tell what he was thinking.

"Your mother said you were in shock. I can see you still are," Dad said as he steered me to a chair.

"I sat down, well I sort of fell into the chair. My legs were wobbly. Anxiety? I think it was shock like they said.

"Beth's accident was unexpected. Drowning in the Mosamic River…" Dad was saying.

"He trailed off. I felt as though I'd awakened in someone else's family. It was Dad that drowned in that river, not Beth. Maybe I was dreaming or having a horrible nightmare, deep in sleep where nothing made sense. I shook my head as though to get rid of the cobwebs. I tried to tell myself to wake up. I even screamed inside my head, 'Wake up, Melinda!' Still I sat in the kitchen looking at my family. Or were these people really my family?

"I looked at my father and asked, "What are you talking about? I spoke to Beth this morning."

"My mom sat down in the chair next to me and took my hand. "We'll help you get through this, honey."

"I snatched my hand out of my mother's and looked at her. She must be an alien or something. She wasn't my mother. And Dad…well, I couldn't deal with any of it anymore. I ran from the room, my head full of thoughts. I tried the nightmare route and that didn't work, so something must be seriously wrong with me. Do I have some weird medical problem that was making me see and hear things? Either that or I was living in someone else's world.

"These thoughts ran through my head as fast as my legs were carrying me up to my room. I slammed my door as hard as I could and rushed to the closet. I pulled out my suitcase, tossed it on the bed, and randomly threw clothes into it. I didn't know where I was going. In fact, I didn't even know until I zipped it up that I even wanted to leave. But I didn't know what else to do. I couldn't stay there with strangers. I had to get away from this place.

"There was a knock on my door and I heard Kyle asking me if he could come in. I didn't respond. I didn't know if I wanted him around me or not. If Mom was acting weird and Dad was all of a sudden alive again and Beth was dead, what or who was Kyle? Certainly not the brother I grew up with. He had just sat there at the table accepting whatever was happening. He questioned nothing. That wasn't like Kyle. If he knew I wasn't feeling well or I was upset, he *always* tried to help me. But not then. He sat there and stared at me. He probably thought I'd lost my mind. I felt like I had. Maybe that's what happened. I flipped out. Went insane. I needed medication or something.

"Mel?"

"I've never heard him call me anything else. No one called me that, except Kyle. To me, it meant he loved me and each time he uttered the name, I would feel that love surround me. Then was no different. Maybe he didn't want to say anything in front of our parents. Maybe he was coming to tell me I wasn't nuts and something *was* wrong. I relented and opened my door.

"He came in and sat on my bed.

"What are you doing? Where are you going?"

"I don't know!"

"I began sobbing hard as I stood in the middle of my room. When I cried really hard, I'd get the hiccups and it would take a while to go away. That's what happened then. Awkwardly, Kyle stood and patted me on the back with both hands in a sort of hug. Then he got me some water from the bathroom.

"Mel, I can't pretend to know what you're going through. I've never lost a friend before…"

"Beth is not dead!"

"He hadn't come in here to tell me he agreed with me, that something was wrong. He was here to prove I was crazy. I sat on the bed and began crying harder, hiccuping the whole time. After my tears began to subside, I looked at Kyle standing there staring at me. I could tell he wanted to flee my room and my craziness, but he didn't.

"Kyle, you have to listen to me. I need to tell you something."

"I'm angry and bewildered. I needed Kyle to be Kyle again, but he seemed to believe the stories that spewed from our parents' mouths. I didn't. I had to reach him, make him understand that it was Dad that was supposed to be dead. Not that I wanted him to be, but it's what I had...we *all* had been living with. The funeral, the grief.

"Tell me what?"

"Last week, Dad died. He drowned in the Mosamic River. Then..."

"Dad's downstairs. He's fine."

"No, you don't understand," I told him. I was frustrated and sighed loudly. "Kyle, I don't know who that man is, but it isn't Dad. Mom seems weird, too."

"Mel, you must have had a bad dream. Beth died in that river this morning. Dad is fine and so is Mom."

"I can prove it. Beth's fine."

"I grabbed my telephone from the nightstand and punched in Beth's number. It rang continuously and I finally hung up.

"I'm going over there."

"Mel, no."

"He grabbed my arm, but I pulled free.

"My room overlooked our back yard, which wasn't very big. We had a bunch of trees between our house and our neighbor's. It was thick and was sort of like a fence made out of bushes and trees. On the other side was Beth's house and we used to weave our way through the trees all the time, creating a path over time. It would take me seconds to get over there.

"I rushed from the room, practically flew down the stairs, past my parents sitting at the table, and out the back door. I ran through the trees and into Beth's backyard. I stopped and bent over, hands on my knees, out of breath. I picked my head up and saw Beth's mother Krissy standing on the small porch off their kitchen. She's holding something in her hands and crying.

"Krissy?" I walked up to her, tears of my own streaming down my face.

"She saw me but seemed to look through me. Then she looked at what was in her hand.

"Beth loved this. It is…was her favorite. She left it on the kitchen table."

"I looked at what she held. It was Beth's bracelet, made of red cord. I remembered I gave that to her some time ago.

"I was going to bring it to you. Here."

"She held it out to me.

"No. I would prefer you keep it. Beth…"

"I'm sobbing harder now from confusion.

"She will want you to hold on to it for her. I don't know where she is, but she'll be back."

"I ran from their backyard and to mine. Kyle stood there at the back door.

"Do you understand now?" he asked.

"Understand? No. Beth is not dead. The truth will come out!"

"The truth? About what, Mel? That Mom and Dad aren't who they say they are? That Beth is alive when we know she's dead?"

"Yes!"

"You're just confused, upset that your best friend is dead."

"No, I'm not. I know what I know, Kyle."

"I'm going to tell Mom and Dad you're all right so they don't worry."

"Worried about what? That I might be crazy? I see it in your eyes, Kyle. You think I am, don't you?"

"No, I think you're sad about Beth and your mind can't grasp the fact she's gone."

"What are you, a doctor now?"

"Kyle shook his head and left. I called after him, but he didn't come back. I ran back inside, past my parents again, and to my room. I pulled my suitcase off my bed and tucked it in my closet. I was going to leave, but I couldn't do it now. I had to wait until they were asleep. I didn't want them coming after me—whoever *they* were. It wasn't my Mom and Dad, and Kyle wasn't Kyle anymore. My brother would have believed me. He knew I wasn't prone to lying or making things up.

"My whole world was falling apart and I didn't know what to do about it."

Chapter Five

Remembering makes me shake again with rage. I wasn't some dumb kid back then and they treated me like I was. The pain comes rushing back. I don't know if I want to cry or scream. Maybe hit something. Instead, I pour a glass of water from the table near the window. I sip it, looking down on the fences that keep us all inside the grounds, wishing I could just jump from this window and over the fence and run to freedom.

I know that's not possible and it makes me more upset. Angry that everything happened the way it did. Angry no one believed me back then. Angry that I'm stuck here when I should be living my life. Angry that I no longer have a family. Angry that I need someone to believe me in order to live my life.

I grit my teeth, close my eyes, and try to get a hold of my emotions. I know that all the resentment I'm feeling will get me nowhere. I can't let Alex see anything less than perfect. Otherwise…well, let's say the staff here will be caring for me for the rest of my pitiful life.

"So, you woke up in this…alternate reality?" Alex asks.

"Yes," I whip back to face Alex. I can hear the bitterness in my voice and am sure Alex does as well. But I can't help it. As much as I try to hide what I'm feeling, I can't. "It was so weird. I can't begin to tell you how I felt, still feel." I take a deep breath, take another sip of water, and sit back down. *Stop, Melinda. Stop letting him see your frustration.* "Sorry," I mumble.

"For what?"

"I was frustrated for a minute, but I'm fine now."

"Don't apologize for your feelings. They are yours and no one should criticize you for them."

I'm surprised. It's okay to be mad?

"But it's not good to feel anger. It was all in the past."

"Yes, it is, because you are still trying to deal with it. Melinda, it's okay if you're upset. You can be mad. I won't think ill of you."

"I'm glad to hear that."

I'm relieved, but still wary. A new doctor comes in and devotes his time to just me *and* he's not upset that I'm mad sometimes? He is a Godsend.

"Do you want to break for lunch? It's about that time now."

"That's a good idea."

I'm not hungry, but if I don't eat, they'll view it negatively. They'll think I can't handle things. Handle life. I have to force myself to get something into my stomach.

"Melinda, what you're doing today is very brave. I think if you continue being honest about everything with yourself as much as with me, you will actually begin to heal. The anger will abate."

"I am being honest. I have been."

"Then continue to do so."

I nod my head and turn to leave.

"We'll meet back here in an hour then."

****

By the time I arrive at the dining room, everyone is almost done eating. It is slim pickings, but I don't really care. I have a little salad and put a half of a sandwich on my plate for good measure. I pick at the salad and eat a few bites of the sandwich. The food here is okay, but I don't have an appetite. My mind is still reeling.

It's like I'm still back in the kitchen with my dead father, weird mother, and a brother who's not Kyle. I manage to eat most of the salad. Nurse Hamilton is standing near the door when I empty my tray. She doesn't say anything, so she must not have noticed I hardly ate. That's good.

I say hi to her as I pass and she smiles. I make my way back to Alex's office and knock on the door. I hear him say come in.

When I do, he says, "You weren't gone long. Did you eat?"

"Yes."

He takes the last bite of his sandwich and wipes his mouth.

"Well, then. We've both had some sustenance and we can move forward."

"I suppose."

I sit back down in the chair and scrunch my knees up to my chest, feeling like that small child from the past. Realizing that I need to present myself as the adult I am now, I pull my legs back down and sit up straight.

"It's okay to be comfortable. Go ahead, relax," he tells me.

I am more comfortable with my legs up, so I pull them back up in the chair.

33

"Let's continue. You were upset when you woke up. You felt like you were living in another world?" Alex prompts me.

I mentally prepare to send myself back to the past again. For a while now, I've avoided it. Now, it's time to hit it head on. I'm ready…I hope.

"Sort of. Kyle was the one person who always believed me. He knew when I was lying and when I was telling the truth. But that time? He stood and looked at me as if I was nuts."

"You never ran away that night, did you?"

"No," I sigh.

I am exhausted from my inner battle of having to relive the past. I slump back in the chair, closing my eyes.

"I see you're tired. I think it best we resume tomorrow."

I open my eyes and look into Alex's. I want to see the truth.

"Dr…Alex, do you really want to see me tomorrow?"

Without hesitation and without blinking, he answers, "I most assuredly do. And before you ask, no I do not think you are crazy. It is actually too early in our discussions to assess you or your psyche."

"So, it's a wait and see?"

"Exactly. I told you I'd be truthful and that is what I'm being."

"Thanks. I guess I can't expect anything more."

"It's still early in the day. Why don't you go out to the garden and enjoy the sunshine."

"Maybe some fresh air will make me feel better," I agree.

"I believe it can't hurt."

"I doubt I'll feel better until I'm out of this place."

"Why don't you concentrate on today? Tomorrow will be here soon enough."

Chapter Six

Alex

When Melinda leaves, I begin ruminating about our first session. She seems of sound mind, but some of the things she claims to remember are hard to digest. Dead people talking to her?

I've studied science and its methods in healing and it left very little room for thoughts of the paranormal. Still, it can present problems. I admit that I believe very little of her story, but it's obvious she believes everything she's saying.

Before dismissing the paranormal, I need to find out as much as I can about the subject. I'm worried it can be a barrier to Melinda's recall. That wouldn't be good for anyone. She needs to remember everything.

Chapter Seven

After leaving Alex's office, I stroll through the beautiful gardens. I take a few minutes and enjoy the many flowers and their smells. Earlier, I heard someone saying we are supposed to get a big storm soon. You can't tell by the clear blue sky. I sit down on a bench and think about how it's a good day for a young couple to have a picnic.

I wouldn't know anything about being one-half of a couple though, only what I read in the books they allow me to have. I've been locked up in here in Skyview Haven since I was fourteen and it can be stifling, to say the least.

I haven't had any visitors in a long while, let alone the chance to meet a boy. My aunt Bet and uncle L came to visit me regularly when I first arrived here. They are my mother's sister and her husband. They stopped coming after I wouldn't stop telling the story over and over, the real one, the one I'm trying to tell Alex now. Aunt Bet and uncle L—it's actually Aunt Betty and Uncle Larry—don't believe me anymore than anyone else and think it best they don't see me until I can come to terms with my psychological problems.

Those are their own words. Even though I wasn't sure at first what 'come to terms' meant, after all I have been through since that time, I certainly do now. Mom will probably be very upset to hear they won't support

37

me. They don't like me much because they think I had something to do with it all. At least I'm sure that's what they think. Why else would they abandon me?

My heart is heavy. I'm tired of being my own company. I stand up from the bench and look to make sure no one is around. I am alone...again. This part of the garden isn't where I like to spend my time. So I figure as long as I have to be alone, I might as well head to the place I really enjoy. I weave my way down an old path and head toward the area I know no one will think to look for me.

I'm pretty sure the doctors and nurses don't want me back here. I found it by accident one day when I was walking, not even realizing I left the garden. I abruptly came to an overgrown area and was turning around to head back when out of the corner of my eye I saw a small area that if I ducked under, I could go beneath the brush. It was as if two trees grew together to form a semi-circle, leaving the other half of the circle open at the bottom. I was curious, so I checked it out. It looked like a little shelter I could hide away in. I'd only been here six months when I found it and since then I would come whenever possible.

I arrive at the thick brush. I duck down and pass through the open arc. On the other side is my place of serenity. A place I can do what I want. I hide the books here they forbid us to read. If they have violence or sex scenes in them, they are taken away. Stupid. How are we supposed to learn anything tucked in an asylum away from the world without any educational materials? Okay, violence and sex scenes are not necessarily educational, but they do help a person to understand the world and grow, don't they?

I used to have a roommate whose sister would sneak those types of books in. Stephanie hid them and showed me where they were if I wanted to read them. I didn't touch them until the day after she left, if you could call what happened leaving.

I was told she was placed in another home, but I knew they were lying. She hung herself in the communal exercise area using a strap she roped around the rod guys did pull-ups on. I knew it happened because she told me she was going to kill herself. One night when she thought I was asleep, she sneaked out of our room and I followed her. I saw her do it and was so shocked I was rooted to the spot where I was hiding. I couldn't stop her. One more death that was my fault.

After Stephanie died, I took her books and brought them here. I would sit and read for hours. The dictionary was my favorite, believe it or not. When I ran across words I didn't know, I looked them up. Over the years, I slipped various things like throw blankets and small pillows into my bag that I was supposedly taking into the garden when I ate my lunch.

Not far from where I stooped under the brush, there was once a house, but is now just a shell with only a brick chimney still standing. It looked like it burned down. I wish I knew what it once held. Not wasting time on questions, I would probably never get the answers to, I stride past the area to a point beyond, to my special spot.

It's a small cottage that beckons to me each time I see it. This is my place. At least, that's what I like to call it. No one knows about it. I made it my little home, acting as if I was the owner of a palace instead of a trespasser. It is set back from what was probably the main house with a maze of shrubs, now overgrown and separate from the large backyard. In its day, if you stood on the small front porch, you could have probably seen right into the second story windows of the larger home. That is, if there was a second story. It does look like there could have been.

When I first found this place, I walked up the short two steps, stood on the small porch, and peered in the window. It was so caked with dirt I was unable to see anything inside. I nervously looked around, hoping no one lived here. It seemed abandoned, but it was too hard to tell without seeing inside. I tried the front door knob and with a loud squeak, it turned in my hand. The noise made me hesitate. Did anyone hear that? What if this was someone's home? Would they come out with a gun pointed at me and demand I leave their property, like the stories I read in my banned books? I waited, but didn't hear anything except the pleasant sound of birds chirping from their claimed tree branches.

Holding my breath, I cautiously opened the door a crack and peered inside. I quickly scanned the area and saw no one. After looking behind me once more, I opened the door wider and stepped over the threshold…and right into a maze of cobwebs. Yelling with disgust—spiders and their webs are not something I consider pleasant—I brushed them aside and wiped my hands on my pants.

To make a long story short, no one lived there anymore. To me, it was like finding the gold at the end of the rainbow. It didn't matter that it was small and filthy. I set to work and after a month of sneaking cleaning supplies and linens from Skyview, I made it my palace. I cleaned the filthy furniture that was partially covered in dust-topped plastic, threw away the dead plants hanging in planters in front of the windows and, using fabric I found in Skyview's craft room, haphazardly sewed together makeshift curtains for the windows. It was one of the things I learned in crafts class.

Now walking into Mel's Place—that's what I decided to call it—I am still delighted with my find. The windows sparkle in the sunlight and the curtains fan back from the gentle breeze. I took to leaving the windows open to air it out and decided it was refreshing. The windows in my small room at Skyview don't open and even if they do, it won't matter because there are bars on them.

It is my secret hideaway. A place I can be without my every step and action monitored. It is somewhere I can sit and figure out who I am. I thought I knew when I had a family, but now? Now, I just feel like I have no identity. All I am is the crazy girl who supposedly killed her family who lives in Skyview Haven. But in Mel's Place, I can be anything or anyone I want. There is no one here to make sure I eat the right food, dress the right way, or read the right books.

I walk to the bookcase that sits in the corner to the right of the window and try to decide which book I want to read. I run my finger along the spines on the top row. I have read most of them, but there are a few I recently added. Sometimes, I sneak into the staff lounge and find books lying about. I take them and bring them here. I don't exactly steal them. Those I read and bring back to where I found them, so really I only borrow them.

I look on the second shelf and see an empty spot

between two books. I frown, knowing I don't leave spaces between books, only at the end of the row. I shrug and figure it's one I returned at some point and forgot. I pick up a book by some female author, sit in my small chair near the window, and begin reading.

I didn't know so much time passed until I realize I can no longer see what I am reading. It is getting dark. Panicking, I stand up with a start, dropping the book on the floor. I pick it up, place it on the sofa, and dash out the front door, heading back the way I came. If they find this place, I know I will be forbidden to come back. I cannot let that happen.

I reach the main garden and quickly sit down on one of the benches to catch my breath.

"Melinda, there you are! We've been looking all over the place for you. Where have you been?"

Nurse Hamilton is standing with one hand on her hip and with the other is pointing her stubby index finger at me. I'm not sure if she likes me and she isn't my favorite either. Okay, that's not true. I do sort of like her.

As usual, I don't respond, just look at her with wide eyes. She scares me sometimes. She often has a scowl on her face and despite her shortness, seems to loom over us with a look of disappointment. She always makes me feel like I did something wrong, even when I know I didn't.

"Well? Answer me."

As a response, I bow my head and look at my feet. She grabs my arm gently and begins leading me through the garden and back to the gloomy prison they call a home.

"It's time for dinner; just five minutes time. You

need to wash up and eat quickly. It's your turn in the kitchen tonight."

Each night, they have those of us who are able take turns washing and drying dishes. I don't mind because it gives me something to do beside sit in the common area watching cartoons or playing card games. I've outgrown those childish things, but at the same time, in the back of my mind, I know my growth is stunted. They don't give us anything in here or let us see anything that has to do with real life. There are no phones. All we have are each other and there are very few girls I like.

While doing dishes later, I start thinking about Dr. Leever. He probably thinks I'm just as nuts as the other doctors did. Most people here think I tell tall tales. So far, I told Dr. Leever more in one day than I told all the other doctors combined. There is something about him that makes me feel I can trust him to hear my whole story, the *truth*. That doesn't mean I'm not still scared. I am scared about what Dr. Leever will do when he hears it all. He'll probably say that I'm more mentally unstable than anyone thought and that I should never be released.

But I have to get out…I *must* get out of here.

Chapter Eight

The Other Side

Blue skies, sunny, but I can't tell where the sun is. It's all around me. It's bright. It's there with no beginning and no end. It's the world I'm in. I observe, but don't complain. There is nothing to grumble about. I feel at peace and have since I got here almost nine years ago.

I may not find fault with anything here, but I'm feeling uneasy lately. You see, my daughter Melinda was in harm's way when I first died. Fortunately, she's safe at Skyview Haven. But in the distance, I see a black cloud. I was told that they are never good to see here. It generally means someone is in danger, someone you love, and left back home. You know it's your cloud because only you can see it. That's how they explained it to me. So, now that I see it, I fear for Melinda. She's my kitten, my baby girl, and I still worry about her and always will, even if I am dead.

With dread, I approach the black cloud. I must peer through and see what's happening. For years, she was okay, safe where they couldn't find her. Now that may all be ending. I realize I'm getting ahead of myself. Maybe it's not Melinda. Maybe it's Larry or Betty. But even as I think it, I know for sure it's Melinda. It scares me.

This is a parallel universe. It's the Other Side. We literally walk next to the living on Earth. Picture a street in any city and then imagine an equivalent street next to it, like drawing two lines side-by-side. Only one line is appealing but contains hidden dangers combined with love, hatred, evil, and everything in between. The other line is nothing but magnificence, peace, and love with a sporadic dash of worry. That dash is the black cloud we see at times, like I'm seeing now. Two similar worlds, one not knowing the other exists until they're thrown into the other street.

Often, we check in on our loved ones, but we have new lives here. Friends and family who have passed before us, with whom we are reunited. Our world is growing every day. However, I don't want Melinda here until she has lived a long, full, happy, and healthy life. It's too soon.

I look across the 'street' to what used to be home. I smile. There's Melinda. She loves that garden. Often, I see her sitting on a bench, face pointed at the sun, the warm rays making her close her eyes and smile. She's there now.

She gets up and heads toward the trees. I know where she's going. 'Mel's Place' is just what the doctor ordered for her. It's her little haven, a place she can be alone to think and be herself. She's getting ready for her real life to start and I know she can't wait.

Melinda looks happy. She looks okay. So, what is this black cloud about? I move my attention to the buildings. I see many people mulling about. There's Nurse Hamilton. She's a good person, really likes Melinda though she tries not to show favoritism. Familiar faces I've seen many times over the years.

So, what's the danger? There is obviously something. This cloud doesn't appear without reason. I summon all the energy I can and walk the halls of the main building. Cafeteria, patients' rooms, common area for the patients, and plenty of offices.

That's it. A new face walking into an office. I follow him through and look at the name plaque on his desk. Dr. Alex Leever. Hmmm...he must be the new psychiatrist Melinda has been ordered to see. I hear that if she convinces the director she's stable and not a danger to anyone or herself, she can finally leave Skyview Haven. I want her to be free and able to live her life, but am also worried that they'll get to her on the outside. I have mixed emotions.

Maybe that's why I'm seeing this black cloud. Perhaps there's no real danger after all, just my fatherly worry. That must be it.

Chapter Nine

The next day, Dr. Leever began asking me questions before I could even sit down.

"How old are you, Melinda?"

"Twenty-two."

"I understand you finished your high school subjects here with a tutor."

"Yes."

I go to sit then decide not to. I roam over to the window. I like looking out it. There are no bars here like in my room. I have a basic room that has nothing in it that can be used to harm others or myself. It's more like a cell. Don't get me wrong, it's not terrible here. They treat us well and take good care of us. It's because as I've said, most of the people residing here have mental problems, we get sterile safe rooms with bars on the window. Stifling for those of us who don't need such close monitoring.

"What subjects interested you the most?"

"I don't know."

"Did any of them?"

"I've always liked reading."

"That's good. Reading has always been one of my favorites as well."

"Why are you asking me these questions? Isn't all that information in my file?" I roll my eyes as I ask.

"Some of it, but I want to hear it from you. Is that

okay?"

I realize I need to let go and say, "I guess so."

"Tell me," Dr. Leever starts tapping his pen on his desk, which I find irritating, "if you could do one thing, what would you do?"

"Leave here."

"Besides that."

Tap, tap.

"I don't know."

"Okay, you said you like to read. So, English interests you?"

Tap, tap.

"I guess so, yes it does. Can you stop that?"

"Sure," he put his pen down on the desk. "Why does that bother you?"

"It's irritating."

"How so?"

"I don't know. It just is. It makes me anxious."

"So, English then. What kind of books do you like to read?"

He ignores my statement and keeps questioning me.

"They don't give you much of a choice here. Most of the books in the library are for fifteen-year-olds."

"What if I brought you some books that are for your age?"

"They would take them away. They say I can't read anything with "bad stuff" in it," I make quote marks with my fingers.

"Like what bad stuff?"

"Sex, swear words, anything scary."

"I see. If you could read whatever you wanted, what would it be?"

"Does any of this matter? Can't we just get on with it?"

"You are edgy today."

I am, and I shouldn't let him know it. He will have to report it and I'll be back to square one. I used to have nightmares a lot about what happened. I haven't had one in years, but I did last night. I learned to hide it when I woke up screaming. When someone ran in the room, I told them I saw a mouse or something. It happened again last night, but no one came in. They must not have heard me and I want to keep it that way.

This doctor is my last hope. If he doesn't agree that I am mentally able to live on my own, it will be Skyview Haven for the rest of my torturous life. I will kill myself like Stephanie if that happens.

"Melinda?" he asks when I don't answer.

"I didn't sleep much last night."

"I see. Do you want to continue today or take a break?"

"No breaks. I have to tell you," I say as I finally take a seat.

I know I sound desperate because I am. I figure when I finally tell him everything, they will want to keep me here for life. But I won't allow it. If Dr. Leever doesn't tell them I am okay to leave, I already plan to end it all myself. I can't stay here anymore.

"All right. Yesterday you were telling me about your talk with Kyle, how he didn't believe you."

"Yes, Beth wasn't dead, Dad was."

"Okay, let's start there."

Chapter Ten

"The entire time was weird. It was June 2005 when they finally had a funeral for Beth. I stood there next to what they said was her grave, but I knew she wasn't in it. I didn't know what was going on and no one would believe me. They all thought I was in denial. *They* were the ones in denial.

"For a while after, I had to see a shrink. I thought maybe if someone like a doctor believed me, then my family would. But I overhead Dr. Raspin tell my mom and dad that I was more out of tune than she realized. Those were the words she used, 'out of tune'. What was that supposed to mean? It didn't matter. I knew then I was alone.

"I went back to school and still no Beth. All my friends stopped me in the hallway to say how sorry they were. Were they? Didn't they know Beth was alive? Why was I the only one who knew the truth? Even Beth's mother was always crying. Mom and I went to visit her a few times after the funeral. Each time, she and Howard, Beth's dad, were either crying or you could tell they had been.

"After a while, I began to think maybe I was nuts after all, especially after seeing my dad alive day in and day out after I was just at his funeral. He wasn't in my head any longer, but *there*, right in front of me. So, if my dad was in my head when he was dead, why isn't

Beth in my head if she's dead? None of it made sense.

"I was just about convinced I really *was* in shock, that Dad was alive the whole time and Beth was really the one who was dead until…"

"Until what?" Dr. Leever prompts.

"I'm not sure if I can talk about it. You're going to think I'm lying."

I fidget in my chair, wanting to get up, but don't want to pace his office again. I want to be outside, breathing the air, instead of being cooped up in his stuffy office.

"Why don't you let me determine that?"

"I don't know."

"I won't pressure you. If you are uncomfortable, we can stop for the day."

"Okay…I mean no, I don't want to stop. It's just I don't…I'm not lying, Dr. Leever."

"Alex, remember? And I believe you when you say you're not lying. If you think it's true, then it is to you."

"That's only a fancy way of telling me I'm messed up. I don't have a college degree like you, but I'm twenty-two now and I do know some things."

"Of course you do. I didn't mean to offend you. Do you wish to continue?"

"Yes, I guess."

Chapter Eleven

"Like I said, back then I thought Beth was dead. After all, everyone kept telling me she was, so it had to be me who was wrong. Only I wasn't. I went to bed like normal one night. Dad stayed up watching TV, Mom went to bed early with a headache, and Kyle was in his room. I tried to fall asleep, but was restless. I didn't know why. These were usually the times I'd call Beth and we'd chat and I even reached for the phone, but remembered Beth was gone. I shut my eyes and must have drifted off because the next thing I knew I woke up and the bedside clock read 3:17 a.m. I was wide-awake and decided to get out of bed.

"I walked to my window and just as I'd done so many times in the past, looked down, hoping to spot Beth. And suddenly, she was there. She was waving up at me to come down. I could see her forming the words, *Come on.* I smiled like I haven't smiled in a long time. I knew it. I knew she was alive. I put my index finger up to tell her I'd be there in a minute. I quickly stuck my feet into some shoes and grabbed a jacket. I tiptoed all the way downstairs and through the kitchen to the back door. I looked out the window first to make sure I wasn't seeing things. Nope. She was there! Right there at the foot of our path. I smiled again, quietly opened the door, and slipped out. I hugged her hard and she pulled away.

"What are you doing?" she asked.

"What do you mean? I've missed you. Where the hell have you been? They said you were dead. I didn't believe them," it all came out in a rush, in one long sentence, hardly a breath in between words.

"I'm right here. Remember? We promised to be in each other's lives for always."

"I know, but..."

"Ssshhh," she cautioned. "We have to be quiet. Come on," she tugged at my arm.

"We walked a short way down the path. Before we got to her backyard, she suddenly stopped and I ran smack into the back end of her.

"What the hell?"

"Shit! I can't..."

She looked at me with a frown on her face then smiled. "Let's go to our place!"

"Okay, but you do know it's the middle of the night. We'll get into trouble if they know we're out here."

"Everyone's sleeping. They won't know."

"She grabbed my arm and tugged at me when I hesitated.

"Beth..."

"What?"

"I smiled and said, "Nothing. Let's go!"

"I was happy and nothing was going to spoil it for me. I *knew* Beth wasn't dead. I knew it!

"'Our place' was a fort that we constructed in the woods. Well, not a *real* fort. We found some wood and leaned them all around a tree, sort of forming a teepee. Then I brought some old curtains my mom didn't use anymore and we draped it over top of the wood. The inside was small, but it was ours. We sat huddled under old blankets she brought from her house a while ago. It was dark in our fort, but we had a flashlight if we needed it.

"We chatted for a while. I told her all about how everyone thinks she's dead, that she'd drowned. After I told her they had a funeral for her and everything, she giggled.

"Why are you laughing?"

"Because it's funny. I'm not dead, I'm right here."

"She laughed again as she pinched my arm.

"Ow! Damn it!"

"If I was dead, I couldn't do that, could I?"

"I laughed with her, but it felt wrong. Something was not right. Then it hit me. If Beth was alive, that meant my dad was dead.

"Beth, you're alive."

"Yes, silly, I *know* that."

"But then what about my dad?"

"What about him?"

"Beth, I think he's dead."

"What?"

"Tears started trickling down my face again.

"What are you talking about? You're dad's fine. I saw him earlier today."

"Where?"

"I knew the answer. Deep inside, I knew the answer and I can't tell you how I knew.

"I saw him on the bridge. At least I think it was him. It was raining pretty hard. But I know it was your car. Hey! Where are you going?"

"As she talked, I got up and left the fort. It started raining, but I didn't care. Beth was here, which meant

Dad was dead. The little pleasure I got seeing Beth again didn't last long. I couldn't win. I felt like I had to choose between Beth and my dad. It wasn't fair.

"Melinda, what's wrong?" she pleaded. "Aren't you happy we're together?"

"Yes, but my dad…" I said, standing there in the rain.

"He's fine. Can we go back under now? I'm getting freakin' soaked."

"I have to go."

"I turned abruptly and began running back home. The rain made everything slick and I fell a few times, getting branches stuck in my hair and plastered with mud. In my backyard, I stopped and looked at our house. Every light seemed to be on. I saw Kyle pass by the kitchen window. I stood rooted to the spot. Do I go back to Beth? Somehow knowing if I did, it meant my dad would be dead. Or do I go in the house and accept the fact Beth was gone?"

Chapter Twelve

Recalling the past makes me both nostalgic and upset. I stare off into space for a few minutes before Alex brings me back to the present.

"What did you do, Melinda?"

Dr. Leever allows me to answer in my own time. He doesn't push me.

"I...I...Can we talk about this another time?"

"Of course. When you feel comfortable, we can continue that discussion. How about we pick up tomorrow and you can enjoy the rest of your day?"

I don't though. Just as it did that night I was in the teepee with Beth, it is raining hard. The storm they talked about did come. They won't allow me outside. I want to go to Mel's Place, but I know I'll have to wait until the weather clears.

Chapter Thirteen

The Other Side

Things were a bit confusing for a while. Did I die in the car or at the hospital? Apparently, the hospital. At first, it was traumatic knowing I left Meredith, Kyle, and Melinda all alone. I missed the warmth of my wife's welcome and the clamoring of the children.

It was some time before I got to the Other Side. Time is actually subjective here, so I can't really say how long. It felt like quite a while before I 'checked' in to my new paradise. It took more time to adjust, but I finally did. Now, it definitely helps knowing I can check in on my family on Earth from time to time.

I'm doing that now.

Melinda just finished another session with Dr. Leever. My daughter is baring her soul, talking about something she should have been confiding in someone a long time ago. Instead, she bottled it up, knowing that her talk of it earlier is the reason she's in Skyview Haven today.

She's smart though. She knows that in order for her to move forward, she must look at the past. She's certainly doing that. It's hard on her. I can see it. The crying, the nightmares. Some nights I appear and comfort her, but she doesn't realize I'm there. To her, it's a dream. It's okay, so long as it helps her.

I have to do more. A few days ago, I found this young man running from his home. For some reason, he was brought to my attention. It dawns on me now that he is the one who can help Melinda. I don't understand how, but I know this, deep in my soul. I must get him to befriend her. Somehow, I understand that she will need him soon.

There's that prick again in the back of my mind. Something is terribly wrong. I must be vigilant. If someone hurts my daughter I will tear them limb from limb.

Chapter Fourteen

The next day, I'm back with Dr. Leever, but the rain stops and he says we can talk outside in the garden. The benches are dry enough, so we sit down. It's cool and damp, but it feels good, invigorating.

"I thought this may be a change from my dreary office. I heard you like the garden."

"I do."

I'm relieved we're outside. His office is okay, but stuffy. I like the fresh air and it's definitely prettier out here.

"I love what the rain does, it clears everything up, and helps the flowers bloom," he is looking at me. "Is that what happened the day after you saw Beth?"

"No. The rain hasn't stopped and all the flowers are dead. At least that's the way it's felt since the day this mess all started."

"Felt? Do you mean you don't feel that way anymore?"

"I'm not sure. I mean, sort of. I've never told anyone this much of my story before. It helps me feel…"

"Free?" he asks while I sit searching for the right words.

"Not free," I sweep the area with my hand. "I want to be free though. Free of this place."

"If you don't feel free, what is it that you are

sensing?"

"I've changed. Like I told you from the start, I know what I know and that will always be the truth. But you're listening to me. You keep coming back. Why?"

"Because I told you I would. I want to know the entire truth as you see it."

"As I see it? Again, you're reserving judgment, right?"

"That's correct."

"You'll believe, too. Give it a chance and you'll understand."

I am suddenly confident he will. Once I get my whole story out, he'll have no choice.

"So, you'll keep talking to me?"

"Yes, because I know you're the person that's supposed to know the story, the entire truth, as you put it."

"Why am I the one?"

"I don't know. I just know you are."

"Here," he leans over and reaches into his briefcase he set on the ground next to his seat. "I brought you something." He hands me a book. "It's a fantasy/sci-fi. I already got it approved by Dr. Allcott. There are no sex scenes and very few cuss words."

Dr. Allcott is the medical director of this place. I'm shocked. Why would he bring me a book?

"I…Thank you. Why did you do this?"

I rub my hand over the top of the hardback book. It's the first time someone cared enough to bring me a gift. He listened when I told him I like to read.

"Because it will bring you hours of enjoyment. If you like it, that book is the first in a four book series and I'll bring you the second one. I think the author is working on more of them."

"I don't know what to say. No one has brought me a gift since I've been here. Especially something that means so much."

He pats my hand that's still on the book's cover and smiles.

"It's my pleasure. Now, it's a beautiful day. Let's stay here until lunchtime and talk. What do you say?"

I smile up at him. "Yes, it's nice out. I'm ready to continue."

Chapter Fifteen

"Remember, I just ran from Beth and I'm standing in the backyard looking at my house. The house is lit up and I see Kyle in the window. I knew I had to go in and face whatever was coming. For some reason, I knew there was no turning back. I couldn't go back to Beth, but I was afraid to go forward. What if they are both gone? Would that mean I killed them? Was it really up to me to decide who lives and who dies?

"I was angry. I wasn't God! This wasn't my choice. Deep in my soul I knew that once I walked into my house, life as I knew it before my father's car accident, before I heard my father's voice, before Beth drowned in the same river as my father, would not be the same. I couldn't turn back time. Choices are made every day and for some reason, I was being forced to make this one.

"I turned around and looked back at our path and whispered, "I love you, Beth. I will see you again."

"Having made my decision, I strode up to the house, my legs getting heavier with each step, and opened the kitchen door. I tried to change my frown into a smile, but it didn't work very well. My eyes still blazed with fury when my mom and Kyle looked up. I could tell Mom had been crying. She rushed to my side, knelt down, and hugged me.

"Melinda! You're soaked to the bone! And muddy.

What in the world?"

"She took my jacket off of me and Kyle handed her a towel. She proceeded to dry my hair, but I took her hand and stopped her. At least her nurturing was changing my attitude, even if I did know what was coming. It felt good to have Mom tending to my needs. I wished I knew then what I know now. I would have let her fuss over me more. Instead I would shrug her hugs off and air-kiss her when I had to.

"Mom?"

"It's okay. You're home now. It's all okay."

"Where's Dad?"

"My mom and Kyle exchanged looks. It confirmed my suspicions, but I needed to hear it.

"Where is he?" I asked again.

"Mel..."

"Kyle walked to me, an anguished look on his face.

"Where is he?" I screamed.

"Melinda, there's been an accident. Your father was coming home. He..."

"Tears rolled down my mother's cheeks.

"He's dead, isn't he?" I quietly asked.

"I wanted them to say it. I needed to hear them say it out loud. My heart was heavy. I just killed my father. It was my fault.

"Mel, he's in the hospital. Mom and I couldn't find you. We didn't want to go there without you knowing."

"In the hospital?" I asked, shocked.

"Maybe I was wrong. I had to be wrong! My dad wasn't dead because I spent time with Beth. It was going to be all right. I was overcome with joy.

"I smiled and said, "Let's go. I want to see Dad."

"I began putting my coat back on, but my mom

stopped me.

"You're in your pajamas. Go clean up and change."

"I began to leave the room, stopped and turned around and told them, "Dad's going to be just fine now."

"I believed that with my whole heart. After all, I left Beth. It really sucked that I had to choose, but there was nothing else I could have done.

"When we got to the hospital, Mom made Kyle and me wait in the hall while she talked to the doctor. They left the door slightly open and we could hear quite a bit. The doctor was telling Mom that Dad had hypothermia. I didn't understand a lot of it at the time. They said something about Dad being confused, he was in cold water, and ended up laying on the side of the river, half in and half out.

"We heard a loud bang and nurses were running in and out of a nearby room. One of them darted into the doctor's office. Within seconds, the doctor flew out of his office and into the other room. My mother was on his heels.

"Mom?" Kyle asked.

"She grabbed us both, one with each hand and pulled us close.

"It's your father."

"He's going to be fine, Mom," I tried to reassure her. I looked up at her and said, "You'll see."

"A few minutes later, the doctor walked out of the room slowly, head down. He looked up at my mother then met my eyes.

"No! No!"

"Melinda, stop."

"She held my hand tightly when I wouldn't stop yelling.

"Everything is going to be okay."

"She hugged me and Kyle closer to her. I was confused. What is going on? I left Beth. Dad is supposed to be alive.

"This wasn't supposed to happen!"

"I was beside myself. I thought—I *believed*—he would be alive if Beth wasn't. It took a while, but Kyle calmed me down while the doctor delivered the bad news. I found out later that the hypothermia was too severe. When the nurse went in to check on him, they found him under the bed. He was delusional. I guess that's a bad sign, something about hibernating like an animal. I didn't understand it all, although now I know a little more than I did, thanks to my reading. I'm sure being a doctor, you know all of this."

****

"Yes, what you said is true," Alex agrees.

"Well, it was wrong, Alex."

I look at the ground in front of me for a few minutes. I still don't understand how it all works, but I do have a better understanding now than I did. I'm getting ahead of myself though. I slip back to the past and continue my horrible tale.

"Does this mean Beth is still alive? I didn't know. When we got home, the first thing I did was go out back by our path. She wasn't there. But I didn't give up. I went out there for the next week, a few times even sitting in our fort just waiting. I even went to see her mother. She was getting better about losing Beth, but I could see when I looked in her eyes, it still haunted her. I knew how she felt, still do.

"I never saw Beth alive again. And…my dad was gone, too."

Chapter Sixteen

I put my hands palms down on the bench, stretch backwards a little, and close my eyes. For many years I was furious about it all. Now, I'm sad and empty and yes, still a bit angry.

Dr. Leever decides it best we cut the session short. It leaves me completely exhausted, having to relive my father and my best friend's deaths in one day. Even the thought of Mel's Place doesn't cheer me. I grab the book Dr. Leever gave me and I go to my room. I want to hide from my thoughts. I start reading the book, but just can't focus. I make myself go into the common area and try to watch television.

Nothing distracts me from my misery. Telling Dr. Leever about that time in my life left a hole in my heart bigger now than back then, if that's possible. It sure feels like it. The rest of the day is miserable and I finally drift off to sleep late that night.

This morning, I rise early and go out to the garden. I sit on a bench, listen to the birds chirp, and smell the fresh, clean air. I need to change my frame of mind. What happened is in the past. I need to move on and I can't if I keep breaking down and being sarcastic. The good doc will tell Dr. Allcott the same thing the other doctors said, that I'm a threat to myself and others. It's best to keep me here. There is no way I can allow that again.

"Before you ask," I tell him the minute I walk in his office, "I'm ready to continue. Alex, I have to tell you. I can't stop now. Please don't make me."

I can hear myself. I'm pleading and I sound desperate. Right now, I don't care. All I do care about is resolving my issues, meeting the past head-on in the here and now. Then let the past be what it is…the past.

"I have no intention of doing so," he reassures me. "Before we begin, I have a few questions, if that is all right with you."

"Okay."

"I know you're in the middle of your story and haven't gotten to everything, but I'm curious about Beth. Where is she now? Is she alive?"

"To answer that, I have to continue with my story. You wouldn't understand otherwise."

"Okay. I'd like to ask about your Aunt Betty and Uncle Larry. Do you mind speaking about them?"

"There's not much to say. They deserted me like everyone else," I plop down in the chair. "They didn't believe me anymore than any of the other doctors did."

"Do you think I'm going to assess you in the same way?"

"I don't know. Probably. Maybe."

"Let's see what we can do about that doubt. But first, tell me about your aunt and uncle."

"When the cops started thinking I murdered my family, they convinced Aunt Bet and Uncle L the best thing for me was to get psychiatric help. My aunt and uncle don't live close by. They flew out here and spoke with the cops and a few doctors. The next thing I knew, they were sticking me in here. They used to come and visit quite often, but not anymore." I frown and continue, "I wouldn't recant my story and they thought I was beyond help. Uncle L actually told me that himself. Needless to say, I was devastated. I haven't seen them since and have no desire to. That's it."

He must sense my anger at them when I firmly state that I don't wish to see them.

"You're still hurting over that and you need to confront it in order to heal. Tell me about your conversations with your aunt and uncle."

He's right, the thoughts still hurt. Not only that, they still make me mad. These confrontations of my past are getting harder than I thought they would be.

I sigh and say, "I'm not sure even thinking about them will help me."

"Thinking? Perhaps not. But talking is healing. I think you're already seeing that."

Once again, he's right.

"All right. Like I said, once they heard the news of the deaths, Aunt Bet and Uncle L flew out here from New York. Initially, Aunt Bet wanted to take me back with them. That is until they spoke with the cops. The police were convinced I murdered my family. Aunt Bet actually confessed to me that Uncle L convinced her it would be best to put me in here for help. She all too willingly agreed."

I shake my head at the memory. Family is supposed to mean something, but not to them.

"They came and saw me a few times. Uncle L kept trying to get me to confess, that I killed them. He'd say that he understood it wasn't me really, that I was sick and needed help. I refused to change my story. I kept saying the truth. Aunt Bet even started yelling at me a few times. Asking me how I could do such a thing.

Their visits came less often and honestly, I was glad about it.

"The last time they came was when they really broke my heart. Nurse Hamilton told me they were here and I was heading to Dr. Allcott's office to greet them. They were in speaking with Dr. Allcott and I happened to overhear the conversation."

****

"Dr. Allcott, I appreciate your concern. My wife and I cannot take in a mentally unbalanced child. She insists others killed her mother, my brother, and nephew. And she keeps saying that the dead came back to tell her. She's not well. I think it's best we don't see her again until she can come to terms with her psychological problems."

"Not having her family support her, can hurt her," Dr. Allcott said.

"Then I guess you people here need to do your job. If you get her well, then you can contact us. Otherwise, we just can't keep going through this."

"May I remind you both that it's your niece that is going through a lot. Whether or not she killed her family has not yet been resolved. The fact remains, *she* believes everything she is saying."

"My husband is right, Dr. Allcott. It's not that we don't love her. We just can't help her. She needs professional help. Contact us when she's better."

"You don't even want reports?" Dr. Allcott asked.

"No," Uncle L said firmly. "It's best we don't."

****

"I ran back to my room. I couldn't stop crying. I never came out of my room that day. I still can't believe they just deserted me and didn't even want to know if I was making any sort of progress."

"I can see how that must have been devastating," Dr. Leever says. "I've spoken with Dr. Allcott on this subject. Apparently, he has been keeping your aunt and uncle up-to-date on your progress. They changed their minds by the time they arrived back in New York and called Dr. Allcott."

"What? Really? Why wasn't I told?"

"They asked Dr. Allcott not to. Does that knowledge alter the way you feel about them?"

I'm stunned. All of these years I've spent resenting my aunt and uncle and they've been getting status reports on me. In their ways, they do care. Except they still have made no contact with me.

"Somewhat, yes. But family is important. Just because they are getting up-to-date information about my progress doesn't mean they love me. I've not received so much as a birthday card from them."

"It doesn't mean they don't love you either."

"I need time to digest this, Alex."

"I understand. We will leave it alone for now and come back to that subject. I think you have enough on your plate right now."

"I do."

"Now, you expressed a desire to continue. Are you still up to it?"

"Yes."

I drink some water then begin speaking.

Chapter Seventeen

"I've been out of school for the summer. It was a relief because I didn't have to face all my classmates. But summer was nearly over and I still didn't have any answers. My father was gone, Beth was gone. I couldn't come to grips with any of it. My father didn't come back into my head or in person—if you can call it that—and Beth didn't meet me at our fort.

"A funeral was held—again—for my father, which was exactly the same as the first one we had. Only Mom and Kyle don't remember that time. Maybe I dreamt it. Maybe I saw into the future. I don't know. I only know I had to put myself through three funerals in the matter of a very short span of time, two of which were for my father. Crazy.

"My mother and Kyle were still introverts. I was alone. Just me. No best friend, no family. I spent the summer by myself. I would sit for hours in our fort, but Beth never showed up. I even walked out to the bridge where my father drowned several times to see if he'd show up. Nothing.

"I was beginning to believe that none of it happened. My father didn't visit or talk to me from the grave like the first time, nor did Beth come and see me from this other side. That is, until things started happening again. I'm not sure how to explain what I'm talking about, but I'll try because it's important.

"It was early August and it was hot and sticky. We had air conditioning in our house, but my bedroom upstairs still felt about a hundred degrees. Of course, that's an exaggeration, but Mom hated running the air at night, so it was stuffy. I put a fan in front of my window and it helped a little. Anyway, it was early morning, around six, I think. Kyle came running into my room, saying he had a bad dream. I have to tell you that Kyle has *never* run into my room about some nightmare."

****

"Mel!" he was shaking me awake and I could hear him yelling it more than once.

"I wanted him to go away and let me sleep, but he wouldn't. I pushed his hand off me and stuck my head under my pillow.

"You have to wake up. Please!"

"I realized his nudging and insistent whining wasn't going to stop, so I threw the pillow off my head and opened my eyes. I was lying on my left side, head toward the door.

"What?" I mumbled.

"He was standing there in his pajama bottoms and nothing else. Apparently, he thought his dream was so important, he couldn't bother putting a robe or shirt on before he barged into my room.

"I had a dream. Dad was in it."

"And?" I prompted.

"Mel, I have to talk to you. Please get up."

"He pulled the covers off me. I sat up and rubbed my eyes.

"Fine, tell me about your dream."

"You already know, don't you? Dad said you did."

73

"What are you talking about? Dad is dead."

"I *know*, but in my dream, he wasn't."

"I was awake then. I mean fully awake. Had he experienced what I did? Was Dad talking to him now? Is that why I haven't seen him or heard him in my head? I was getting excited that maybe finally someone will believe me and I won't be so alone.

"I stood up and pulled a robe over my pajamas then sat back down on the bed Indian style. Kyle sat next to me.

"Tell me what you're talking about."

"Don't think I'm crazy. I'm not. I swear to you. I can't go to Mom with this. You are the only one who will listen to me."

"I'm listening. Are you going to get to the point?"

"I was waiting, breathless and anxious. I hoped he was going to validate me when I said Dad was talking to me and that Beth was alive. If he did that, I'd know I wasn't nuts.

"Is this about when I tried to tell you Beth wasn't dead?"

"What? What are you talking about?"

"Clearly he didn't remember me wanting to run away when they tried to tell me Beth was dead, back when I thought Dad was still alive. At least, he was in our kitchen then.

"Never mind. So what about Dad?"

"I had a bad dream. He came to me and told me his death was no accident. He did drown, but someone was the cause of it. He was murdered."

"I sat there and stared at him. It was almost exactly what Dad told me.

"Uh, huh," was all I said.

"Kyle didn't realize I had even spoken because he just continued on, without even looking at me.

"It must have been a dream, but I remember going to the bathroom and coming back to my room. Maybe I was sleepwalking, who knows. All of a sudden, Dad was talking to me. I didn't see him, I only heard him. It was a dream, right?"

"I didn't answer and I don't think he expected one.

"I had this warm feeling all over me the minute I went back into my room. I heard him in my head, but it was almost like his voice was everywhere."

"Uh, huh."

"He started telling me all kinds of stuff."

"Like what?"

"Like they were coming to the house to get *it*. I asked to get what, but I don't think he answered me. I can't remember. It's sort of fuzzy. Anyway, he did keep telling me to warn Mom."

"Who was coming?"

"It was a question I had asked and never got an answer to.

"I don't know. I didn't ask. At least I don't think I did. Dreams are like that, I guess. Weird, huh?"

"Yeah, weird. What else did Dad say?"

"That was it. I wanted...I *had* to come in and tell you. I don't know why. Sorry I woke you."

"It's okay. Did you tell Mom?"

"No, I came right to your room. I'm not telling Mom about my dream. She'll think I'm nuts. You do, too. I can tell."

"I was looking at him in a new light, wondering if I should tell him about my experiences. He must see me looking at him oddly and think it's because I don't believe him.

"No, I don't think you're crazy. As a matter of fact…"

"I was interrupted by Mom's bellows.

"Kyle? Melinda? Are you awake? I made breakfast!"

"Mom's awake? *And* she made breakfast?" I asked, shocked.

"Weird dream, weird Mom."

"That's for sure," I agreed.

"Come on, let's go eat."

"Wait, Kyle. I have to tell you something."

"Later. I'm hungry."

"He stepped out of my room and then popped his head back in.

"And don't tell Mom about my dream."

"Kyle, please. Wait."

"But he didn't stop. I heard him bounding down the stairs. I stayed there sitting on my bed. So, Dad was reaching out to Kyle now. I couldn't help it. I felt a little jealous that Dad stopped talking to me and went to Kyle instead. I couldn't blame him. I kept telling him to go away. I decided to see if I could get Dad to talk to me again. It was better than all of this quiet in the house.

"Dad? I whispered.

"No answer. "Dad? Kyle said you talked to him. Was he dreaming or are you real?"

"It was crazy, *I* was crazy. Did I really ask if my dead father was real? I shook my head and left my room.

"Mom and Kyle were in the kitchen. Mom was the happiest I'd seen her since Dad died. I look at her

76

warily and sat down at the table. She put a plate of eggs and toast in front of me.

"Bacon is up in a minute," she said in a singsong voice.

"Mom, are you okay?" I asked.

"Sure, honey. Why wouldn't I be?"

"Uh, because you haven't made breakfast for us in a long time. And you're smiling. And you're out of bed before noon."

"Kyle was busy shoveling food into his mouth and didn't join in the conversation.

"I know. I've been a bit down lately. After your father…"

"She got quiet for a minute then continued. "Anyway, things are good now. I'm feeling better. Your father wants me to be happy."

"He *wants* you to be happy?" I questioned.

"You know. He wouldn't want me to be so upset. Life has to go on."

"I looked at Kyle, who was looking at me. He stopped eating, fork halfway to his mouth. Something finally got his attention. He knew what I knew, which is that Dad got to Mom. Only Kyle probably thought he came to Mom in a dream, but I knew differently. It wasn't a dream. Dad was trying to get through to Kyle and now he was trying with Mom. I was still wondering why he didn't talk to me anymore. Despite the fact I didn't want him in my head, and wanted him to go away, I felt abandoned all over again.

"After getting dressed, I decided to walk to the bridge. I went to Kyle's room to see if he wanted to go. I knocked on his door.

"Yeah?"

"Kyle, it's me. I'm coming in."

"I opened the door. Kyle was standing in front of his window. His room was across the hall from mine and he had the view of the street. At least he was dressed now.

"What are you looking at?"

"I thought I saw… Never mind. What's up?"

"Saw what?"

"Nothing. Figment of my imagination, I'm sure."

"I let it go. I've had enough of seeing things myself. I didn't need to know about his craziness.

"I'm going to take a walk. Wanna come?"

"Sure. Nothing better to do."

"After leaving the house, I led the way to the now familiar path toward the bridge. There was a shortcut at the end of our street. If you cut through the woods and went left up a long hill, you ended up walking adjacent to the river.

"At the opening of the woods, Kyle asked where we were going.

"The bridge."

"Kyle stopped walking. I noticed and stopped, too.

"Why?" he asked.

"Why not?"

"Because that's where Dad died. You know that."

"I do know that. Kyle, I need to tell you something, but before I do, let's walk for a ways."

"I'm not sure I can go there, Mel. I haven't been there since…well, since Dad died."

"You have to face it sometime."

"It was like I was the older sister trying to help a younger brother, instead of the other way around. He was more scared than I was. I could see it written all over his face. He frowned and looked forward then back the way we had come. I understood his fear.

"Even from there, I could hear the rush of the river as it flowed up near the bridge. Or maybe it was my imagination since I'd been up here so many times over the summer. I really don't think anyone can hear it from the bottom of the hill. I don't remember hearing it so loudly before. As odd as it sounds, the water almost seemed angry; rushing to a destination only it knew about.

"I started walking again and I could hear Kyle following me, leaves crinkling under our feet.

"Mel?"

"I didn't turn around when I answered, "Yeah?"

"Have you been to the bridge since Dad died?"

"I know that Kyle used to go there a lot with his friends. I followed him once. They all hung around, feet in the water, sitting on larger boulders near the edge of the river.

"Yeah, a lot."

"Why?"

"Looking for answers."

"To what questions?"

"Let's just get there and I'll tell you."

"I started trudging up the long hill, my calves aching from the effort even though they should be used to it by now. I heard Kyle breathing hard behind me. I slowed down and let him catch up.

"I can hear the water," he said.

"So it *wasn't* me and my imagination.

"We didn't speak the rest of the way. At the top, we walked parallel to the water. It was loud, just as I heard it below. Its spray seemed to spit out quite a distance, sort of what I imagined would come out of a whale's blow-hole. I had learned in school that's what it was called. I remembered laughing out loud in class when I heard that term. I never forgot it.

"The water looked rough, much like you'd see after a good rain. It flowed quickly toward the bridge and down the small hill before it reached the underpass. They were more like rapids. I've never seen it this wild.

"Kyle and I slid down the small hill next to the bridge. I sat down on a boulder near the water's edge like I'd seen Kyle and his friends do. Kyle sat next to me. Neither of us spoke. We stared at the water, feeling its spray on our faces and arms as it rushed over rocks in its path. I don't know if it was the intensity of the river, but I was beginning to feel anxious. Almost like I was waiting for something, but I didn't know what.

"Kyle, what you told me this morning about your dream, was it a dream?"

"What does that mean?"

"I mean, things are different, aren't they? You saw Dad last night…"

"That was a bad dream. It made me miss him even more."

"Okay, you saw Dad *in your dream* and Mom acted weird this morning."

"What are you getting at?"

"I've seen Dad and heard him."

"You had dreams, too? Why didn't you tell me?"

"They weren't dreams, Kyle. It was daytime and I wasn't sleeping and I saw Beth and Dad warned me to tell Mom like he did you."

"It all came out in a rush of words, one after the other. I couldn't stop talking until I told him everything, even the part he didn't remember about me wanting to run away. He didn't interrupt me and let me chatter on.

"When I was done, he sat there with his mouth open, looking at me. After a minute, he averted his gaze to the water, almost as if he didn't want to look at me anymore.

"He didn't say anything for a while and I was starting to panic.

"Kyle? You don't believe me, do you?"

"He stood up and started throwing pebbles into the water.

"Kyle? Damn it, answer me."

"I heard you, Mel. What can I say to that? That I think you're crazy? That you're letting your imagination run away? I can't say any of that."

"He walked up the river a bit. He slipped a few times on the rocks and got his sneakers wet. I didn't follow him. I was worried he was going to tell Mom and they'd put me in a…well, a place like this. I guess it happened after all."

Chapter Eighteen

Sure enough, here I am. The place I dreaded back then, still do. I sigh and look down at the floor.

"You've stopped talking. Did you not want to tell me more of Kyle's response?"

"I do. This is so exhausting. I've never bared my soul this way before, you know. I never told the other doctors half of what I'm telling you. And honestly, it brings all the hurt back. Not that it ever really left, it's just, well, now I have to really think about everything. I've been avoiding it."

"This is best for you, Melinda. Avoidance is never a good thing. It's best to meet your problems head on. You'll understand that more as we go along."

"It's painful."

"I'm sure it is. And I feel honored you've shared this with me. Do you need a break?"

"I guess I do. I could use some air."

"Very well. Let's do that. When would you like to resume?"

"I want to do it later today, but I think my mind needs to forget for a while. Can we resume tomorrow? I can probably answer your question about Beth then, too."

"Tomorrow it is."

Chapter Nineteen

Alex

It was all I could do not to shake her from her insanity. Melinda is a nice girl, one who can possibly have a future. However, she's stuck in the past no matter how much she thinks she's living in the future.

And it's the past I'm interested in. She talks constantly about this paranormal subject. Her father's dead. Then he isn't. Then Beth is. I shake my head in confusion. It's all so strange and not what I expected to run into when I took this assignment. But there's no way I can stop now. Not yet.

Melinda also said she told her aunt and uncle everything and they insisted she needed help. Just what did she tell them? If it's the same from the police report, it's nothing that's going to aid in getting Melinda to recall everything. But maybe they know more than everyone thinks.

When speaking to Dr. Allcott about her aunt and uncle, he indicated they won't come back to California to see Melinda until she's completely healed.

And healing begins with remembering everything.

Chapter Twenty

The Other Side

As a father, it's so difficult to see your children crying and in pain. I watch as Melinda tells the doctor about Larry and Betty. I knew about that conversation and knew Melinda knew about it, but now she's reliving the deception again. She also tells the doctor about my death and of Beth's. Then she relays how I visited Kyle that night, when he thought it was a dream. It wasn't a dream. I was reaching out to him. I tried to get my family to listen to me back then. They finally did, but it wasn't enough and it was too late.

Just as I felt before, the sense of dread is overwhelming. After all this time, something is happening. Melinda needs protection. I'm not sure how the danger will come or what will exactly happen, but that black cloud is ominous. I'm staring at it, wishing it to give me answers when Meredith walks up.

"You're tense," she tells me as she put her hand on my shoulder. "What is it?"

"I'm not sure. Something is wrong. I hadn't wanted to worry you, but I believe it has to do with Melinda."

"What aren't you telling me, Paul? Is it the same business from the past?"

"I believe so. I think they found her."

"In Skyview? She's been safe there all this time.

What makes you think she's in danger now?"

Her voice rises a little. She's probably feeling the same fear I am.

"Don't you see the black cloud?"

"Yes, and I know what it means. But it can't be Melinda."

"Then who?"

Meredith stays quiet in thought for a minute before answering, "We have to do something, Paul. What can we do?"

"I'm not sure yet. I'm devising a plan, but it may be risky."

"For Melinda?"

"No."

"You? Why? You're already dead. He can't hurt you."

"You know the rules about going over and staying too long."

"Paul, you're not considering going for good, are you?"

"Not on purpose."

"Tell me your plan. I want to help."

"You're not going to like it. I'll need Kyle."

"We have one child in danger on the Earth. You're not endangering the one we have here."

"Let me explain before you quash my idea."

She's going to be furious. I don't know if it will work, but Kyle's influence can mean everything.

"Kyle and I need to go over. We need to try and stop this man from hurting Melinda."

"How are you going to do that? Even in human form, you can't hurt him."

"Actually, I can. Regardless, I don't want to hurt

him, well not kill him anyway. I want him to leave this area. I've been talking to a few people here. Others have gone over and swayed the living to do what they want them to."

"But how you will convince him of anything?"

"Not me. Kyle. Remember, they only saw how we were when we died. Kyle was only fifteen. That's what he'll see. A fifteen-year-old come back to life. Scare him. Many are scared of the dead."

"And?" she knew me well, that there was more.

"And that's where I come in. Once Kyle gets him to believe he's not dead after all, he might think twice about a lot of things. Me, specifically. It's one thing to see a kid that you believe you've killed is 'alive,' it's another to see a second person come back. It may be enough to scare him straight."

"Then I can help. I can go, too."

"No, it's too dangerous. It could take longer than we have. I can't risk anything more happening to you than it already has."

"But you'll risk our son?"

"No. The minute he sees Kyle, I'm sending him back. You know I won't do anything that could harm our children. It will be only me running the tight time line."

"I don't like it," she states, her mouth set in a grim line.

"I knew you wouldn't. Unless you have a better plan, it's all I have. We have to protect Melinda."

"I know, but I still don't like it."

Chapter Twenty-One

After I leave Alex's office, I decide to visit Mel's Place. I haven't been there in a while and am anxious to see it again. Once inside my little abode, I sit down and breathe slowly. I ran the entire way. I am in a tizzy, needing to be here. But now that I am, I don't know why I have such a burning need.

I look around and everything is pretty much as I'd left it. The cozy atmosphere immediately quiets my anxiety. A sense of belonging comes over me. And pride. I cleaned the place up and made it into a home...or at least as close as I could get. I hadn't realized until now, but this place is important. I don't know why, only that it is.

I step outside onto the small porch. The afternoon sun covers my face and I close my eyes to the warmth. I stay that way for a few minutes. I hear a noise off to the right, on the other side of the cottage. Is it an animal? Is it a person? Oh no! What if it is the owner coming to check things out? I'll be arrested for trespassing. I know my imagination is running away from me.

I take a deep breath and hold it, listening for another sound. I hear nothing. I finally stop holding my breath and gasp for air. I decide to explore beyond the little house. I've never gone further than the cottage. At the time, it was all I needed. There is no back door to the cottage so I never explored behind it. But hearing the noise makes me think about what may lay beyond my house of escape.

I step off the porch and round the right side. The bramble and weeds are taller than I am and I can't see anything. I don't feel like trying to scoot through all the bushes, so I go to the other side of the house. There are stones set down in the ground to form a walkway. Most of it is overgrown with weeds, but I can still see most of the steppingstones. I walk down the path past the house and into the back.

My eyes widen in amazement at what I find. There is a large tree with boards nailed to the trunk to form a ladder. My eyes follow it up and find a big tree house. I look left, right, and behind me then back at the tree house. I don't see anyone, my curiosity wins out, and I start climbing the boards.

I poke my head up into the man-made quarters. There is a small table sitting in the middle. I pull myself up inside and look around. There is one chair pulled up to the table and a candle sitting on the tabletop. A part of the tree trunk had been cut away and a flashlight and book sit on the ledge. I briefly wonder if it is the book that was missing from the cottage's bookshelves, but I don't bother to look, feeling it's not important right now. I turn to look at the other side and notice a sleeping bag with one pillow lying in the corner.

The entire place is dust free and tidy. It looks like someone comes up here often. I start to panic, wondering if whoever stays up here knows I visit the cottage. They must know, it's only a stone's throw from this tree. Another thought hits me: Whoever it is, may tell on me.

I quickly scurry down the tree and run back toward

the front of the cottage. Should I stay? I desperately want to be here right now. I don't want to leave, but what if whoever went into the tree house comes back and finds me here?

I have no choice. I must leave. I run back toward Skyview. When I enter the gardens I slow down to stroll and act like I am just enjoying the day. When I see that no one is around, I sit on a bench, my heart still pounding in my chest. I can't hear anything else over the noise it's making. I can almost feel the blood pumping to and from my heart as fast as the water flowed down the river the day I was there with Kyle.

I finally get myself under control and walk back toward my room. A million questions are running around in my head. I am afraid of the answers and not sure if I should ever go back to Mel's Place. It isn't my house and it isn't my tree, but someone is visiting it other than me. Who? And they must have noticed me before. So, why haven't they told on me yet?

It gives me a creepy feeling to know that someone in the tree could have watched me every time I went there. They can't see into the cabin, but from where the tree sits, they can see me coming toward it. I don't know what I will do if I can't go there anymore. It's my safe haven. It's where I can go to be alone with my thoughts and my books. Now what do I do?

Chapter Twenty-Two

The Other Side

"It's time. It's dark and it will make it scarier for him, hopefully. We need that advantage," I tell Kyle.

"I'm ready. Mom isn't too happy about this."

"I know, but I don't know what else to do."

Kyle and I find the portal and wait until we see him exit the building. When he does, Kyle crosses over. He waits for him to get into his car and turn the headlights on. Then he steps in front of the car. The man revs the engine and slips it into gear. Then hits the brakes instantly before he moves. I see the taillights.

Perfect. It's working. Kyle stands there for a moment then approaches the car.

"Who's there? What do you want?"

"You thought I was dead. I've come back to deliver a message," Kyle tells him.

"Damn animals," I hear him say.

Animals? Doesn't he see it's Kyle? Hear him?

He honks the horn.

"Get out of the way. I'll run your ass over, you fool dog."

Dog?

"Kyle!" I yell over to him. "Come back."

"Dad, what's going on? Why does he think I'm an animal? Can't he see me?"

"I don't think he can. Something is stopping him from seeing you. Let me try."

Kyle stays on the other side of the portal as I go over. The man is already moving forward in his car. I gather all the strength I can muster and block his path. I manage to stop his car.

"What the hell? Damn dog."

He thinks he's hit the animal. I move to the driver's door and smash the window. I'm able to do it, but for some reason, he can't see me anymore than he could Kyle. What's blocking his view? Is it his disbelief? I've heard that can happen.

I see him leaning over toward the passenger seat. Glass is all over the inside of his car, in his hair and on his clothing.

I start screaming at him, "Leave. You must leave this city at once."

He throws open the driver's door and gets out. He has a gun in his hand. He brushes the glass from himself and starts looking all around, his head whipping from left to right and back again. He walks around his car looking into the night.

"Who's there?" he yells out.

I grab the gun from his hand and he screams in surprise.

"What the hell?"

He backs up around the car to the driver's door, facing forward the whole time and squinting his eyes like it would help him see better into the darkness. But he still doesn't see me. A slash of fear crosses his face. *Good.*

He tries to get back into his car, but I pull him by his arm and he sprawls on the ground, landing on his stomach. I hear him grunt as he rolls over onto his back. He props himself up on his elbows and I kick them out from under him and he falls on his back again.

Quickly, he gets to a standing position. I tap him on the shoulder and he whirls around.

"What the fuck is going on? Who's there?"

I laugh. I can't help it. I hear my summons. I have to go. One more try.

"Leave this town. You hear me?"

He shakes his head and backs up to his car again. I let him get into the driver's seat and close the door. Through the broken window, I reach in and turn his windshield wipers on. This is fun. I'd enjoy it more it if didn't involve my daughter.

"Holy shit," the man says.

"Dad! Hurry up!" I hear Kyle saying.

I'm running out of time. I hear my last warning.

Hopefully, that was enough to scare the bejesus out of him and he'll leave.

He practically slams the car into drive and peels away. I don't try to stop him. I hope I didn't fail. I won't let him hurt Melinda. I go toward the portal. I see Kyle beckoning me. I reach out, the opening is slowly closing. I *have* to make it back.

Chapter Twenty-Three

The next day, I am on my way to see Alex again when Nurse Hamilton stops me.

"Have you had your breakfast?"

"Yes, Ma'am."

"Good. You're needed in the kitchen. Stella is...no longer here."

"Did she get to go home?"

"Don't ask questions. Just please do as you're told."

"Yes, Ma'am."

I walk into the kitchen and find the counters piled high with dirty dishes. Manuel, the cook and all-around kitchen guy, is scrubbing pots at the sink.

He turns and sees me and says, "Thank God someone is here to help."

I smile at him and walk over. I've always liked Manuel. He is nice, gives me extra biscuits, and snacks when no one is looking. He never asks what I am doing with them and I don't volunteer the information that I am taking it all to Mel's Place to munch on.

"Hi, Manuel. What happened to Stella? I heard she wasn't here anymore."

"All's I know is she left. Home I guess."

I pick up a dishtowel and start drying dishes he has stacked in the drainer.

"I wish they'd put in a dishwasher. Would make

my job easier," he grumbles.

He complains a lot, but I doubt he will ever leave. He was here when I arrived nine years ago and had been for some time before that.

"Got ya a little care package over there," he nods toward the counter on the far end of the kitchen.

I start walking over to it, but he stops me.

"Can't have it 'til we're done here, though."

I roll my eyes at him and smile. We work together in silence for a while. The only noises the click and clatter of dishes and splashes of soapy water.

"So what ya doin' with the stuff I give you?"

It is a question I'm not expecting. He never asks.

"I'm hungry."

He looks at me and raises an eyebrow.

"Doubt it. You eat all that in one sittin' you'd at least have some meat on them bones. I see you eat in the lunchroom. You eat like a bird. So, you savin' it all and eat it somewhere else?"

"Maybe."

"Where? Garden?"

"Sometimes."

"You're not goin' tell me, are ya?"

We are almost done with the dishes. There are only a few left on the counter.

"Can you get the rest here? I have an appointment I'm late for."

"Yeah, go ahead. Take your stuff over there."

I smile and thank him, telling him I'll come back and get it later.

"I'll put it in the closet. You know where it'll be."

He always leaves things for me in the furthest corner of the pantry. Half the time he doesn't say anything, I just look and there it will be for me. He is the only one here I will miss when I leave. Well, probably Nurse Hamilton, too. And mark my words, I *will* leave here. One way or the other.

I rush up to Alex's office.

"Alex, I'm sorry I'm late. I had kitchen duty."

His office is empty. He didn't wait for me. Probably went to see another important patient. Someone who isn't quite as nuts as me. I walk over to the window and look outside. My mind goes back to my secret place. Who is staying in that tree? Is it safe to go back there?

I sigh loudly.

"What's weighing so heavily on your mind today?"

I whirl around to find Alex standing right inside the doorway. I am startled but relieved to see him.

"I thought you left because I was late. I had to do dishes with Manuel."

"I was told and I didn't leave nor would I without letting you know. Now, what were you sighing about?"

"Another time for that," I answer.

He closes the door and walks further into the room.

"Have you started the book I gave you?"

"I tried, but I was too upset to get into it. I will, though. I appreciate you bringing it to me."

"You're welcome. I think you need a change of scenery for a few hours. How would like to go to lunch off-campus today?"

Off-campus? Sounds like I'm in college.

"Really? Will Dr. Allcott let me?"

"I've already asked and he said yes. I will be responsible for you. We're only going into town and I promised to have you back in two hours. I know this little cafe I think you just may like."

"Why do you want to take me to lunch?"

"Because I like you, Melinda. I want to see you make as much progress as you can. It's in you. You just have to let it come out."

"You really think so?"

I'm beyond happy. Does this mean I might get to leave here some day? Will he tell them all I'm fine?

"I do. So, would you like to go?"

"Yes!"

Without thinking, I run to him and hug him. Then I realize what I'm doing and quickly detach myself.

"I'm sorry, Alex. I'm just excited and well…it won't happen again." I feel my face turning red.

He laughs softly. "It's okay, Melinda. No, you shouldn't make a habit of that, but I understand and take it for what it is. Your happiness."

"Thank you for understanding."

"How about we pick up where we left off yesterday?"

"I suppose."

Alex's offer of lunch out of this place helped get my mind off the tree house. Now I need to concentrate on where in the story I am. I must continue before Alex gets tired of me.

He walks around and sits behind his desk.

"Whenever you're ready."

I go and sit in the now familiar chair, curling my legs under me. When I'm ready? I'll never be ready, but I must do what I must in order to get what I want. So, here goes.

Chapter Twenty-Four

"We were talking about the river where Dad drowned in 2005. Kyle and I were there. I told Kyle everything and was waiting for him to announce that he thought I was crazy. But that's not what happened.

"I was trailing after Kyle as he walked down the river and when he finally spoke I was so shocked at his words that I slipped and almost fell into the water.

"I believe you, Mel. About everything. I didn't tell you everything about the dream last night. Dad told me so much. I didn't think you were ready to hear it all, but I guess you've been through more."

"You believe me?"

"After saving myself from a good drenching, I sat down on a rock and stared at Kyle.

"I said I did. I don't know what's going on with Beth, but having Dad back from the dead is enough to make me believe anything."

"I was quiet for a minute, letting his words sink in. It was hot that day and I wore shorts. I remember feeling the water spray on my bare legs and it felt good. If I could just concentrate on that, maybe I could forget everything else that was happening. But I knew it was impossible.

"Tell me everything that happened with Dad last night."

"He joined me on the rock and looked out at the

97

water.

"Like I told you, he talked to me. It seemed important to him that I warn Mom about someone coming to get something."

"I agree that he really wants us to tell Mom. Do you think she already knows? She seemed so much better this morning and she mentioned Dad."

"But if he came and warned her, she wouldn't be all smiles."

"Unless all she could think about was he was with her and maybe he didn't get to tell her about the other people."

"Maybe," Kyle agreed. He dug into his pocket and pulled something out. "Dad gave me this last night. I think maybe it's what he meant by someone coming to get something."

"He handed me a folded up envelope. I opened it and took out a sheet of paper. It had a lot of numbers on it and I had no idea what it meant.

"What is this?" I asked.

"I'm not sure. I think maybe account numbers."

"To what?"

"Banks? Maybe Dad hid someone's money or something."

"And they're coming to our house looking for these numbers?"

"I handed the paper and envelope back to Kyle, jumped up off the rock, and walked toward the bridge again. I was scared, *really* scared. For me, for Kyle, for Mom. Even for Dad. He was dead all because of money?

"Kyle came up behind me.

"We can give them this paper and they'll leave us

alone," he suggested.

"Give it to who? We don't know *who* they are."

"Okay then we can leave it on the front porch or something. That way they'll go away and leave us alone."

"I thought about it and realized it wasn't such a bad idea.

"Okay. But how will we know they took it and not some random person?"

"I don't know."

"He looked as frustrated as I felt. But I didn't quit pestering him with my questions.

"And how do we know that's what they even want?" I asked.

"They do."

"Oh my gosh, Dad was back!

"Kyle," I whispered.

"I know," he answered. "It's Dad."

"You hear him?" I asked, still ignoring my father.

"You two need to listen to me. I don't want you dealing with any of this. Give it to your mother."

"Did you talk to her? Is that why she's so happy this morning?" I asked.

"I tried, and yes, she knows I'm around. I'm not sure how much she believes."

"What's going on, Dad? This is freaking me out," Kyle admitted.

"I've been listening to the two of you talk. These people are dangerous. I—"

"If they're so bad, why were you dealing with them?" I retorted, cutting him off.

"I was angry. My father ruined our whole family. At one time, we were a happy family of four. He got himself killed and made us a miserable family of three.

"It wasn't by choice. I didn't realize what was going on until it was too late. I didn't get involved on purpose."

"Involved in what?" Kyle asked.

"It's not for you to worry about. Do not leave that envelope just lying around. Give it to your mother. I will tell her what to do with it."

"We can go to the police," Kyle said.

"And tell them what? That Dad is dead and he's telling us what happened to him, and he gave you an envelope? Wait...how did Dad give you an envelope? Dad, you can do that?"

"Yes. I had enough energy to move the envelope into Kyle's room last night. I put it where he could see it."

"Why are you talking to us in our heads? Why not out loud?" Kyle asked. "Better yet, why not appear in person like you did to Mel?"

"Listen, right now the only thing that matters is that you are all safe."

"I'm not putting Mom in danger," Kyle said. "If I give her this, they'll come get it from her. Then they'll kill her and we won't have any parents. No."

"Kyle sounded firm and for emphasis began walking up the incline to the top of the hill. He stuck the envelope in his back pocket.

"Kyle," I yelled after him. "Wait! Dad, stop him."

"I can't. Get him to do as I asked."

"Dad, please. I don't want them to kill Mom either."

"I didn't get a response. The water slowed and was suddenly flowing calmly, like it typically did. It was then I realized the rapidly churning of the water was because Dad was there. It must have been his energy.

"Kyle!"

"He stopped walking and waited for me to catch up.

"Dad, can't you do something else?" I asked.

"He didn't answer and I knew for sure he was gone.

"Kyle, what are we going to do?"

"I know what to do and it's *not* giving this to Mom."

"Then what?"

"We're going to hide this. Then the three of us are leaving that house."

"What? Where would we go? Mom's not going to want to leave."

"I'll convince her. In the meantime, we need to put this someplace safe."

"Why not give it to them?"

"Dad died because he had this information. I'm not going to let them have it. They ruined our lives and I hope theirs is ruined by not having these numbers," Kyle said.

"He was obviously upset. I could tell by looking at his face. It had turned red and he was scowling. He was beginning to scare me. Kyle started looking around the area. I saw his eyes dart to the bridge, then down the slope to the water and then he turned around in a circle, surveying the area.

"What are you looking for?"

"A good place to hide this."

"You mean you want to bury it out here?"

"Sure. They wouldn't think of looking for it here."

"But it will get wet and moldy. Wait! We can put it in a plastic bag to bury it," I suggested.

"Good thinking. I'll go back to the house and get something. You wait here."

"No. Let me go. I don't want to be here alone. Besides, while I'm gone, you can find the right place."

"The place was starting to creep me out for some reason. It never did before, but now it was like being alone with death. Dad died here and then he talked to both of us here.

"Fine, but hurry," Kyle agreed.

"I ran as fast as I could home. When I got to the porch, the door was wide open. I knew that when Kyle and I left earlier, I closed it. I wished now I let Kyle come. I was scared. Did Mom leave and not shut the door? No, she would never do that. Besides, her car is in the driveway. Was she inside? Was someone hurting her?

"I didn't want to go in the house so I crept off the porch and around the side to the backyard. I glanced around and at first, didn't see anyone. Then I noticed that at the end of the path Beth stood there waving to me. I couldn't believe my eyes. Beth? I was conflicted. Did I run to her or did I go inside and make sure Mom was okay? Of course, Mom won out. Family always did.

"A thought dawned on me. Beth appeared before when Dad died. Does that mean Mom's dead? No! I must go check *now*.

"I have to see you later," I yelled out to Beth.

"That's when I realized I may have given myself away to whoever was in the house and quickly clamped a hand over my mouth. My eyes darted to the back door. I crept up to the stoop and peered through the kitchen window. It was empty. That was a good sign. Well, it all depended on how you looked at it. Was Mom in the living room? Who was in our house?

"I turned the knob on the kitchen door. Locked. Now what? I wondered. I'd have to go through the front door. Maybe I could get Beth to go with me. I looked back toward the path, but she was gone. If she was even there before. The thought of Mom being dead ran through my head again. Please, God. Not again!

"I thought about running back to get Kyle, but it could be too late if Mom was injured or something. No, I had to check on Mom. I had to know she was okay after seeing Beth. And I needed that plastic bag. I was the one who insisted Kyle let me come here. I know I wasn't thinking straight. I was too frightened and my mind was in a thousand different places with just as many scenarios as to why our front door was open.

"I sneaked back around to the front. The door was still open and I couldn't see anyone. I was sweating now and it wasn't from the heat. My mouth was dry and I licked my lips. Swallowing hard, I tiptoed onto the porch. I peeked through the doorway into the living room. No one was there. I walked further into the house.

"Mom?" I whispered.

"I checked out the rooms downstairs. No Mom. I slowly walked up the stairs, trying not to make any noise. I got to the top, rounded the corner, and ran smack into my mother. She was carrying a box and it fell to the floor.

"Melinda! What in God's name are you doing slinking around?"

"Mom?"

"Well, who do you think it is?"

"I don't know. The front door was open."

"I opened it. I've been in and out with boxes of clothes I'm taking to the women's shelter. What are you and Kyle doing?"

"Hanging around."

"My mind was definitely full of imagination. Here I thought someone broke into our house and hurt our mother and it was just her loading the car with boxes.

"Help me with these. I have one more box. Take this one out to the car. It's light. I'll get the other one."

"Okay."

"I had to get back to Kyle. I put the box in the car and ran back into the house before my mother could even come down the stairs. I went into the kitchen and found some plastic baggies. I grabbed three of them and darted out the back door. I didn't want Mom to make me do anything else.

"I ran around the right side of the house, opposite of where our driveway is. I checked and Mom wasn't out there. I dashed into the woods at the end of the street. At the bottom of the long hill, I finally stopped to catch my breath.

"I leaned forward putting my hands on my bent knees and…that's all I remember until I woke up near the bridge with Kyle standing over me looking worried."

Chapter Twenty-Five

"Did you faint or is it something you blocked out?" Alex asks, bringing me back to the present.

"I don't think I fainted, at least not at the bottom of the hill. Kyle said we buried the envelope, but I don't remember it. I must have blocked it out. Maybe I don't want to know where it's buried."

"Perhaps your subconscious is shielding you. You may not have been ready before now. Did Kyle tell you where it is?"

"No. At the time, he said that if I didn't remember it, it's probably for the best. I agreed with him."

"Total recall is important, Melinda. Have you ever considered hypnosis?"

Of course I know what that is, but I don't know anyone who's experienced it and I don't think I like the idea.

"No. I don't think I'm ready for that."

"I've already spoken to Dr. Allcott about the idea. He feels like it would be beneficial for you."

"I don't know. It sounds dangerous."

"It is not perilous in the least if it is being performed by a professional. I've done it several times before. It has helped many patients in the past."

"I don't know."

"My recommendation is you consider it. It can help you move forward. That is what you want, isn't it?"

"Of course. Okay, I'll think about it."

The thought of being under someone else's control makes me nervous. What if I tell him things he shouldn't know? Then again, I'm already giving him the ins and outs of my entire life. By the time I'm done, he'll know everything anyway. Maybe he's right and I should try it. I'll talk to Dr. Allcott about it since he already knows. Maybe he can help me make up my mind.

Still, I'm apprehensive. But like I told him, I'll consider it.

"Excellent idea. Now, tell me how you felt having your father there with you and Kyle."

"It was creepy, just like it was the first time. Only the time with Kyle, he was in both of our heads." I shuddered. "I never got used to it."

"Does that mean he spoke to you since then?"

"Yes, many times."

"And he didn't see from above or wherever he is where you and Kyle hid the paper?"

"I don't think so. He never said and honestly, I never thought to ask him."

"Do you still speak with him now? Perhaps you could ask."

"I haven't heard from him by voice or in-person since I was put in here."

I lower my head and frown, my heart breaking all over again.

"And your mother?" Alex asked. "Did she get better?"

"She started taking care of us again. We were like a family, minus Dad. It was good, but weird."

"How much did she know about your father

speaking to you and Kyle, if anything?"

"She knew. She just didn't want to talk about it."

"Melinda, so far you've told me a part of the story that created the situation that put you in here. I want you to continue telling me in your own time, in your own way, but I feel that you are skirting around one real issue."

"Which is what?"

"Your feelings. You're not really saying how you felt throughout any of it."

"What do you want me to say? That it all sucks?"

"If that's how you feel, yes."

"Well, it does and it did. I lost my father that year. At this point in the story, I lost my mother and Kyle for a while *and* I lost my best friend. I was alone with no one to talk to. When Kyle and Mom started to get back to normal, I was still alone. I mean, yes, I had them to talk to, but not about what happened to Dad and Beth. Well, except for Kyle anyway. So, how do you think I would feel?"

I can't believe I said what I did. Not once before did I admit to any of it out loud. Then again, not one doctor ever asked how I felt. Now I know I can trust Alex.

"Speaking of Beth, did you see her again after that day?" he asked, ignoring my little outburst.

"Yes," I answer quietly. I am getting tired, but there is one last thing I have to tell him today. "It was that night and several nights after."

"Go on."

Chapter Twenty-Six

"The familiar tapping at my window woke me up that night. Beth was there tossing pebbles. She used to do that a lot before...well, before she died. She was standing in the backyard. When she saw me, she began beckoning to me.

"I immediately threw on my robe and slippers and ran down the stairs and out the back door. I flew into her arms and hugged her tight.

"I've missed you. Where have you been?" I asked.

"It's a long story. Come on," she grabbed my hand. "Let's go to the fort."

"We ran to the fort. I'm not sure why we didn't walk, but at the time, I didn't question it. I was just really glad to see her.

"I wouldn't let her off the hook. I wanted to know where she had been, what was going on. I asked her questions as I slipped out of my robe and tossed it in the corner. It was August and it was warm out, even that late.

"So, where were you? You're here one minute and gone the next."

"Yeah, for a while it works that way."

"What do you mean? What works what way?"

"Being dead. You know I'm dead, Melinda."

"I really didn't know that. I mean, yes, I knew everyone said she died, but I know I spent that time with her earlier before Dad died. I was so confused.

"How did you die? What happened?"

"Things are fuzzy. I can't remember everything and I don't know why. I've tried, but all I remember is gasping for breath and being in water."

"The way she said it was ominous sounding. I felt like she might know something more and wasn't telling me.

"If you're dead, how are you here? How are you talking to me?"

"It's the Other Side. You get to come back, I guess. They said that's part of the rules."

"Who said? Where is this other side?"

"Where dead people go. Don't you know anything about it? I guess you wouldn't. You're not dead. You'll understand when you are."

"I don't want to die, but I want to know now."

"It's my new home. I run into your dad sometimes. He..."

"What?" I interrupted her. "You saw my father?"

"Coupla times. He always seems so worried. They said you're not supposed to be worried there, so I was surprised. He asked if I came back to see you. I said once. He was starting to tell me to tell you something, but my protector interrupted him and I had to go."

"Beth, you aren't making any damn sense. You saw my dad and you *talked* to him?"

"Yes."

"You don't know what he wanted me to know?"

"No. My protector said it was time for me to get settled with my family."

"What the hell is a protector?"

"Beth giggled and said, "Someone who watches

over you and guides you. Kinda like a social worker in your world."

"My world? Beth, this is your world, too."

"She frowned and looked down at the ground.

"Not anymore, Melinda. But hey, I get to come see you!"

"She turned her frown into a smile. I think it was really for my benefit, so I wouldn't feel bad for her. She was always like that. She hated pity.

"She stood up and walked to the doorway of the fort, looking out into the black forest.

"What aren't you saying?"

"Again, I had that feeling that she was hiding something.

"Nothing."

"I didn't pursue the subject. When it was time, she would tell me.

"You have a family there?"

"Yeah, everyone who passed before me and there are even some relatives I never met. They're great, but I miss mine here. They said it's hard at first, the transition. After a while, it's supposed to get easier."

"So, what you're saying is when you die, you go somewhere else and start all over?"

"Sort of."

"Where is it? Can I come visit you there? Hey! I can visit my dad!"

"I was starting to get excited. The thought of actually seeing Dad again and hugging him made me so happy I almost started crying.

"No, you can't go there. You're still alive. Only dead people can go there."

"I was crushed. I ached to see my father again. It

wasn't fair.

"Why hasn't he come to visit me lately?"

"I don't know."

"I still don't get it. You can come here to see people, but I can't go there. Dad came to see me and Kyle a few times and we've heard him, too."

"You hear him?"

"Yes. Kyle, too. Sometimes, he just talks to us. It's like in our heads. Other times, he's shown up like you."

"I'm still learning the rules myself, but from what I know, you get to come back and visit with people you left behind. Only some can see you though. Most don't believe. If you don't believe, coming to visit is a waste of time for us. Like my mom and dad."

"You can't visit with them?"

"I can, but they don't know I'm there. I've tried. Like I said, people of Earth have to believe. They don't."

"My heart was breaking for her. At least Kyle and I've heard from Dad, so has Mom. It must be killing her—no pun intended—every time she tried to talk to her parents and they didn't know it. How sad.

"Then why doesn't Dad get to see us more often? Kyle and I believe."

"Anger. They said if you can't get over the anger of being murdered, if that's the case, you can't go back until you do. I heard a rumor though that you can talk to people, but you're not supposed to. Your dad is probably breaking the rules."

"I think he's pissed. He told me he was murdered, it wasn't an accident that he drowned."

"Beth came back and sat down next to me. She grabbed my hand like she's done a million times before.

111

The familiarity calmed me and I enjoyed the moment.

"So, what happened to you?" I asked her.

"I think I fell into the river. I guess I hit my head on a rock when I fell."

She used to always avert her eyes from mine and become fidgety when there was something she wasn't telling me. She was doing that now.

"What are you leaving out, Beth?" I asked again, knowing I probably wouldn't get an answer.

"Nothing you need to worry about."

"I don't believe you."

"Fine. I just can't tell you, but it's not important right now. What is important is that we get to see each other."

"True," I let the issue go for the moment, but knew I would get all of the facts out of her eventually. "How many times can you come back?"

"I don't know yet."

"How do you get back and forth?"

"Listen, I have to go. I hear my protector calling me."

"Wait! Can you tell my Dad something?"

"If I see him."

"Tell him Kyle and I want to help. Ask him what we need to do to help. He said we're in danger."

"Okay."

"She got up and started walking out of the fort. I began following her when she stopped me.

"You can't follow me. Stay here for a few minutes then you can leave."

"Why?"

"They don't want you knowing where I go."

"It's not like it will do me any good if they won't

let me in."

"If you get in before your time..." She stopped speaking and cocked her head to the left, ear upward, like she was listening. "I have to go."

"Okay. I hope I see you soon. And tell my dad I love him!" I yelled out as she left.

"After that, Beth came every couple of days. Each time, I asked about my father and she said she hadn't seen him. Neither Kyle nor I had heard from him."

Chapter Twenty-Seven

"At the time, I was worried I wouldn't hear from my dad or see him again," I tell Alex as I stand and stretch.

"Did you ever talk to your mother about it?"

"Not right away," I say through a yawn. "She would change the subject anytime Kyle or I brought up Dad."

"Did you tell Kyle about Beth's visits?"

I start pacing his office between the window and door.

"Yes. We both visited with her. She told us all kinds of things about the place they call the Other Side."

"Like what?"

I ignore the question and stop talking and look at Alex to see if he believes this last bit of information I give him. He appears to. At least I don't see doubt written across his face like the other doctors before him.

"Do you believe me, Alex?"

"I believe that you do. Isn't that enough for now?"

"No. You said you'd be honest with me, that if you thought I was crazy, you'd tell me."

"Yes, I did say that. And I am being honest. You believe it and that makes it real to you. Melinda, you have to give me time to digest this "other side" you're telling me about. It's not a typical story I hear all the time."

"I know."

"The doctor in me needs some kind of proof it exists. But the human in me knows there are things out there we don't understand. This could be one of those things."

"So, do you believe that it could exist?"

I walk over to the table, pour some water, and drink the entire glass down. I am thirsty from all the talking.

"Like I said, right now, I know you believe it. That's enough for me. To be honest, Melinda, I will be researching the probability. It's how my mind works. I don't discount anything without looking into it as much as I possibly can. Back when I said I would always be honest with you, I also said that it would be your decision as to whether or not you wish to continue to see me. Knowing how I feel, do you want to end our relationship?"

I look at him for a few minutes. No one else has ever been this forthright. At least he didn't immediately discredit my story before he checked into the possibility. And relationship? Yes, I feel we have one. We are becoming friends, at least in my opinion. I decide to ask him.

"Alex, do you think we are friends or could be?"

"Would you like that?"

"Yes, I would." I am certain of that. "I've never been able to speak so freely with anyone before."

"I think right now, we have a good, candid working relationship. Yes, I do believe you need friends. I would be happy to be yours."

I smile. I am glad. He is the first real friend I've

had since coming here. I had a few along the way. Stephanie for one, but she killed herself. Others, but they are more like acquaintances because we live in the same home. I even like Nurse Hamilton. But a true friend that I could say anything I wanted to? Alex is the first.

"I believe it's lunchtime. Are you ready to go?"

I smile. Lunch away from here!

"Absolutely!"

"Very well. We have to stop by Dr. Allcott's office to sign you out."

We walked to the office and Alex signed me out. Dr. Allcott reminded him that he needed me back here in two hours. Alex agreed and we left.

We walk into the back parking lot. I've never been back here before. When I was brought here, we arrived in the front parking lot and I was ushered through the main entrance. The back is fenced off and the patients don't have access to anything past the garden on the side. Well, at least we aren't supposed to.

Alex unlocks his SUV and I jump into the front seat. Weird. I haven't even been in a car in years. This particular road ends at Skyview Haven, so after we pull out of the front gate, we drive straight for a little ways. He makes several turns onto back roads before we end up in Banning. It's not far from Skyview, just minutes. He turns into a small parking lot next to a building boasting the Best Cafe in Banning. I hope so. I'm looking forward to some food not made at the institution.

A little bell tinkles over the door when we walk in.

"Counter or booth?" a hostess asks walking up to us.

"Melinda?" Alex asks.

"Booth?" I question hesitantly.

"Booth it is."

We follow the lady to a booth next to a bank of windows overlooking the parking lot. I can see Alex's SUV. She hands us some menus and says she'll be back with some water.

"So, what do you feel like having?" Alex asks. "You can have anything you want."

I look at the menu. There are a lot of choices and it's hard to make up my mind. The waitress comes back with some water and asks if we know what we want.

"Can you give us a minute?" Alex asks.

"Have you eaten here before?" I ask.

"Yes, many times. I recommend the French onion soup. The turkey club is also good."

"Then I'll have that."

"Are you sure?"

I am actually too nervous to keep reading the menu. My eyes keep darting all over the restaurant. People smiling, kids laughing, couples sitting together. I haven't been out in the real world in years.

"That sounds good, yes."

He motions to the waitress and places our order. He ordered a salad and half a pastrami sandwich.

"Tell me how you feel being out," Alex says after the waitress leaves.

"Overwhelmed is the first word that comes to mind. Also happy. Thank you for this, Alex."

"You're welcome. Any anxiety?"

"Maybe a little. This is sort of new to me. I haven't been out to eat in a restaurant since my family was alive."

"I just want to make sure you're comfortable. If you're not, we can leave any time."

"I'm okay."

And I really am. I watch a few cars going in and out of the parking lot before speaking again.

"Alex, tell me about...about the world out there. I was a teenager when I left it and I know nothing about it. Have things changed much?"

"Tremendously. Most people, as you can see," he waves his hand to encompass the restaurant, "are more into texting and talking on their cell phones than they are talking to the people right in front of them."

I didn't notice before, but he's right. It seems like several people are doing just that. I've never owned a cell phone, but yes, I of course, know what they are. I'm not that out of the loop. Nurse Hamilton has one. I've seen her use it.

"I think it's sad."

"It is, indeed," Alex says. "Real communication between individuals is rare these days. They'd rather text and tweet."

"Tweet?" Now I have no idea what he's talking about.

"Twitter is a social media site. When chatting via Twitter, they call them tweets. Facebook is another of those sites. The kids these days spend all their time on them."

"Why not just call the person?"

"Why not is a good question. Let's see, what else has changed? There are more people around, which means more traffic. Even in the small towns around here."

"What about Beaumont?"

"Ah, where you grew up. Still small, but getting overpopulated, like here. But quite charming, all the same."

"I liked Beaumont. I don't know much about Banning."

"It's very similar to Beaumont. Do you know the city well?"

"Kyle and I traveled all over that place. I know almost every area there is. Well, I did. I'm not sure now."

"The river where your father died? Did you go there often?"

For just these few hours, I don't want to think about my past. I want to enjoy the present.

"Do you mind if we don't talk about any of that stuff right now? This is like a nice break for me."

"Of course. I understand."

"Tell me about you," I say.

"There's not much to say. You know I'm a doctor. I live here in Banning. I like the small communities like that."

"Do you go to church or anything?"

"On occasion. Actually, on religious holidays I do. I admit I'm not an every Sunday attendee."

"Don't you believe in God?"

"Yes, I do. What about you?"

"I did. I guess I still do. I just get angry a lot with him. He could have helped me in the past and now, really, but he hasn't."

"Perhaps he did help and you just didn't know it."

"Maybe. Actually, now that I think about it, maybe he's helping now. He brought you to me."

Alex smiles and says, "Yes, maybe he's here with

you now."

The food arrives and we eat in silence. Alex is right. The french onion soup is delicious. So is the sandwich. I can't believe how hungry I am. I haven't eaten this much in one setting in a lot time.

I finish my entire meal and feel like I can still eat, but I don't want to take advantage. It's nice of him to take me to lunch. Alex must be reading my mind.

"How about dessert? They have some wonderful pies here."

I order banana cream pie and he orders apple. It tastes great and I eat the whole slice. I'm finally full. After we're done, he pays the check and we leave.

Heading to the SUV, he asks, "We still have time. Would you like to do anything while we're out?"

I can't think of anything because it's been so long since I've even been off Skyview's grounds. Parks are out, as we have one. I don't have money to go shopping. Although, that would be nice.

"I don't think so. I don't know what's around here we could do."

"We don't have time for a movie," he says looking at his watch. "How about a bookstore?"

"Well, I don't have any money, so that's okay."

"Nonsense. I can buy you a book. There's a used bookstore just down the road."

He drives us to the store and we head inside. It's huge and I try to take it all in. I roam the aisles just smiling as I run my hands along the books' spines. I end up in the fantasy section and start reading titles. They all look good.

Dr. Leever comes up behind me. "Anything look interesting?"

"Several, but I don't know what I'm allowed to have. I don't know any of these authors."

"Let's take a look."

We spend the next half hour going through them. We settle on one that we think Dr. Allcott will approve of and he pays for it.

Back in the car, he says, "We'll have to show the book to Dr. Allcott to make sure it's appropriate, but I think it'll be fine."

"Thank you, Alex. For everything. For lunch, for this day. I've had a great time."

I feel like my face is going to freeze into a smile, which is so much better than the frown I was used to wearing.

"You're welcome. Perhaps next I can get approval to take you out to a movie. How does that sound?"

"Fantastic. Do you think Dr. Allcott will let me?"

"As long as he approves of the movie."

"Why would you want to spend your time with a patient? Isn't this unorthodox?"

"Yes, actually it is, but I strongly feel this is going to go a long way for your healing. It will help get you ready for the real world. As to spending time with you, I enjoy it. It's sort of like having a niece."

That was the nicest thing I've heard from anyone in so long, I almost cry tears of joy. Instead, I agree with him about getting me out in the world again.

When we get back to Skyview, we sign back in and have Dr. Allcott look at the book we chose. He agrees it's fine. Then Dr. Leever suggests we resume our normal session tomorrow morning.

Chapter Twenty-Eight

The next morning, Nurse Hamilton tells me that Alex called and said he won't be able to see me until later in the afternoon. I decide to go see Dr. Allcott about Alex's hypnosis idea. I knock on his door and he agrees to speak with me.

He's just getting up from his desk when I walk into his office. He's a big man with a stomach that sticks out quite a bit. Most of his hair is gone and what is left is gray.

"What's on your mind, Melinda?"

"Well, Alex...Dr. Leever thinks I should be hypnotized to see if it will help my memory."

"I'm aware of his suggestion. How do you feel about that?"

"I'm not sure. That's what I wanted to talk to you about. He said you thought it would be good for me."

"I do. It will help with your healing process. It's important you remember everything about your past in order to move forward. Confront it."

"That's what he said."

"You cannot be forced to go under hypnosis, but I think you would be making a mistake not to do it. Like I said, total recall is of the utmost importance."

"I will think about it then. Thank you for giving me your opinion."

"You're welcome. Let Dr. Leever know what you

decide, and I think you should do it sooner rather than later."

I leave his office feeling like I'm missing something. Why do it sooner? He seems to be pushing me toward the idea. But I'm sure Dr. Allcott has my best interests at heart, just as Alex does.

I still have time before lunch and consider going to Mel's Place, but am apprehensive. I don't want someone to turn me in if they see me again. At the same time, I am curious about who is going there. Maybe they don't belong there either, which would make sense because whoever it is obviously hasn't ratted me out yet.

I go outside and find it's windy and cool out, so I walk back to my room and grab a sweater. I also bring the book that Alex gave me as a gift. The fantasy one that's the first in the series. I sneak my way out of the gardens and to the small house. Approaching, I look up toward the tree. It makes me wonder how I've never seen it before.

I stop on the path. I don't see any movement in the tree house, so I keep moving forward. Instead of going into the cabin, I walk to the back. I stand at the foot of the tree for a minute before climbing.

Once at the top, I look around and see that the sleeping bag is rolled up in the corner. The book I saw there is gone. Now I wish I had taken the time to look at the title to see if it was possibly one of mine. Everything else is the same as I last saw it.

I climb back down the tree, walk back around to the front of the cottage, and enter through the door. Nothing has been disturbed. I don't know whether I should stay or go. I decide to risk it. If I hear a noise or see someone, I will leave right away. I am not going to let whoever is hiding in the tree house scare me away. I have as much right to be here as they do.

I notice it is getting dusty again, so I go into the kitchen and grab the rag from under the sink and start cleaning. It feels good, almost as if I was cleaning my own place. It gives me a sense of pride. After I finish, I pick up my book and sit down on the sofa.

I don't know how long it is that I am reading before I hear the noise. The steps on the little front porch creak. There it is again. I am startled and stand up quickly.

Heart hammering, I rush to the front door, and calling upon all the courage I can summon, yank it open. There stands a tall, skinny boy. He looks younger than me, maybe sixteen, if that. He's wearing tattered but clean jeans and a blue t-shirt. He seems as frightened as I am. He doesn't move, like he's rooted to the spot. We stand staring at each other for a few minutes before he takes flight.

He runs around the side of the house and to the back. I follow him. By the time I get around to the back, he is already up the tree. I see his foot disappear inside.

At the bottom of the tree, I yell out, "Who are you? What are you doing here?"

I don't get a response. For some reason, I'm not scared. I start climbing the makeshift ladder. I poke my head into the opening and look around. He's sitting in the corner on the sleeping bag, knees drawn up to his chest, arms wrapped around his scrawny legs. I go all the way in and stand looking at him.

It is warmer in here, despite the unclosed sides.

The wind is lessened up here, too.

The kid stares up at me with wide eyes.

"Who are you?" I repeat my question. When he doesn't answer, I say, "It's okay. I won't tell that you're here."

"Don't care if you do."

He sounds like he's trying to be brave and uncaring. But his demeanor shows me that he's worried. I'm not trying to scare him, so I sit down at the chair next to the small table. It seems to make him more comfortable.

"Yes, you do. Otherwise, you wouldn't have run," I tell him.

He shrugs his shoulders.

"Do you live here?"

"I guess."

"What's your name?" I ask.

"Trent."

"I'm Melinda. Where are your parents?"

"Gone. What are *you* doing here?"

Hiding from the world, but I don't tell him that. Instead, I say, "Hanging out. I don't live here."

"Where do you live?"

"At Skyview."

"That big house on the other side of the trees?"

"Yeah."

"So why do you come here?"

"To get away."

"From what? That's a big house. I hear you get fed there and have your own room."

"Yeah, but that's about it. I can't do much else."

"So, you come here to do it? What do you do?"

"Read mostly. What do you do? You said your

parents are gone. Where to?"

"Just gone. You sure you're not going to tell on me?"

"I won't as long as you don't tell that I come here."

He smiles and says, "Deal."

I'm relieved. It's not someone who's going to turn me in for being here. It's obvious to me that he isn't supposed to be here either.

"I have to go. They're going to be missing me at Skyview and I don't want them to come looking for me."

"Okay. Are you sure you're not going to tell on me?" he yells out as I'm climbing down.

I look back up and see his face poking out, looking down at me expectantly.

"No. We made a deal, right?"

He smiles and pulls his head back in.

I leave and go back through the garden. When I get back inside, I look at the clock. It's time for lunch and then I have my appointment with Alex. I make myself a plate then sit down and eat. Nurse Hamilton is once again in position near the door. I guess she's making sure we all eat. She's had that position since the day I came here.

After lunch, I haul myself upstairs to Alex's office. I think about Trent as I open the door.

I don't tell the doctor about Trent that day and I may never. I'm not sure why. It is another secret I am not prepared to share yet. It is enough I have to bare my soul about my family and everything we went through. Something inside me tells me to be cautious and not divulge anything about Trent's appearance in my life. Besides, I don't want him to send Trent away. I am hoping he can be my friend. That will make two. And that's if he's even friend material. I don't even know that yet. We just met and it wasn't on the best of terms. Maybe over time. Who knows?

"So, how are you today, Melinda?" Alex asks.

"Okay."

"Have you given any thought to my suggestion of hypnosis?"

"I talked to Dr. Allcott. He seems to think I should do it as well, but I don't think I will. Can't we see how it goes in our sessions?"

"Absolutely. I'm not pressuring you into anything. If you change your mind—and I hope you do—let me know. Fair enough?"

"Yes. Thank you."

"What do you feel like talking about today?"

"I'm not sure where we left off. I know I told you about Beth's visits."

"Yes, you did. You also said Kyle visited with her as well. Tell me about Kyle. How did he react to seeing Beth and hearing about this other side?"

"At first, he couldn't believe it, but after the first time, he had no choice."

Chapter Twenty-Nine

"By this time, it's September and school was due to start soon. I wasn't happy about having to go back. I had other things to worry about besides studying.

"Kyle and I visited with Beth every time she came. It didn't take long for Kyle to believe. After all, he'd had the same experience with Dad that I did. Honestly though, it was hard for both of us to wrap our minds around the fact Dad visited and spoke to us from the grave and Beth came from someplace called the Other Side, too.

"Actually, when I think about it, what are the chances that both my father and best friend die and both come back to see me? It's weird. Even when I say it now, it feels implausible. So, I can't blame you if you don't quite believe my tale."

"I haven't said I don't believe you yet, Melinda," Dr. Leever reassures me.

"I know. But even to me, it sounds farfetched."

I pick at my fingernails instead of meeting his gaze. I don't want to see it if he actually thinks I'm a habitual liar. And I'm sure it will be written all over his face, just like his predecessors.

"Look at me," he instructs.

I do and the look on his face surprises me. He's smiling.

"It does sound fanciful, at the very least. However,

it does not mean it's a lie. If you are to gain acceptance of yourself, you must first be able to speak frankly. You cannot do that if you don't have faith in the doctor you are talking and sharing deep, dark secrets with. I hope with time, you'll come to see that you can trust me and that you'll garner the ability to speak freely, without fear of reprisal."

"I have been, for the most part. I haven't shared a fifth of what I'm telling you with anyone else before. That's trust."

"It is. But you are holding yourself back."

I realize he's right. Okay then, I will speak frankly.

"Well then I need to change that," I smile at him. "I'll continue and I'm not going to worry about your reaction. Okay, that's not true either. I will worry because I need your approval, but I'll keep telling you everything."

"The only approval you really need is your own. But I do understand what you are concerned about. I know Dr. Allcott said that essentially I am the doctor who would decide your fate. In all honesty, Melinda, *you* decide your fate. Are you willing to take the risk to overcome the obstacles you are throwing in your own path?"

I see that he's right. I have been holding myself back. I'm standing in my own way. I must face everything, no holds barred.

"Yes, I am. I will take that risk. Are you ready to hear it all?"

He moves his hand in front of him as if he is telling me the floor is all mine. I take the spotlight and continue on.

****

"Back to Mom. She was happy again, so I know she'd been talking to Dad. She wouldn't say a word though. I wonder if she was worried about frightening us or concerned we'd want to try to lock her in a loony bin. If we hadn't had our own experiences, we probably would have.

"Kyle and I walked by the river constantly, hoping to hear or see Dad. We'd finally heard from him. It was a few days before Labor Day. We were sitting on rocks next to the water. I was swinging my legs back and forth, hitting the water with my bare toes, having kicked off my sandals earlier.

"Hey, kids."

"His voice startled me at first and I almost fell off the rock. Kyle appeared to be taken by surprise as well. He looked all around like he'd actually see the face that went with the voice. By this time, I'd learned that if we heard his voice like he was talking directly into our ears, he wasn't in person, but in our heads.

"Dad?" Kyle asked.

"Yes. Listen, I've been talking to your mother. She's finally starting to take me seriously. She was going to go look for you kids, but I told her I would get you to go home. So, you both need to go home. Now."

"Why? What's the urgency?" I asked.

"Your mother is taking you out of town today. Please don't ask questions and don't put up any kind of fuss. This is best. I want you all safe. So, get home."

"Kyle's eyes widened with alarm. He jumped off the rock and started heading up the hill. I joined him.

"Dad? What's going on?" I asked.

"Just as I told you and your brother before, you're in danger. I can't talk any longer. Please get home, and

I will visit with you again as soon as I can."

"That was it. Silence. Kyle and I looked at each other. I was scared and worried and I could tell Kyle was as well. We ran as fast as we could.

"Mom!" Kyle yelled as we both burst through the front door.

"Up here!" we heard her yell.

"We both ran up the stairs and into her bedroom. She was throwing clothes haphazardly into a suitcase.

"I need you both to go pack. Five minutes. We need to leave."

"We know," I said. "Dad…"

"Never mind that right now. Just go!" she insisted, never taking her eyes from what she was doing.

"I ran to my room while Kyle ran to his. I pulled out the suitcase from the closet. I emptied it after I realized I couldn't leave my family, even though they were weird back then."

I scoff at what I said. Back then? It's still weird. I dismiss my thoughts and continue telling Dr. Leever the story.

"Anyway, I put the bag on my bed and quickly put clothes in it. I didn't pay attention to what I was packing. I ran into the bathroom and grabbed toothbrushes, toothpaste, and some other toiletries and dumped them all in my bag. I was back in the hallway in three minutes. I left my suitcase at the top of the stairs and went to Kyle's room.

"I already have your toothbrush," I told him.

"Okay, I'm ready."

"He put his suitcase with mine and we both went into our mother's room.

"Mom?"

"She wasn't there. Her suitcase was still on the bed, clothes hanging off the sides. I looked at Kyle. I could feel the hair on the back on my neck stand up.

"Something's happened, Mel."

"I know."

"We rushed down the stairs and outside. She was not in the car. We ran back into the house and checked the kitchen, living room, and downstairs bathroom and didn't find her.

"The office," Kyle suggested.

"We had a small office in the back of the house Mom and Dad used to pay bills. We went in there. A man with a gun in his hand stood over my mother, who was on her knees in front of the closet trying to open the safe.

"I screamed. The man whipped around. I could hear Mom sobbing. The man hit Kyle on the side of the head with the butt of the gun. I screamed again and he lunged for me. I darted out of his way and in my blind panic, ran to the other side of the desk. It was a very small room and contained a desk, the chair, and a small table near the closet. You could cross from the closet to the desk in one stride.

"The phone, I remember thinking. I reached my hand out to grab it. The man snatched the handset out of my reach before I could pick it up. I jerked away. I picked up the stapler from the desk and threw it at him. It hit him on the side of the head.

"You little bitch!"

"A paper. Have you seen a piece of paper with numbers on it?" my mother was asking me through her tears.

"I knew what she was talking about, but I didn't

have it. I couldn't think. A man with a gun was trying to kill us.

"Just run," Mom was saying. "Leave my daughter alone!"

"The man backhanded her in the face. Kyle was still lying on the floor, inert. I couldn't help him or Mom and it killed me to be so helpless.

"I picked up the tape dispenser from the desk and threw it at the man. I didn't waste time to see if the object connected with him or where. Instead, I quickly bolted out from behind the desk, jumped over Kyle, and ran out of the room and through the back door of the kitchen. Before I knew it, I was in the fort. I didn't even realize I was heading there.

"I began bawling and the hiccups started full force again. I didn't know what to do. The man hurt Kyle and he could seriously hurt my mother. I needed to get help. I stifled my tears and ran to Beth's house. It was right behind ours and the closest one. I banged on the door repeatedly yelling for help.

"A few seconds later, Krissy opened the door.

"What in the world?"

"A man hurt Kyle! He has a gun on Mom! Please call for help!"

"Get in here, come on."

"She grabbed my arm and literally pulled me into the house. She let go of my arm and went right to the phone. I heard her telling whoever answered the nine-one-one call my address and hers.

"Please tell them to hurry!"

"After she hung up the phone, she hugged me to her. After a minute, she stepped back and steered me to the kitchen chair. I sat down. It was more like I fell into the chair. My legs were shaking. My entire body was shaking.

"Krissy peered through her window like she was making sure the man didn't follow me. I hadn't thought of that until I saw her checking.

"He's not out there, is he?"

"I stood up and rushed to the window to look for myself. I didn't see anyone.

"No, it's all right. No one is there. Come on," she steered me back to the chair. "Sit down. The cops are on their way. Please try to calm down and tell me what's going on."

"A man had a gun on Mom, he…hit…her and Kyle," I was sobbing again.

"What did he want?"

"A paper. I…don't…know."

"I couldn't stop crying. I couldn't stop seeing the man holding a gun to Mom's head and him hitting Kyle with it. I didn't know if he killed Mom and Kyle. Krissy gave me a bottle of water to help with the hiccups. She knew what happened when I cried hard, too. And I was close to hysterical at this point."

Chapter Thirty

"It's okay, Melinda. You're not there anymore. It's over," Alex is trying to comfort me.

I guess I start crying while telling the story to him. It seems like it was happening all over again.

"I know," I take a deep breath. "I'm okay. It just brought me back."

"Are you okay to continue?"

"Yes. I need a minute. May I use the bathroom?"

"Of course."

I go in and splash water on my face. I look at myself in the mirror, but see only my family. Those images will never go away. Neither will the ones from what happened later. I know I have to face them all, but it isn't going to be easy.

I dry my face and hands and walk back into Alex's office.

"Are you sure you want to proceed? We can pick this up tomorrow."

"Tomorrow, the next day, the day after... It won't matter. The pain will never get easier. I need to do this now, Alex."

"Continue when you feel up to it."

Chapter Thirty-One

"By the time the cops got there, I was near hysteria. Krissy tried to calm me down by holding my hands and whispering to me like a child. I would cry then go into a rage.

"Damn it! What is taking the police so long?" I lashed out as if it were a defense mechanism designed to make everything all right. "That man better not hurt my family! I will kill him if he does!" It was hard to imagine me alone, no family. It made me all the more mad. "Where's Beth when I need her?"

"I felt my face turn instantly red, realizing what I said and to whom.

"I'm sorry, Krissy. I'm so sorry."

"She was looking at me with her mouth open, then I saw sadness touch her eyes. She closed her mouth, shut her eyes, and took a deep breath.

"I know how much you miss her. So do I."

"How could I tell her that I see her all the time? I couldn't. I stood there and let her grieve when I could have done something, said something."

"It's not your fault," Alex interrupts. "As you said, if you don't believe, you can't see your loved ones. It wasn't up to you to make Krissy believe enough to see her daughter again."

"How do you know? What if I had talked to her and told her everything? Maybe she would have believed."

"You will never know that, Melinda, and it's in the past. You can't go back and change that. I believe things happen for a reason. Perhaps Krissy couldn't believe at the time for some reason. How do you know that after all this time, she hasn't started to? She may be visiting with Beth right now as we speak."

The thought made me feel a little better. He was right. I didn't know. I hadn't seen or talked to Beth in years. Maybe by this time, Beth got her parents to believe enough to see her.

"Thank you for that perspective. I hadn't thought of that."

Alex nods and I run my hand through my hair. It's getting long, but not fast enough, at least where my bangs are concerned. Oh well, in time. My mind leaves my looks and goes back to the past.

****

"After Krissy reassured me I hadn't made her mad, I stood looking out her window again. I couldn't stand not knowing what happened. I ran from her kitchen and back to my house before she could stop me. The cops were talking to my mother in the living room. I didn't see Kyle. My mother's face was red and looked like it was starting to swell. I started tearing up again. Thank God they were still alive. At least Mom was.

"Where's Kyle?" I asked before I could go into a full-blown bawling/rage session again.

"He's okay," Mom replied. "The medics are treating him in the office. Just a bang on the head. The other police officer is talking to him."

"Do you believe Dad now?" I asked almost in a scream. "He tried to warn you…warn us."

"I was angry at everything. At everyone. Things were getting out of control and I didn't anticipate the events getting anything but worse.

"Excuse me," the officer interrupted. "Did you say your father tried to warn you about something?"

"Yes."

"No."

"My mother and I answered simultaneously.

"Ma'am?" the officer asked my mother.

"Her father passed away. Drowned. Melinda is still very upset about it. Distraught. I'm sure you understand, Officer Rayn."

"My mother threw me a look that screamed 'shut up' and directed her attention back to Rayn. But he was looking at me.

"Is that correct?"

"Yes, she's right," I conceded.

"I remained quiet while she told the officer what happened.

"My kids and I were getting ready for a short vacation. I left the front door open, going back and forth to the car with things. This man came in and demanded money. I was getting it out of the safe when the children came in."

"I knew the man wasn't after money, but I stayed quiet.

"Can you describe him?"

"White, medium build, blonde hair. I'd say he was maybe six feet."

"Any physical characteristic stand out to you? Tattoos, scars."

"No."

"He had a tattoo on his hand. I noticed it when he

grabbed the phone away from me. It was here," I indicated the web between the thumb and index finger.

"Could you tell what the tattoo was?" the officer asked me.

"A cross, but it wasn't a good one."

"What do you mean?"

"It looked like he did it himself. That kind of thing. I need to see Kyle."

"So you were in the room when this all happened?" the officer stopped me from leaving the room.

"Yes, Kyle and I were looking for Mom."

"Anything else you can add?"

"Not really. Mom described him. And there's the tattoo. I've never seen him before."

"Have you?" he asked Mom.

"No."

"Okay," the officer stood up. "If you remember anything else, give us a call." He handed her his business card. "We'll let you know if we find the perpetrator."

"I quickly went to the office. The medics and the other cop were leaving the room as I walked in. I went right to Kyle. He had a bandage on the side of his head. At least he didn't shoot him.

"Are you okay?"

"Bad headache, but yeah, I'm fine," he said.

"What did you say to the cop?"

"Described the guy. He asked if I knew him and I said no."

"Anything else?"

"No, why?"

"Mom lied," I whispered.

"I told him that Mom lied to the cops, saying the

man wanted money, when it was really the piece of paper he was there for.

"We've got to give them the paper, Kyle. They could have hurt Mom or you."

"Or you. But no, Dad said not to."

"What do we do?"

"Leave like Dad said. We'll talk to Mom. Come on, let's go."

"Mom agreed and still wanted to leave. After the cops left, we finished packing as quickly as we could. I notice the boxes she was going to take to donation were still in the trunk. I guess they will have to wait.

"Mom went to Krissy's to talk to her while we waited in the back yard. She didn't want us near the front of the house in case the man came back.

"After Mom came out of Krissy's kitchen, we all got in the car and Mom drove down the road.

"Mom, where are we going to go?" I asked.

"I know of a place. Your father and I used to go there before you kids were born. No one will find us there."

"Don't you think it's time to talk about it?" Kyle asked her.

"About what?"

"Dad. You know as well as we do, he's the one making us leave," Kyle responded.

"It's not something I want to talk about with you kids."

"Mom, we already know," I chimed in. "Dad talked to us before you. He tried to get me to warn you. He said he'd already tried, but you wouldn't listen."

"Let's get to our destination where I know we'll be safe and then we can talk."

"Kyle didn't listen.

"We know what the paper is all about. Mel and I hid it."

"You what?" she screamed, looking in her rear view mirror at him.

"I was sitting in the front and I looked back at Kyle, too. I was surprised he told her. He said we shouldn't tell anyone.

"We hid it," he repeated. "No one will think to look there."

"You must tell me where it is immediately," Mom pulled over the side of the road. She turned in her seat to face Kyle. "We have to give it to these people. They're going to kill us if we don't."

"Not if we go to the police," I said.

"We won't live long enough. Tell me where it is right now."

"Why did you lie to the police, Mom?" I asked.

"What are you talking about?"

"You told them the guy broke in looking for money. You know it was the paper with the numbers on it because you asked if we'd seen it."

"Same thing. They're account numbers. Money held in an offshore account. Your father told me."

"We were on a desolate stretch of the road. I heard a car drive up the road from behind us. I turned to look, but it zoomed past us. I hadn't realized I was holding my breath until it all came out at once in a huge sigh. My nerves were shot. Apparently, my mother's were too, because she closed her eyes and let her breath out slowly right after I did.

"Why didn't you tell the police about the damn account numbers?" I asked, frustration coming out in my voice.

"Watch your mouth, young lady. How would I explain knowing about the account numbers? That your father's ghost told me?"

"It was the first time she actually admitted it. I was relieved. It was all finally out in the open between the three of us. We all knew that Dad talked to each of us and tried to warn us that something like this would happen. We were lucky we weren't dead.

"My mother turned back around and put the car back in gear. "We'll finish discussing this later."

"We can't run away," Kyle said. "We know what they want, but they won't find it. We should go to the police like Mel said. Maybe they can set up a trap or something for them."

"It's too dangerous. You don't know the whole story, you just know about a list of numbers on a piece of paper. There's much more than that. Your father told me everything. Now, no more talk right now."

Chapter Thirty-Two

"Mom drove us up to a bed and breakfast in the mountains above Palm Springs to a small town called Idyllwild. I guess she and Dad used to go there for long weekends."

I scrape my fingers on the chair's armrest, picking at a non-existent piece of dirt.

"What I'm curious about is what Beth has to do with any of this," Alex says.

"Nothing, except she died the same way Dad died. She's the one who gave me information on how he was doing when she saw him, which wasn't often."

"And she came and went as she pleased and your dad couldn't?"

"He did appear sometimes, but mostly in our heads. From what I know, you can come back to see people, but that's only if they're open to seeing you. Most people aren't. They're scared of the unknown."

"And you're not?"

"I never had a chance to think about it before it all happened. It was just sort of thrown at me. Somehow, Dad found out how to speak to us from...over there. After that, I took it all for granted. When you die, it's not the end of things."

"Have you seen or spoken to any of your immediate family since you've been here?"

I drop my head to my chest.

143

"No. It's as if they all deserted me. Beth too. I don't know why. Something must be terribly wrong over there. Or maybe they gave up on me, too. I don't know."

"Let's go back for a minute to this sheet with the numbers on it. Whatever happened to it?"

I shrug. "I don't know. I can't remember where Kyle and I hid it."

"So, possibly it's still there?"

"Probably. Kyle and I never told anyone. At least, I didn't and I doubt Kyle did before he died."

"And you still won't consider hypnosis? It can help you remember."

"Where would that get me? Remembering? I don't care about that damn piece of paper. It's what started this whole mess."

I can't believe I swore in front of Alex, other than relaying the story, that is. I wonder what he must be thinking. In my defense, I'm angry. I know my face is red, it gets that way when I'm really mad. I pick at my fingernails again, wondering if I'll be in trouble for displaying my irritation and swearing. I'm surprised though when he doesn't mention either one.

"All right. We'll let that go for now. Are you ready to talk about the deaths of your mother and Kyle?"

I sigh and say, "Not today. Probably not tomorrow. I'm not sure when I'll be up to that."

"No rush. We can discuss that when you're ready."

"Alex? This whole thing about Dad talking to Kyle and Mom, do you believe it? Do you believe someone can come back from the dead like my Dad and Beth did?"

"Like I said before, it's something I'm researching.

I have to reserve my opinion until I'm more fully informed."

"I guess that's fair."

"We should stop for the day," he says as I yawn. "You are tired and I believe you need a break. It's just about your dinnertime anyway."

"All right." I stand up and start walking toward the door. I stop and turn back around. "Do you know anyone who died?"

He looks caught off-guard with the question, his eyes widen for a moment.

"Yes, I do. A few, actually. Why do you ask?"

"Have they ever come and talked to you?"

"No, they have not."

"Maybe you're just not open to it."

I leave him with that thought and walk back to my room. We won't be eating for another half an hour and I want to lay on my bed for a bit. It has been a long day.

Chapter Thirty-Three

The Other Side

It was a very close call, but I was able to gain entry back through the portal just in time. When Meredith finds out how close I came to being stuck on Earth forever, she is understandably upset. She warns me not to try something so stupid again. We were warned that going through portals is risky. If we stay too long on Earth at any given time, we will be trapped with no way to again enter the Other Side. The danger in that is we will be unable to look out for our families. We will only see what is in front of us *and* our families will still not be able to see us.

What's worse, we wouldn't be able to communicate with them, we'd be stripped of our abilities to speak to them. When I asked how long is too long, they said the first alarm is our protectors calling us, so to speak. If we ignore them, a second warning will be given before we feel the pull of the Earth. If gravity holds us too long we will be trapped on the side of the living forever. So, essentially, it's very risky to come back, but with practice, it does get easier to understand the calls for return and we must abide by them, no matter what.

After all Kyle and I did that night, it didn't work. We weren't able to scare him into hightailing it out of town. What is it going to take?

I come up with a plan to help Melinda in such a way that these people will be done with once and for all. I share it with Kyle. He argues with me that we should tell Trent who's trying to hurt Melinda so that he can warn her. I point out that if Melinda knows, she can inadvertently reveal her knowledge and they would get away, instead of being apprehended. If that happens, they will be a threat to her for the rest of her life. This has to end. But it must to be done right if Melinda is going to live her life freely, without looking over her shoulder. Kyle understands and agrees.

I've tried to reach Melinda on more than one occasion, but I can't. I don't know why, so I ask a few others on this side about it. They say it's because sometimes evil can actually block us. Apparently, evil lurks on Earth more than the living realize. If someone is after Melinda, without even realizing they're doing so, the evil inside them can be enough to hinder us from reaching out. That must be what's happening now. For years, we've watched over her, but now that we need to contact her, we can't.

Hence, Trent. I finally reach him and lead him to the tree house. It is a good thing. I am concerned because of what I am seeing Melinda go through, dredging up past emotions. And that cloud is still hanging around. It's not going away.

It's important to make the boy understand that Melinda needs him. I don't want to use the boy, but there is no choice. The risk must be taken. Meredith is worried about the time we have on Earth, concerned we won't have enough. But we must get through to Trent. Kyle and Meredith agree that we have to try. We wait until Trent leaves the tree house. We think if he sees us go through it, it will be more traumatic for him. We don't have any idea how long he is going to be gone, but we are limited on time.

Unfortunately, he is away too long. I see him frolicking down at the water hole he found. I send out thoughts to get him to come back, but it doesn't work. It took us a few trips to draw him here in the first place. It was as bad as when I called someone on their cell phones when I was alive. Only with this, I can't leave a message.

We end up having to enter the tree house when he is there. We wait until after he is asleep, hoping he won't see us enter. He doesn't. After the three of us are standing in the small space, I wake Trent up. Understandably, he is confused.

"What's going on? Who are you?"

His eyes are wide and I read fear in them.

"There is no reason to be scared. We're not here to hurt you."

He pulls himself up from the sleeping bag on the floor, but stays in the corner.

"Who are you? What do you want?"

He tries to leave. Kyle actually physically stops him from climbing down the wooden boards.

I think Meredith's presence is what finally calms Trent. After Kyle finally subdues him to a point where he's not physically violent, she takes his hand and speaks softly to him.

"Trent, it's all right. We're sorry we alarmed you. Can you listen to us and let us explain?"

He stares at Meredith with wide eyes. He's still scared, but I can tell he's not as frightened as he was.

"Trent?" Meredith questions again.

He slowly nods his head and Meredith smiles at him. While I tell him who we are and why we're here, Meredith keeps her hand in his. He doesn't pull away.

He doesn't believe me and it takes a while for him to accept what I tell him. The kid is probably frightened. I can't blame him. I would be, too if a dead stranger—or family for that matter—approached me and started talking to me.

"If you're Melinda's dead family, why are you coming to me and not her?"

I can tell he is starting to believe us, so I explain to him about being blocked from contacting her. I leave out the part about evil stopping our communication. I figure it will only get him riled up again. Some people believe in good and evil. Others believe in one or the other. And some don't believe anything at all. I don't know yet what Trent believes.

"I need you to watch out for our daughter," Meredith says. "She is in danger. It would be much too risky for us to appear to her in Skyview Haven."

"What is she in danger from? Or who?" Trent asks.

I explain almost everything to him, leaving out parts I don't want to be shared with Melinda. And I don't tell him names because I'm worried for his safety. If he knows who it is, he may try to confront them and that's not a good idea. These men are violent and there's no telling what they could do to him. I don't want Trent joining us on the Other Side. He needs to be on Earth for Melinda.

After telling Trent as much as I could, I ask him, "Will you help her?"

It takes him a while to accept us and the fact three

dead souls are speaking to him.

"What do you need me to do?"

I tell him and he agrees that he won't divulge it to Melinda until the time is right.

"If she ends up hating me, I'll kill you." When he realizes what he said, he starts laughing. "Okay, that was stupid. She just better not hate me."

I assure him that Melinda is reasonable and everything will be okay.

Chapter Thirty-Four

After meeting Trent, I sneak out of Skyview as much as I can. We spend a lot of time together and become friends, just as I hoped. I learn that he is seventeen. His parents were killed when he was seven and he had been in foster care until about six months ago. He was transferred to a new home because his previous foster parents were arrested for fraud.

He ran away and was hiding out in the tree house. He said he thought someone lived in the little cottage. He had nowhere else to go. He snuck food from the garbage bins from behind our kitchen. He found the sleeping bag in town in a dumpster. Before he found the tree house, he stayed in town and begged for change on the street. He used the money to wash the sleeping bag and his clothes and used what he had left to buy what food he could.

I tell him where I'm staying and that my parents are dead. I don't elaborate how they died any more than he tells me why his parents are dead. I tell him about how boring Skyview is and how they don't let me do anything. I tell him I had a brother named Kyle, who died, too. He doesn't ask me how or why, which makes me curious. But I guess boys aren't as nosey as girls are.

He says he didn't have any brothers or sisters. I ask him why he ran away from foster care. He says they didn't care about him, just the money they got every month for having him there. He shared a room with three other boys. The littlest one was four and he slept in Trent's bed. Apparently, the little boy wet the bed all the time, so Trent ended up sleeping on the floor.

After each of my appointments with Alex, I practically run to the cottage. Trent meets me there and we have lunch together. I sneak food out for him to eat. What else is he going to do? I am afraid he'll get caught if he keeps sneaking around our dumpsters. I also bring him another pillow for his sleeping bag.

I try to get him to sleep inside the little house, but he is worried about being found. He makes a good point when he says that even I don't know who the house belongs to and that the owner can come back at anytime.

Because I haven't had a best friend since Beth and have never had a good friend who was a boy, I'm not sure how to act with him. I soon find out it's just as easy with him as it was with Beth. We hang out, chitchat, and even go for walks close by, never going too near Skyview. We find things in the woods we bring back for the tree house or cottage. Things like pinecones we dream about using at Christmastime and rocks I think look pretty on the windowsills and that Trent laughs at me about. We grow close and I quickly come to think that I don't want a life without him in it. He's a good friend and we have a lot of fun together. I forgot how nice is to have a best friend. I'm smiling again these days and I know it's because of Trent.

I talk a lot with Alex. Mostly telling him silly stories about my family and Beth. I avoid the real topics and I think he knows it, but lets me do so. Today, though, he finally starts pushing things.

"We've been meeting now for what? Almost two months?"

"I think so."

"You've shared a lot with me since we began our sessions and I admire your courage to do so."

"I told you, I need to get out and live my life. I can't do that unless someone says I'm not nuts."

"You've been skirting issues for a little while. I think it's time you address them head on."

"How?"

"Stop avoiding what you want to talk about."

"I'm not. Okay, I am, but I'm worried about your reaction."

"I thought we already discussed that and you agreed you wouldn't worry about what I thought."

"I know."

"Why don't you let me be concerned about what I'm thinking? I can't help you if you don't share everything."

"I'm trying."

"You've been hiding something lately."

"I'm not. Why do you say that?"

"You're apprehensive, anxious. You can't wait to get out of here early most days. At times, you act like you don't want to be here."

Uh, oh. Does he know about Trent? I hope not.

"It's probably because like you said, I've been avoiding talking about things."

"Okay, how do you feel about discussing them today?"

I don't really have a choice. He's right. I have to stop skirting around the issues and tell him everything.

"Okay." I walk over to the side table and get a drink.

"Let's start with your mother taking you and Kyle away."

Chapter Thirty-Five

"It was past six by the time we arrived at the bed and breakfast. Mom said not to bother unpacking because she wasn't sure if we were going to be there long. But I heard her book a room for a week. What about school? We were supposed to start the next day. I figured if Mom wasn't worried, I wouldn't either.

"We all shared the one room. Mom said she didn't want us to be apart. It was a relief because I didn't want to be alone. What if that man followed us?

"Mom said she was going to the car and would be right back. I wanted to hear from Dad. So, while Mom was out of the room, I tried calling him.

"Dad?"

"What are you doing?" Kyle asked as we sat in our room.

"Trying to reach Dad. We have to tell him what happened."

"He probably already knows."

"Well, maybe he can give us the name of the person who wants the piece of paper."

"One way to find out. Dad?" Kyle now started calling him.

"We both tried a few times, but we never heard a response. Mom came back in with our bags and told us she was going to town to get some dinner for us.

"Can't we go with you?" I asked, scared to stay in

155

a strange place without her after what just happened to us.

"No. Wait here and don't go anywhere."

"While Mom was gone, Kyle and I still kept trying to contact Dad. Nothing.

"What do you think we should do, Kyle? I mean, we have what this man wants."

"At first, I agreed we should give the paper to them or even go to the police, but not after the man killed Dad and hit Mom and me. No. They don't deserve it."

"Then what?"

"I'm not sure. I have to think."

"Mom wants to give it to them."

"I heard her. I was in the car, too," he remarked sarcastically.

"You don't have to be mean about it."

"I'm sorry. I'm just scared. And if you tell anyone I said that, I'll deny it."

"I'm scared, too."

"Mom came back with burgers and French fries and we all ate. I don't remember even tasting what I ate. Food was sustenance that we had to have, but I honestly couldn't have cared less. After we finished, I started in on Mom.

"We can't keep running, Mom."

"We won't. I just need time to think."

"You're waiting for Dad to tell you what to do, aren't you?" I asked.

"It was what we were all waiting for.

"Maybe. Listen, about your father, it's rather peculiar. It's not something you kids should go around talking about. People will think you're nuts."

"But we're not nuts. Neither are you. Dad's voice

is real. *Dad* is real."

"And Beth," I said.

"Mom looked at me quizzically. "Beth?"

"Yeah, she's been coming back. We spend time together in the fort. With Kyle, too."

"Really?"

"I didn't expect her to be so shocked. Not after knowing Dad was talking to all of us.

"Yes. In person or whatever it is. At least I see her in person."

"You see her too, Kyle?"

"Yes. I know it's weird. I don't understand any of this. I just know I don't doubt any of it any longer. It's like, uh, paranormal or something."

"I told you. Beth said they can come see us almost any time. She said Dad is still mad about being dead."

"Not mad," Mom sighed and said, "worried for us."

"She seemed accepting of the fact that her dead husband was still around and that my dead best friend came around, too.

"Mom? What are we going to do if Dad doesn't come back and tell us what to do?" I asked.

"I don't know yet. As I said, I need some time to think. I'll keep you safe, that's my first priority. I love you both."

"I love you, Mom," I said.

"Yeah, me, too," Kyle echoed my sentiment.

"She told us she was going for a walk, hugged us both, and told us to get some sleep. I don't know if she ever made it back to the room because Kyle and I fell asleep. She must have been kidnapped outside because we would have heard the commotion if it happened in our room. Besides, they didn't take Kyle and me. All I know is Kyle and I were woken up in the middle of the night by Dad.

"Kids! Wake up. Your mother is gone."

"What?" Kyle asked.

"I rubbed the sleep out of my eyes as I sat up. At first, I was disoriented. Not sure where I was. Then I remembered. Somewhere in the mountains, running from a man who tried to kill us.

"Get up. Wake up."

"I got up and flicked our light on. Kyle was now standing, eyes wide and completely alert. At least I think he was. I'm sure my eyes were just as big. I could feel my stomach drop. I know I heard my father say Mom was gone.

"Mom's gone?" I asked, looking around the room.

"Yes. They've taken her. I'm not sure where she's at. I know you kids shouldn't be involved, but I need you to go call the police."

"I looked at the clock next to my bed. 3:17 a.m. Weird. It was the same time I first woke up back home and saw Beth as a live 'dead' person. Then again, everything about what was going on was weird. Time was just another of the oddities.

"Get your mother's cell phone. It's on the nightstand."

"I dashed to the other side of the bed, picked it up, and dialed the numbers that would change many things for Kyle and me.

"911. What is your emergency?"

"My mother is missing! You have to send the police quick," I yelled into the phone.

"Calm down and tell me your name."

"Melinda James. We're out of town in a bed and breakfast. I don't know the address."

"Mel, tell them we're in Idyllwild."

"I repeated the information.

"Can you tell me the name of the place you're staying at?"

"I was so nervous I couldn't think. I couldn't remember what the place was called. I looked for a brochure or something. I didn't see anything.

"Kyle, what's the name of this place?"

"Kyle grabbed the phone from me and told the operator where we were staying.

"She must have asked him if we saw anything because Kyle told her, "No, we were sleeping. We woke up and she was gone. I don't know. Mel," he addressed me. "Go see if the car is here."

"I ran outside to the parking lot. Our car was where Mom parked it last night. I sprinted back in and told Kyle.

"The car is here. Is someone coming or not?" Kyle asked. "I'm almost sixteen, my sister is thirteen. No, it's my mom's cell phone… No, we didn't wake up the owners yet. I will. Okay, we'll stay in our room."

"Kyle hung up and told me what they said, as if I needed him to. I sort of got the gist from listening to his end of the telephone call.

"We need to wake up the owners and then they said to stay in our room. The police are coming."

"I don't know which room is theirs," I said.

"My heart was racing and I was sweating. I couldn't think. All I could feel was fear. Our mother was gone and we had no idea where she was. We knew she was in danger because Dad said so. The idea Mom

159

could be gone for good was not something I wanted to consider. God couldn't possibly take our mother from us so soon after our father was killed.

"We'll try the front desk. Ring the bell."

"We went out to the front and rang the small bell that sat on the counter. It was dim in the lobby, lit only with a small lamp near the front door and an overhead one behind the counter.

"I was shaking all over. Kyle didn't look much better. Clad in nothing but pajamas and with bare feet, we stood and waited for someone to come out. When after a few minutes no one appeared, I went over and hit the bell again and again and again. Kyle came over and put his hand on mine to stop me.

"Mel, it's the middle of the night. Someone will come, give them a minute."

"I was close to tears. Here we were, two teenagers somewhere in the mountains at a bed and breakfast where we didn't know anyone, and our mother was gone.

"I'm scared," I told him.

"So am I," he hugged me. "It will be all right. I'll take care of you."

"Our family went from grieving alone, hiding from each other and the world, to one big nut case in a matter of months. Sometimes I thought I'd lose my mind. Maybe that's what actually happened. But no, I didn't believe that then and I don't believe that now. I was sane then and still am."

"I'm glad you see that. It's important to your recovery," Alex says.

I stand up and walk around the office, trying to exercise my legs. They were asleep. Little needles are poking me everywhere. I shake one leg, then the other.

"I know. It's what I've told everyone all this time, but the problem was that no one believed me. At times, I thought it was because I *was* crazy. But moments like that passed quickly. Other than that, I've never really doubted it."

"That's good to know," Alex says.

I decide to stand for a while and move back and lean against the wall.

"Back to the newest dilemma. Somebody finally came out."

****

"Can I help you," croaked a sleepy man.

"He wasn't the one who checked us in. He was also wearing pajamas with a robe hanging loosely around his shoulders.

"Kyle explained to the man what happened and that the police were on their way while I stood there looking like the lost child I was.

"Okay. I want you both to wait right here while I get my wife. She'll stay with you in the room until the police show up. Then I'll show them which room is yours." The man was nice. "In the meantime, I'll make you both some hot chocolate and bring it to you."

"We thanked him. He left and it was only a few minutes before a woman came out and told us her name was Thea. She walked with us back to our room. She sat down in a chair and tried to reassure us that everything was going to be all right, but I couldn't believe her. Not after everything we'd been through.

"I sat down on the edge of my bed, put a pillow on my lap, and bent forward. I know it didn't help really, but the pillow felt like a piece of security. Like I could grab onto it and it wouldn't leave.

"Kyle sat down next to me and put his arm around me. We were still in that position when there was a tap on the door. Kyle answered it.

"The man was holding two steaming cups of hot chocolate with marshmallows. He brought them in and set them on Kyle's nightstand.

"Are you two okay?"

"We will be as soon as they find our mom," Kyle replied.

"He was trying to be brave. I could hear it in his voice.

"As soon the cops get here, I'll let you know." He turned to Thea and said, "I'm sure it won't be long before the cops get here." He kissed her on the forehead and started for the door, but seemed hesitant to leave. He turned back to Kyle and me and asked, "Are you sure you're okay?"

"What I wanted to say was no, we're not and haven't been for a long time and I can't see us being all right again, but instead I said, "Yeah."

"Where's your dad?"

"Dead. But of course I didn't say that.

"He died a few months back," Kyle said.

"The man cleared his throat and looked around, clearly uncomfortable.

"I'm sure they'll find your mother. Maybe she went for a walk."

"Yeah, probably," Kyle muttered.

"Neither of us believed it, but we didn't say anything. The man was trying to make us feel better and I liked him because of it.

"Well, I'll be in front if you need anything at all."

"Thank you," I told him, "for the hot chocolate."

"After he left, I walked over and picked up my cup. All of sudden, I needed the warmth. It wasn't cold in the room, but my insides felt like ice.

"Kyle, what are we going to do if they don't find Mom?"

"He sighed loudly, "I don't know yet, Mel. We'll be all right."

"How can you say that?" I was angry. "We're both underage. They'll probably stick us in some foster home!"

"No. I won't let that happen! You hear me? Mom is coming back!"

"Thea stood up and walked over to us.

"The two of you will be fine. Your mom will be back. You'll see."

"How could she say that? She didn't know anything. She certainly didn't know we were on the run from someone who wanted us all dead.

"Tears were streaming down my face. I couldn't handle the desperation, the worry, the anger.

"What if she doesn't?" I asked wiping the tears from my face. "What if they hurt her?"

"Neither Kyle nor Thea responded to my questions. They didn't have answers any more than I did. Kyle just hugged me again. It made me feel a little better. At least I had Kyle.

"I calmed down a little and sniffled. Kyle got me a Kleenex and I blew my nose. Then I started hiccuping, so Kyle got me a glass of water from the bathroom.

"We all sat and waited. There was nothing else to do. I was too frightened to go look for her. I didn't know the area at all. I wouldn't let Kyle go even if he wanted to. There was no way I was taking the chance of losing him too.

"Thea left when the cops showed up. It seemed like hours since we called them, but I know it wasn't that long. Every minute Mom was gone felt like an eternity and made me worry more.

"Detective Lewis introduced himself. When he entered the room, he stood by the open door. That was good. I didn't want him to shut the door and I didn't want him too close to me. I was afraid of trusting anyone except Kyle.

"After we gave him the particulars like Mom's name and her description, he started asking other questions.

"When was the last time you saw your mother?"

"Right before bed. We all ate dinner in here then she said she was going for a walk," Kyle said.

"Did she?" The detective wrote in a small notebook each time he asked something.

"Yes. Later, we woke up and saw she wasn't here. We found her cell phone and that's what we used to call you."

"Can you tell me what she was wearing?"

"Jeans and a blue shirt. Oh, and white sneakers," I said.

"More scribbling then, "Was it a t-shirt? Long sleeve?"

"Short sleeves," I said.

"Did she have a jacket on?"

"I didn't know the temperature outside. When I ran out there to check for her car, all I felt was my heart racing.

"No," I said thinking back to when we were all

164

having dinner.

"You wouldn't happen to have a photo, would you?"

"Kyle and I looked at each other before shaking our heads.

"And the car is still here?"

"Yes, I checked when the 911 person asked."

"And your father? Where is he?"

"I was so sick of that question, but I knew the detective had no idea. Kyle explained about his death.

"Do you live around here?"

"No. We came up here to get away," I said.

"Get away? From what?"

"Kyle looked at me. He answered the question.

"A short vacation, before school starts."

"Yes, after Labor Day," I told him.

"He frowned and said, "Which would be tomorrow…today."

"We didn't answer. He wrote in his notebook again.

"Do you know your home address?"

"Kyle told him and he wrote it down.

"Do you think your mother could have…maybe…just left?"

"Left? As in leave us? No way," Kyle stated. "Mom wouldn't bring us here then leave us."

"Mom loves us. She wouldn't go anywhere without us," I firmly stated.

"I was annoyed that he even suggested it.

"I can imagine how hard this must be on you. And I'm sorry, but I have to ask these questions."

"I calmed down, knowing he was right. It didn't make me feel any better though. I know for a fact Mom

165

would not do that to us.

"So you just both suddenly wake up in the middle of night and realize your mother is gone?"

"How do we explain that one? Do we tell him we knew because our dead father woke us up to tell us? Oh, and that we couldn't see him that time, only hear him? I let Kyle answer.

"I couldn't sleep, so I got up and walked to the bathroom for a drink. I must have woken Melinda when I got up."

"Good one. I didn't know Kyle was such a good liar.

"And that's when you noticed she wasn't here?"

"Yeah."

"So you immediately call 911?"

"Yeah."

"Did you look around for her? Did you think maybe she went for a drive or something?"

"She didn't go for a drive. Her car is here."

"I understand that, but you didn't know that right away. What is it that you two aren't telling me?"

"The cop was smart. It made me nervous. Maybe we should tell him everything. Yeah and he'd probably think we were nuts and have us committed.

"Nothing. Listen, I know Mom wouldn't go anywhere without telling us," Kyle said.

"Detective Lewis looked from Kyle to me and back again. He did that a few times. He closed his notebook and put it in his pocket.

"All right. You two stay here. I'm going to have a look around."

"I shut the door and turned to Kyle.

"In a whisper, I said, "Maybe we should tell him

166

about the guy. He can help us. Kyle, I'm worried about Mom."

"He looked thoughtful for a minute, then said, "Me, too. Okay, we'll tell him what happened at our house, but no mention of Dad. No one will ever believe that we're talking to a dead man."

"We waited until the cop came back in the room. He was holding a black purse.

"Is this your mother's?"

"I recognized it as hers.

"Yes."

"Are these the keys to the car?"

"They look like it," Kyle said.

"Where were they?" I asked.

"On the ground by the car. Another officer found boxes of clothing in the trunk of the car. Can you explain that?"

"Yeah. She was going to donate them to a charity. I helped her carry them to the car. She didn't get a chance before…"

"I stopped myself. How do I say before we were all almost killed because of a sheet with account numbers?

"Yes?" Detective Lewis prodded.

"I couldn't answer him. I didn't know what to say. Kyle intervened.

"Um, officer? We kind of lied. We're sorry," Kyle said.

"About what?"

"We didn't come here on vacation."

"I cut him off, rushing my words out. "Yeah, this man tried to hurt us. He hit Mom and Kyle. The police came and…"

"I started crying again.

"And what?" he asked gently.

"A guy broke into our house," Kyle explained. "Mom decided to take us away for a few days."

"The man took out his notebook again.

"This occurred at your residence?"

"Yes."

"Tell me what happened."

"Kyle told him, leaving out the information about the sheet with the account numbers and how Dad was involved.

"I'll check with the police department there. Is there anything else you're not telling me?"

"Nothing of importance," Kyle said.

"You may not think so, but something you think is small could turn out to be huge. What is it?"

"I was tired of all the lies. I wanted them to stop. I wanted my life back.

"The guy wasn't looking for money like we said. He wanted a paper that had account numbers on it."

"Kyle glared at me. I knew he was mad.

"Do you know this person?"

"No."

"How do you know what he wanted?"

"Uh…Mom said that's what he asked for."

"I could tell the officer didn't believe me.

"Right. Then why say he asked for cash?"

"I didn't know how to answer that at first.

"I figured that's what it was for," I remembered Mom saying it was practically the same thing. "Must be a bank account with money in it. Same thing."

"Not really. Where is this piece of paper?"

"Kyle was quiet until now. He answered before I had a chance to say anything.

"We don't know."

"But you do know what he's talking about, don't you?"

"No," Kyle said.

"Look, it seems like you kids keep coming up with new information. I think you know about this paper, why someone broke into your house, and why your mother is missing."

"No, we don't," Kyle said.

"Do you mind if I sit down here?" he motioned to my bed.

"Okay," I said.

"At least he was respectful. When he spoke next, his voice was soft, gentle.

"I understand you both are frightened. I would be, too. I have children about your age and I wouldn't leave them, so I believe you when you say your mom didn't walk out on you. I'm trying to help you, to help find your mother. I can't do that if you're not honest with me about everything."

"I knew he was right. At least he made sense. However, there was no way he would believe us if we told him about Dad.

"Neither Kyle nor I spoke. We didn't even look at each other. I think Kyle was still mad at me for saying what I did. I was afraid to say more, but I wanted Mom back. I didn't know what to do.

"Okay," Detective Lewis stood up. "I'm going to check out the car more thoroughly. If you want to tell me anything else, I'll be back. And it's okay. We're going to do our best to find your mom."

"He patted me on the arm and then Kyle on his shoulder.

"Another officer is coming soon to take care of you."

"We don't need taking care of," Kyle said. "We're fine until Mom gets back."

"The officer looked at us, frowning.

"Like I said, I have two teenagers about your age. I know you are more independent than we parents would like, but you are not adults."

"I'm almost sixteen," Kyle insisted.

"I can see you're a young man and I'm sure you're capable of taking care of your sister, but the law won't allow it. I'll be back. Please stay here."

"When he left again, I said, "Kyle, is he going to put us in a home?"

"No."

"From the way he said it, I knew he wasn't sure. He was trying to make me feel better. I hate being shielded from the truth. I was old enough to know when things were bad. And you couldn't get much worse than right now. At least, that's what I *thought*."

Chapter Thirty-Six

When I stop talking, Alex gives me a few minutes to collect myself. I am actually shaking remembering all that happened and what came next. And it is the *next* part that was even worse.

"So, did you tell the officers about the account numbers? Where to find the paper?"

"No. It was the least of our concern at that time."

"What do you mean?"

"Do you mind if we stop now? I'm getting a headache and would like to rest."

"Of course, Melinda. Like I said, we go at your pace. We can resume tomorrow."

"Thank you."

I initially planned to sneak out and go see Trent after the session, but I am exhausted and my head is pounding. This session has been more than trying. I really do need to lay down.

Chapter Thirty-Seven

I wake up so early the next day that I doubt the birds are even up yet. I roll over and look at the clock on my nightstand. It is only four thirty. I know I can't sleep any longer. Too many things are rolling around in my head from yesterday's talk with Alex.

I dread today's session. I know I'll have to talk about what happened after Mom disappeared. Every doctor I spoke to all said the same thing: I can't heal unless I confess everything. Of course, they meant that I should come clean about lying the whole time. To them, that may make sense, but if they actually hear my entire confession, they will want to keep me here indefinitely. Label me insane and then the pity will start.

I don't want anyone to feel sorry for me. I just want *out*. I know I keep saying and thinking the same thing and I'm being repetitive, but it's my goal. My *only* goal.

I used to dream about seeing Dad, Mom, and Kyle again, but I know now that isn't going to happen, not as real people anyway. The only thing I can do is move forward. Have a life outside of these grounds that doesn't involve talking about what happened in the past.

Right now though, I am also thinking about Trent. He must be hungry. I didn't bring him any dinner. In fact, I didn't eat supper either. I told the caretakers I wasn't feeling well and went right to bed. I guess that's why I'm up so early now.

My stomach is grumbling, so I get up and dress. I decide to sneak into the kitchen and see if Manuel has left me anything. Sure enough, I find a package for me in our hiding spot. I open the small basket holding the food and peek inside. Rolls, separate pieces of Tupperware filled with peanut butter, jelly, and canned peaches. There's a bottle of water and a Kit Kat. My favorite candy bar. I smile and silently thank Manuel.

I take everything and sneak out the kitchen door. It's cool outside and I notice I was wrong about the birds. They are already singing and chirping even though it is still dark out. Maybe they don't sleep at night like I thought.

I find the ground soggy as I run across the side lawn and toward the front. It must have rained quite a bit sometime last night. I keep on the paving stones until I reach the outskirts of the garden. Then I have no choice but to walk on the ground. It is slippery from the wet leaves and I can hear my sneakers making sloshing noises in the mud. I slip a few times and drop the basket once. Fortunately, the food doesn't fall out.

I run right to the tree, knowing that's where I'll find Trent. I call up to him. His head appears at the opening and he smiles. It starts raining and I don't want to leave the food outside, so I put the handle of the basket over the crook of my arm and grab the wood planks and start up.

My foot slips a few times, but I make it safely. It is dry in there. I wonder who made such a sturdy tree house that the roof doesn't even leak.

I can tell Trent is still half-asleep. I probably woke him when I called out his name. He rubs his eyes and yawns.

I put the basket on the small table.

"Did I wake you?"

"Yeah. It's early. How come you are here so early?"

"I couldn't sleep. I brought breakfast for you."

"Good, I'm starved!"

"So am I, but I'll have breakfast soon. You eat."

He eats in silence. I do nibble on a roll, but leave the rest for him.

After the last roll is gone, he asks, "Why do you keep helping me, bringing me food?"

"I don't know. I like you, I guess."

"Yeah, me too."

I suppose that means he likes me as well.

"And it's not like I have many friends. You and Alex are it."

"Who's Alex?"

"The doctor I told you I see."

"He's your friend?"

"Yes. He's nice. He gave me a book and took me to lunch in town. And I think he believes me."

"About what?"

I never told Trent what Alex and I discuss or that I'm there to talk about my weird past.

"Just stuff. So, what do you do when I'm not around?" I ask in order to change the subject.

"Read the books you brought. Sometimes, I go walking in the woods. Oh, yeah! I almost forgot to tell you. I have to show you what I found." He starts toward the opening and says, "Come on!" with so much excitement, I couldn't help but follow him.

"Is it still raining?"

"Only sprinkling."

"Okay."

I look out and see that it's getting light out. I'd been here longer than I thought.

Down on the ground again, I ask, "What did you find?"

"You'll see."

He grabs my hand and tugs me along. It is the first time I'd been touched by a boy that wasn't Dad or Kyle. It feels good and makes me smile.

"What are you smiling about?"

"Oh, nothing. Where are we going?"

"Further into the woods."

"I can't go far. I have to get back before breakfast or they'll wonder where I am. The last thing I need is for them to come looking for me."

"How long do you have?"

"I don't know. I don't have a watch. But from what I can tell, I've been here a little while. I should probably get back soon."

"Okay, I'll show you later then. It takes a while to get there."

"How about tonight?"

"Okay, we can use flashlights."

"I'll sneak out after dinner. I'll bring food."

"I still have the peaches I can eat at lunch. Thank you for the food, Melinda."

"You're welcome. I wish I had more to leave with you."

"It's okay. It's more than I had before we found each other."

Before we found each other—that's nice to hear. I smile and thank him for being my friend.

He smiles back. I tell him I'd better get going. I am walking toward the path when he stops me by putting his hand on my arm. I turn back and he leans down and kisses me on the cheek.

I'm shocked. Other than my family, no one ever kissed me. Because he is younger than I am, I know it isn't a boyfriend-girlfriend thing, but it feels good anyway.

I put my hand on the cheek he kissed and smile. I don't know what to say or do, so I just leave.

It turns out I have plenty of time before breakfast. I clean the mud from my sneakers. I don't want them to see it and ask where I'd been. I eat quite a bit at breakfast since I missed dinner and didn't want to eat Trent's food.

I'm still not looking forward to my session today. I mean, I do want to tell the story. After all, someone needs to hear the whole truth, but it brings back all the bad memories. Ones I've tried to stifle over the years. It's time to go continue the healing process.

"Good morning, Alex."

"Good morning, Melinda. I trust you are doing well today?"

"Yes. Headache is gone."

"I'm glad to hear it. You are ready then to pick up where we left off yesterday?"

"Sure, I guess so. We're at the point where Mom is missing."

Chapter Thirty-Eight

"Another detective came in after Detective Lewis went to check out Mom's car. Before she got there, we took turns changing into regular clothes in the bathroom.

"The other detective's name was Brandi something. I only remember her first name because I thought it was so different.

"Anyway, she asked us a lot of the same questions the other detective did. Then she explained that until my mother was found, Kyle and I would have to visit a group home. Visit? That was the word she used. Funny, I can't imagine any kid visiting a home. That was bullshit and we all knew it.

"Kyle told her there was no way he and I were going to be split up. He said he heard horror stories about things like that. I didn't know where he heard them, but I didn't care. I was in agreement with him. No way. I couldn't lose Kyle, too. She assured us they would do everything they could to keep us together, preferably back with our mother.

"Hopes. Dreams. Wishes. That's what we left with that day. No mother, no other family."

I start playing with the leaves of the little plant that was sitting on the small table next to me. It looks fake, but I can see from touching it that it's not. I realize I'm fidgeting because the thoughts of the past bring with them the feelings of overwhelming sadness I had that day and many days after.

"I'm sorry for the pain you must have suffered."

"Still suffer, but it's getting better. Anyway, we were left alone in our room again while Brandi went to talk to Detective Lewis.

"Kyle grabbed my arm and said, "Come on."

"What? Where?"

"Anywhere. I'm not letting them take us to some home. Mom's out there. We need to find her."

"How?"

"I don't know. I'm hoping Dad can lead us."

"I picked up my bag that I never unpacked. I was all for the plan. It wasn't much of one, but it's the best we had.

"Wait," Kyle said as I headed for the door. "We'll leave by the window."

"Thank goodness we were on the first floor. Kyle pushed the sash up and it groaned. We waited to see if the sound would bring anyone running. When no one came, he poked his head outside and didn't see anyone. Fortunately, our room faced the side of the house, not the parking lot.

"He threw both of our bags on the ground and hopped out.

"Come on," he whispered.

"I lowered myself to the ground. Kyle grabbed my hand and we ran toward the woods away from the house. Several feet in, we stopped. No one was around.

"It was a bit after eight. I knew that because the last I looked at the clock in the room after the female detective left, it was 8:05.

"What are we going to do?" I asked.

"I'm not sure yet. I didn't want them to take us some place where we'll be split up. Besides, what if Mom comes back and finds us gone? She won't know where to look."

"He had a good point. Even though I doubted Mom was coming back to the bed and breakfast.

"We have no money, no place to stay," I told him.

"I have a little money. I've been saving my weekly allowance. We'll be fine."

"How much do you have?"

"Twenty dollars."

"That won't get us too far."

"It'll buy us food. We'll sleep in the woods. It won't be long before we find Mom."

"For some reason, I didn't believe him. I wasn't sure we would see Mom again. The thought of being an orphan made me cry.

"It's okay," Kyle tried to reassure me.

"No, it's not. I want Mom back."

"So do I, but I'm here. I'm not going anywhere."

"I sniffled and stopped more tears from falling. I had to be strong, like Kyle.

"I'm all right. What should we do first?"

"We need to get away from here. They'll start looking for us soon."

"I squared my shoulders and looked around us. I refused to be anything but tough. I would keep my emotions at bay. Save them for later when Mom was back. It was a promise I made several times over the years, and rarely kept.

"Let's head that way," I pointed further into the woods. "We'll be harder to spot."

"Good idea."

"We walked for a long time, stopping only to rest when we absolutely needed it. We passed cabin after cabin. Kyle said we shouldn't stop at any of them because if there was anyone in there, they'd probably call the cops on us.

"Finally, we came to the outskirts of the small town. I peered past the trees down what looked like the main street. It was riddled with what appeared to be tourists. People going in and out of shops.

"We should avoid it. The cops might look there," Kyle said.

"It was almost noon by then and I realized we hadn't eaten since the night before.

"I'm getting hungry."

"Me, too. But let's wait a while."

"We could try and blend in with the others. If we don't look lost, maybe they won't notice us."

"He looked thoughtful for a minute, eyeing the street.

"Okay, see that restaurant there?" he pointed to a place not too far down the street. "We can go in there, see if we can find a back booth. But order light and something we can eat fast." I start to step forward, but he stops me. "Better yet, maybe you should wait here. I'll go get us something and bring it back."

"I didn't like having him leave my side, but I remembered my vow to be strong. He was only going just a short way and I could see the area clearly.

"Okay, but come right back."

"He looked around. I assumed he was looking for cop cars. He darted to the street and then slowly and with purpose, walked into the restaurant. My eyes stayed glued on the door until he came back out. When he did, he strode just as slowly. I figured he didn't want to draw attention, but I wanted to scream at him to hurry.

"We took our food a little way into the woods. He got a bottle of water, a tuna sandwich, a cup of soup, and some crackers to share. It was enough. I knew we had to watch what money we spent.

"Kyle, do you have a plan? I mean, we've been walking all morning to avoid the cops. When do we start looking for Mom? And where do we start?"

"I've been thinking about that this morning. Chances are, they'll tow Mom's car and take her things from her room. I wish we had thought of taking her purse, or at least the money. Anyway, it's too risky to watch the place where we were staying. So, I'm thinking if we can somehow find our way home…"

"Home? But Mom is around here somewhere," I interrupted him.

"Okay, true. Then we find a place around here to stay. Somewhere that's away from the main part of town, but we have to be able to see it. Then we'll know if Mom is in town or if that same guy that broke into our house is."

"That's a good idea. I remember what he looks like. You think it's him?"

"Maybe. It's worth a shot."

"I didn't have a better plan, so we went with that one. We walked into the woods bordering the small town to see where the best and safest viewpoint would be. We finally found a spot on the other side. It gave us a view of most of the main street, but we wouldn't be hidden that well.

"How about we take turns sleeping tonight? Here,"

he moved our stuff twenty feet into the woods, "we can sleep here. Whoever is keeping watch can see the street and the person sleeping."

"The ground he selected was filled with pine needles and had a large tree next to it.

"Why? It's not like Mom or that guy is going to come down the middle of the street in the middle of the night."

"Probably not, but you never know."

"All right. I wonder where Dad is. Why hasn't he contacted us again?"

"I don't know."

"What are you doing here?"

"I jumped at the sound. A man had come up behind us from the other side of the woods nearest the street. He must have crossed over and seen us. I scooted behind Kyle, eyes wide. I know I said I'd be strong, but brave I wasn't.

"The guy was not much taller than Kyle and skinny. Actually, he didn't look much older either.

"We were playing. Mom and Dad are in the stores. They know where we're at," Kyle rambled on.

It sounded like he was nervous because his voice was a little shaky.

"Uh, huh. What store?"

"Don't know. They said we could play, but to stay here and not go any further."

"Then what's with the bags?"

"We were picnicking," I said.

"He held what looked like a rolled up skinny cigarette in his hands. "Wanna get high? It's better than fried chicken and all that."

"Drugs. Great.

"Uh, no thanks."

"But thank you anyway," I said.

"He laughed at us.

"Couple of squares, huh?"

"We just looked at him. I was ready to bolt, but I wasn't going to leave Kyle alone with this guy. I nudged him, trying to tell him silently that we should leave. He got the message.

"We better go find our parents now."

"The guy laughed as we grabbed our stuff and headed toward the street. I wanted to run as fast as we could away from him and even tried to, but Kyle grabbed my arm and made us slowly walk away. I assumed it was so that we didn't show fear of the guy, but I was afraid. My insides were running while my body leisurely strolled next to Kyle.

"The main street was the last place we should probably have gone, but I didn't see we had a choice. The first side street we came to, Kyle pulled my arm, and we ran down it and didn't stop for five blocks.

"Gasping for breath, I bent over and put my hands on my knees. I was sweating. The long sleeve shirt I put on this morning wasn't helping. I pushed my sleeves back. I looked around us. I saw a few houses and an inn on the left side of the street and on the right was a large, empty parking lot. We headed that way.

"It was filled with empty beer bottles, soda cans, and tons of trash. Crumpled fast food wrappers, a rusted metal bed frame, and even an old shoe. I didn't see its mate. I kicked one of the cans as we walked.

"I guess we'll have to find a new place," I said.

"Yeah."

"He didn't suggest anything. We kept walking. On

the other side of the parking lot we ran into a RV. It looked like the front part of the cab had caught on fire. The front was black and the entire thing was rusty. Someone must have driven it here and abandoned it as the engine went up in flames. We inspected the outside and the rest of it seemed somewhat okay, at least from what we could tell. At least it was still standing.

"Kyle pulled open the side door and it practically fell off in his hands. It hung by the lower hinges, and it didn't look like that would hold for much longer. I jumped back and he laughed.

"It's just a door."

"I didn't want it hitting me."

"He tried to prop it up so we could enter without getting scraped by its rusty edges. He poked his head in.

"No one."

"I figured. If there was, we would have known the minute you tore the door off."

"I laughed. It felt good to have a smile on my face for a few minutes.

"We tentatively entered the RV, worried that with each step, we'd fall through the floor. There was a galley kitchen with a small refrigerator with its door hanging open, and a few cupboards. Two benches facing each other sat beneath a window that had long since been smashed. There used to be a table between the seats and that was gone, too. It looked like kids had been there with spray paint. There were black squiggly marks and weird pictures all over the cupboards.

"Empty beer and soda cans and bottles were on the counter and floor, along with other garbage. It looked like a smaller but messier version of the parking lot we just walked through.

"The floor creaked with every step we took. We ambled toward the small room in the back. It was big enough to fit a double bed. There were no sheets or blankets and the mattress was filthy and torn in spots.

"I doubt anyone lives here anymore," I said.

"Just rats probably."

"Yuck!"

"We should stay here tonight, but we'll come back later."

"Yeah, we're not going to find Mom if we stay here. I have an idea. I'll go to town. I have my hood on my jacket. I can put it up. I want to see if I can spot that guy or Mom."

"Not a good idea, Mel. If you see him and you're alone, he could take you, too."

"We have to do *something*!"

"I know, okay? I don't know *what*."

"Frustrated, I flopped down on the bed. Dust flew everywhere. I coughed, waved my hands in front of my face, and stood back up. I was getting mad. At the situation. At Mom being gone. At letting Kyle talk me into leaving the bed and breakfast—well, that wasn't true. He didn't make me. I agreed to his plan. But I was mad at having to hide from the cops. At two kids being alone, trying to find their mother. At everything.

"I stomped down the very short hallway through the miniscule galley, kicking cans and garbage out of my way as I went, and out the door. Kyle followed me.

"Where are you going?"

"I don't know. I want to find Mom. I want that...that *bastard* who took her arrested. I want to talk to Dad. Where the hell is he? Why isn't he helping us?"

"I sat down on the short stoop, crossed my arms

over my knees, and started crying.

"I know, Mel. It will be all right."

"Will it?" I shouted and stood back up. "No, it's not going to be all right, damn it! How can you say that? You don't even know what the hell you're talking about!"

"I took off at a run back across the parking lot and up the street. I didn't look back and I didn't stop until I reached the main part of town. I didn't care. Let the cops see me. I hoped they did. Maybe they had news on Mom.

"Kyle didn't follow me. I stood on the corner alone. Not knowing what direction to go in. I didn't know this town at all. I had no idea if it was big or small. All I knew was that this seemed to be the center of town. Tourists were still flocking the streets.

"I saw a family across the street. It looked like a mother, father, and two kids. It reminded me of what I used to have before Dad died. I sucked back my tears, wiped my face, and crossed the street.

"I fell into step behind them so that if anyone looked, they would think I was part of that family. The children were skipping and laughing. At one point, they turned around. They were excitedly pointing to a bike in a window of the store as their parents took their hands and dragged them away. They were younger than Kyle and I.

"My heart ached. I missed my family. And now I'd run off and left Kyle back at the RV. What was I doing? I had no idea what I thought I would accomplish. That's the problem, though. I didn't think.

"I ignored the family and started looking at men and women. I looked into shops and down alleyways. I must have walked the small street half a dozen times, up one side and down the other. Nothing. No Mom.

"I was getting tired. And hungry. I figured I'd better go back to the RV. Kyle had all the money to buy food. I walked back to the rusted piece of tin. Kyle wasn't outside anywhere. I went in and found a bag on the counter. But no Kyle. I opened the bag to find a cheeseburger and fries. The water bottle sat next to the bag. The food was cold, but I didn't care. I broke the meal in half and put the rest in the bag for Kyle.

"I sat on one of the benches and ate, taking small sips of water. After finishing, I went back outside. I didn't see Kyle anywhere. Remembering he said we'd stay here the night, I sat and waited for him, figuring he'd come back.

"I felt bad about my actions. This situation wasn't Kyle's fault and I took it out on him. I left him there, not caring what he would do. Not thinking that he would be worried about me.

"I'm sorry, Kyle. Please come back," I whispered to the dusty, stale air.

"To pass the time, I looked all around the outside of the RV to see what else was there. Nothing but trees and trash. The street ended not far past the RV and there was nothing but trees beyond that. I wasn't about to go into the woods alone and didn't want to stray too far from our home away from home."

"Hours later, Kyle still didn't show up and I was frightened."

I pause when my stomach starts rumbling and I realize I'm hungry and need to use the bathroom.

"Do you mind if we take a break. I'm getting hungry," I tell Alex.

"Good idea. It's almost lunchtime. Go ahead and come back when you're done. I'll be here."

"Okay."

I go to the bathroom then to my room. I have about ten minutes before lunch. Nurse Hamilton hates it when we get there early and will shoo us away. She says there's no need to get there early because the food will not be served early. She has a point.

I sit down on my bed and my thoughts stray to what my life will be like when I get out of here. I close my eyes and dream about having a place of my own where I can read whatever I want and watch whatever I want. I will take cooking classes. The only things I know how to cook are the things I help Manuel make. The easy stuff like pancakes, bacon, sandwiches, soup, and stuff like that. I smile thinking about all the freedom I will have.

I open my eyes and look around my sterile room. I realize that right now, all my fanciful ideas of a free future are only a dream. Soon, it will be a reality.

I go down and fill my tray with food. I decide to eat outside because it looks pleasant with the sun shining. I see others in short sleeves, so it must be warm. There are a few others out there with their lunch. I carry my tray outside and sit at one of the picnic tables set to the side of the garden area. I sit on the opposite side so I can see the flowers and grass.

I take my time and enjoy lunch in the sunshine. Another patient comes and sits down across from me. Her aide is next to her. It's Lucy. She's probably one of the worst here as far as medical conditions go. The aide has to be with her at all times. Otherwise, she'll wander around. She'll pick things up and put them in her mouth every chance she can get.

Doesn't matter what it is, rocks, dirt, whatever she can get her hands on. Mealtimes are good for her because she can put things in her mouth without getting into trouble. I feel sorry for her as I do many of the patients here.

Lucy doesn't talk to me. She rarely talks to anyone. I've only heard her say a few words, and that includes the word 'no' when they take from her whatever it was she was going to stuff down her throat.

Grudgingly, I finally get up and take my tray inside. I'd rather stay out, but I have to go back in. Nurse Hamilton smiles at me on my way out of the cafeteria. I smile back and proceed on to Alex's office.

When I go inside, he has what looks like a recorder in his hand.

"Do you tape our sessions?" I ask him, surprised.

I didn't think he did. Actually, I never thought to ask.

"I don't usually, unless I think it's necessary. For some patients, it's important for me to go back and listen to everything again. You don't have to worry."

"Oh, okay."

"Would that bother you?"

"Well, sort of, yes. I wouldn't want anyone else hearing what I'm saying to you."

"It's for my ears only. So, are you ready to pick up where we left off?"

****

"Yes. I was telling you about being alone in that run-down RV in Idyllwild. It was creepy and scary.

"Kyle hadn't come back yet. It was getting dark and I panicked. Where was he? I entertained the idea of

189

looking for him. Maybe he was in town somewhere. But I knew that would be stupid. He obviously knew I'd come back here because he left the food. I knew I should stay put.

"Time was wasting. I had no plan on how to find Mom and now I was alone inside of a singed, rusted, rat-infested trailer with Kyle doing God knew what.

"It was late. I had no candles, no flashlight, or anything. There were no streetlights outside anywhere nearby. I sat in the pitch black willing Kyle to return. I started getting sleepy. I pulled my jacket tightly together and using my bag as a pillow, lay down on the sagging, disgusting mattress. Kyle would wake me when he came in.

"I fell asleep to owls hooting and the wind blowing the tree branches, causing them to scrape against the side of the vehicle. It was eerie, to say the least.

"I woke in the middle of the night screaming. I'm not sure why. I was alone and it was pitch black. I clung to myself, wrapping my arms around my body, having nothing or no one else to hang on to. It took me some time to fall back to sleep. I kept hearing small scratching noises, thought of rats and worried they'd scurry onto the bed, and bite me while I slept. Then I started worrying about someone coming in and hurting me. I never needed my mother more than I did at that moment.

"I'm not sure how, probably from pure exhaustion, but I didn't wake again until morning. I jerked awake and immediately looked for Kyle. He wasn't on the bed or anywhere inside. The bag of food and water bottle were still on the counter. I walked outside and found the sun shining. I took off my jacket and tied it around my waist.

"Where was he? Why didn't he come back? Had something happened to him? I went back inside. I was starving and decided to eat half of what I left Kyle. That way if...no, *when* he came back, he'd have something.

"After munching, I thought about Kyle's bag. I used mine as a pillow last night. I looked around for it. I found it under the bench I was sitting on. I checked it. I didn't know if everything was there or not because I didn't watch him pack. I knew he had the money in his wallet, which was in his jeans pocket.

"I became scared. No...terrified. Why hadn't he come back last night? Did the man get him? I was close to hyperventilating. I remembered Dad making Kyle put his head between his legs at an amusement park when he almost passed out from being frightened on a ride. I did that now and it helped.

"After calming down, I thought about what I should do. Wait here? Go looking for him? I figured I'd wait a little while longer. After another hour passed, I couldn't stand it any longer. I decided that if I couldn't find him anywhere I would check back and if he wasn't here and there was no sign he had been, there would be no choice but to go to the police.

"I roamed the town and went down side streets. I went quite a ways into the woods around the town. I decided to check the other side where we first entered it from the forest. I didn't see any sign of him. I walked back to the RV. His bag was still there and so was the uneaten food and water. I drank some water and sat down for a few minutes.

"I knew I was going to cry again, but I stopped myself. I had to be strong like I said I would be. It was time to talk to the cops. I had no idea where the police station even was.

"I hauled myself up and forced myself to walk the five blocks back to town. I was tired from all the walking I did already, but there wasn't anything else I could do.

"Once I got on the main street, I went into the first shop I saw, hoping the owner could tell me where the police station was. The bell tinkled when I walked in and the older lady who sat behind the counter barely looked up from her magazine.

"Enjoy browsing. Let me know if I can help you."

"I walked up to the counter and gathered the courage to speak.

"I said, "Actually, I need help."

"What can I do for you?"

"Can you tell me where the police station is? I'm not from here and I don't know." I was again near tears, my voice was shaky, and I had to swallow the lump in my throat.

"Are you in trouble? Where are you parents?"

"Um, I'm not sure."

"Are you lost?"

"Can you tell me where to find the cops?"

"I'll call them for you. They can come here." She dialed the phone and told me, "Come around here, honey."

"I guess my face said it all: my sadness, my worry, my downright terror at being alone.

"I walked behind the counter she indicated and stood next to her. She told whoever answered the phone that a young girl was in her shop needing help.

"They're on their way. Are you hungry? Can I get

you anything to eat? I don't have much here, but I might have something in the back."

"No, thank you. I'm fine."

"Drink? Here," she handed me a can of unopened soda she had sitting by the register. "You can have it."

"I thanked her. She was so nice. It didn't take long before a cop showed up. It wasn't either of the detectives that had come to the bed and breakfast.

"Okay, young lady, tell me what's wrong."

"It all came pouring out along with the day's pent-up tears. I couldn't stop the words or the waterfall. The woman kept saying "awww" like she was sorry for me. The cop took notes. I started hiccuping and took a drink of the soda the woman gave me.

"So, you're the missing girl from the bed and breakfast? That's quite a long way up the road. How did you get here?"

"We walked," I muttered, putting my head down.

"And you say you don't know where your brother is?"

"I sniffled and the lady handed me a tissue.

"No. I was mad at him, well, not really at *him*, but at everything and I stormed off. I haven't seen him since."

"And this was yesterday?"

"Yes."

"Where did you stay last night?"

"I told him and said that Kyle was there yesterday because he left me food.

"Have they found my mom yet?"

"I don't think so. I'm going to take you down to the station. I'm sure the detectives would like to talk to you."

"He got on his radio and asked the dispatcher to contact Detectives Lewis and Horn. He must mean Brandi.

"You'll be okay, honey. They'll take good care of you and find your mother and brother. Don't you worry," the lady tried to reassure me.

"I smiled at her and thanked her as the cop led me out to his car. I can't explain to you how scared I was. I've never ridden in a cop car before and even though at the time, I knew I wasn't in trouble, I was still anxious.

"I wanted Kyle. I wanted Mom. And I wanted Dad."

Chapter Thirty-Nine

"I think we should stop for the day."

I didn't realize I was crying as hard as I was. Again. Gosh, will the tears ever stop? I feel like a big crybaby. It happened the last time, too, when I stopped talking and realized I was bawling. I get up and drink some water when the hiccups start. I must stop acting liked a child. Alex must think I'm nothing but a weak kid by now. Tears are pouring down my face and I am shaking. It seems like that's all I've been doing since my family and Beth died.

"That's a good idea."

"I think you need some time alone."

"I think so, too. Thank you."

I can't even talk. I grab a tissue, blow my nose, and try to regain my composure.

"It's okay, Melinda, to feel sad and be upset. You've been through a lot. And I do believe that you have never shared most of this story. It's hard to do that, especially for the first time."

"I know."

I leave and go back to my room. He is right. I do need time alone. I don't want to face everyone else and have to plaster a smile on my face and pretend everything is all right.

Life sucks.

And apparently, so does death.

Chapter Forty

Alex

I was beyond frustrated by the time Melinda left. I feel like she'll never heal enough to remember everything. That will be to her detriment.

I decide to replay the last three sessions. There must be something in there that can help. After listening to the sessions four times, I shut it off and slam the digital recorder down on my desk. I'm going to have to report to him soon and I have no idea what to say.

It's unfortunate, but I think Melinda is doomed. I guess time will tell, but I fear she's running out of it.

Chapter Forty-One

The Other Side

I knew that black cloud was hanging around for a reason. Now I see why. It's him. Damn it! After all this time, he's found Melinda. How? I watch him walk toward a car. I must stop him!

I walk through the portal and confront him. He doesn't see me. Why can't he? I scream at him and he keeps walking. I try to block his way and am unable to. What is going on? Why can I appear to Trent and to my family before Meredith and Kyle died and not him now?

I have to find a way. He is going to get to Melinda.

He is on his cell phone speaking to someone.

"Well, figure it out. Get her away from there. I don't care what you have to go through. Get it done!"

He hangs up and I try again to get him to hear me.

"You leave my daughter alone!"

I try to push him, but I fall to the ground. I'm so frustrated. I was able to make physical contact before. Now? Nothing? Damn it!

"I won't let you near her! You hear me?"

I know he doesn't. For some reason, he has no idea I'm there.

I'm being summoned. I have to get back.

Chapter Forty-Two

Later that night after dinner, which I eat in my room, I decide to sneak out. I need to bring Trent something to eat. I go to the kitchen and again, there is a little package from Manuel. I think he knows I am feeding someone else. He's started leaving double the food.

The cottage is a welcoming sight. To me, it represents a piece of me. Something I would have if I was able. A place of my own to do as I please. Neat, tidy and organized.

Trent must have seen me coming because he meets me at the front of the cottage.

"Let's go in here and eat," I suggest.

He goes in ahead of me and lights the candles. It is comfortable in the dim flicker, but a bit stuffy. I open the window, hoping the evening breeze will find its way in. I set out the food.

"How was your session today?"

I often share parts of my long-running memory sessions with him, but nothing in detail. I don't think he'd believe in the 'other side.' Mainly, I tell him about trips with my family.

"It was okay." I don't say anything about all the tears I shed...again. "What did you do today?"

"Not much. Are you ready to go to the place I found?"

I'd forgotten all about that.

"Sure. We have the flashlights here."

We finish eating and Trent jumps up from the sofa like he's on fire.

"Ready?" He's smiling with excitement, his face almost glowing. "It would be better during the day to see, but I can't wait anymore to show you. You're going to love it!"

He is beaming from ear to ear and his good mood makes me happy. He makes me feel better.

"Okay, let's go," I say, smiling with enthusiasm.

He leads the way through brush, weeds, trees, and bushes.

"I hope you know how to get us back. I'm lost."

"I do, don't worry."

We seemed to walk for a long time. I am getting worried.

"How much farther?"

"Not far. It's just up the next hill."

Of course, I can't see any hills, it is too dark. I barely see in front of me, but for some reason I trust Trent.

"It's up ahead."

I can hear the excitement in his voice. He's probably still smiling. He stops so suddenly, I run right into him.

"Ow!"

"Are you okay?" he asks.

"Yeah, but why did you stop like that?"

"Sorry. We're here." He takes my hand. "As soon as we're through these big bushes, I want you to aim your flashlight straight ahead. Got it?"

"All right."

I do as he asks and notice he does the same. I look and in front of me is a nice sized pond. I open my eyes wide in surprise. Trent doesn't say anything. I guess he is waiting for me to say something.

It looks serene. Because it's dark, I can't really tell how big it was. I hear water flowing from nearby. I wonder why I couldn't hear it before now, but in my defense, it isn't that loud.

"Wow. Is there a waterfall?"

"Yeah, you can't really tell in the dark and it's not that big, but it's cool. It's on the other side."

"How big is the water hole?"

"Kinda big. The water from the falls pool here. It doesn't go anywhere else."

"I want to see it in the daytime. Is it for swimming or fishing?"

"The water is clear, so swimming. And it's not that cold. See?"

I feel water splash on my arms and face.

"Hey!"

I am not expecting it.

"Sorry. It's not bad, huh?"

"It's sort of cold."

"But it's nighttime, too," he reminds me.

"That's true. We need to come back during daylight hours."

"We will, but come on," I hear the sound of a zipper.

Oh my God! He is taking his pants off!

"Let's go swimming," he says.

"Are you crazy?"

"Let's have some fun. Who's here to see us? We can't even see us."

He has a point there. I shrug even though he can't notice the movement.

When I hesitate, he says, "You never do anything fun. You told me that yourself. So, who's to stop us?"

"Fine, but no peeking!" I can't believe I say that. "Okay, that was a stupid statement."

We both laugh. I take my shoes, jeans, and top off and walk tentatively in the water clad in nothing but my bra and underwear. It's cold and I shiver, but it still feels good. I haven't been swimming since before my dad died.

I hear and feel a splash next to me. The rough ground tickles my bare feet. It feels good. Because I can't see, I don't venture too far from the embankment.

We end up staying there for a few hours, at least. I don't even think about time or getting back to the house, only about all the fun I'm having for the first time in a very long time.

We laugh and splash each other. Trent would go under the water and tickle my toes with his fingers then come up laughing. I would swim around him and scare him from behind. Once, because it's so dark, I ended up in front of him and almost hit him in the head when my arm came up to grab him. I can picture having a float of some kind, lazing under the sun next to Trent and having a picnic on the water's edge, enjoying life. I smile so much my face hurts.

I haven't had this much fun since Kyle and I used to play in the river.

The thought sobers me, but I don't want to bring Trent down with me, so I try to dismiss it. But I can't. The laughter is gone. Reality is sinking back in. It always does.

"We better get back. I wonder what time it is."

"No idea," he says.

"It must be late. Let's go."

I start walking out of the water and he grabs my hand.

"Thank you for coming here with me."

I smile, even though he can't see it, and say, "It was fun. Thank you for taking me here. I won't be able to find this place on my own, so you'll have to bring me back. And next time, in the daylight, okay?"

He laughs. We both get dressed. My clothes cling to my wet body, but it feels good. I left my flashlight on the entire time we were in the water so we could find our clothes when we get back out. I purposely pointed it away from the water. I didn't want him seeing me get in or out of the water in my undergarments.

We finally make it back to the little cottage. I have no idea how late it is. I figure the next item I smuggle here should be a clock.

"I should go."

"Why don't you stay until morning? You can sneak back in at daybreak."

"I'm not sure that's a good idea."

"You can have the bedroom and I'll put my sleeping bag on the couch or I'll sleep in the tree house."

"I've never stayed out all night. What if they find I'm missing?"

"Are they really going to check on you in the middle of the night?"

"I suppose not."

"Well?" he asks.

I can use some company. I am tired of being alone.

I've been by myself since Mom and Kyle disappeared. Well, at any rate, I'm sure Trent is lonely, too.

"Okay. But as soon as dawn arrives, I have to leave. And you are not sleeping in the tree house."

"Okay, the sofa it is for me then. I always wake up as it's getting light out, so I'll get you up."

Trent runs to the tree house to fetch his sleeping bag. I go in the bedroom and see there are no sheets or blankets. I go back out and grab the small throw blanket I previously brought to use as a cover. It will be enough.

Trent comes back and I suggest, "If you'll be comfortable, you can sleep on the floor in the bedroom."

I didn't want to be alone in a room. Just for tonight, it will be nice to have some company. He agrees and pulls his sleeping bag into the room.

We chat for a while, almost in whispers as if someone from Skyview will hear us. I feel like a misbehaving child not wanting to sleep at night and talking low so our parents won't hear us. If you think about it, it's silly because I'm almost twenty-three. It's actually pitiful.

"When I was in that foster home near here, I started to learn to drive. I never got my license, but I probably could if I had a car. Did you ever learn?"

"No. Skyview won't allow that. After all, most of the patients wouldn't have the skills needed to be able to drive. I think I'm really the only one…well maybe a few others probably could."

"Too bad. I can teach you some day."

"That would be nice. I'll need a car first. After I get out of there, I can probably get one. My parents left me money according to my lawyers."

"That's good. Mine didn't, but that's okay. As soon as I'm eighteen, I'm going to get a job."

"Sounds good."

I hardly hear him anymore. My mind is getting tired and my eyes are already closed. He says something else, but I really don't know what.

As I drift off to sleep, I can't help but finally feel at peace. At least for tonight, I'm not alone.

Chapter Forty-Three

I wake to Trent nudging me and telling me insistently to get up.

"I've been trying to wake you for ten minutes now."

I sit up and rub the sleep out of my eyes.

"You have?"

"Yeah, you sleep like the dead."

"Ha, ha."

He has no idea how ironic that statement is.

I look out the window and see dawn is approaching. I can hear the birds in the trees chattering away. I yawn and stretch.

"Did you sleep all right?" I ask.

"Better than I have in a long time. Thanks for staying last night."

"You're welcome. I slept well, too." I know it's because I had someone in the same room with me. "I better go. I have to change before breakfast."

"When can you come back? I want to show you the water and the falls when it's light out."

"I can come back later, but probably not until dark or close to it. This weekend we can go there. I don't have sessions with Alex on the weekends unless I ask and I won't."

"Okay."

"I'll bring food later, too. I'm sorry I don't have

anything now."

"It's all right. I'll be fine."

I feel bad. I know he is hungry, but he won't complain. He never does.

I quickly make it back to my room. It wasn't a moment too soon because as I am changing my clothes, there is a knock on my door.

I slip my shirt over my head and say, "Yes?"

Nurse Hamilton sticks her head in.

"Oh, good, you're almost ready. Manuel needs help preparing breakfast this morning. Go help and I'll excuse you from doing dishes after you eat."

"Yes, Ma'am."

After brushing my teeth, I make my way down to the kitchen.

"Where's Claudia?" I ask Manuel when I enter.

Claudia is the older woman that helps him cook.

"Called in sick. Here," he hands me a spatula, "start flipping pancakes when they're ready and finish making them until the batter is gone."

I do as he asks. It is a huge bowl of batter, so I know it is going to take me a while. We work together in silence for a while before Manuel speaks.

"So, tell me what you're really doing with all the food."

"I told you."

"I know what you said. Now, how about the truth."

I don't answer him because I am afraid to tell him about Trent. What if they send him back? I didn't want to lose a friend. He and I are starting to make plans; we're going to do things together. Plus he says it is terrible where he lived. He won't want to go back to foster care. I don't blame him from what he told me.

"Anything you tell me is between us," he encourages me.

"You promise not to tell?"

"Promise."

"I'm bringing it to a friend. He doesn't have any money to buy food."

"And where is this friend?"

This I know I won't tell him. That will mean he will know about my secret place as well.

"Around."

"Uh huh. Hey, you're burning the pancakes."

"Damn!"

"You swear now?"

I don't even realize I do until he says something. I guess some of my past ways are creeping back into my life. Well, that may be part of it, but mostly, I haven't really sworn around Manuel before. I don't feel like he will judge or condemn me. I'm very comfortable around him. He makes me feel needed and like a person, not a patient.

"I'm sorry."

"Don't be," he laughs. "You're finally becoming a little human."

I smile. We chitchat about mundane things like the weather. He doesn't ask about my friend again. We finish making breakfast for everyone. I eat in the kitchen with him then announce I have to go to my session with the doctor.

"When you come back later, a goodie basket will be waiting for you."

"Thank you, Manuel."

"Uh huh."

I rush out the swinging door, letting it flap back

and forth behind me. I approach Alex's office door and hesitate. I don't know why, but something makes my steps falter. For the first time in a long time, I don't want to continue my story. I keep thinking about Trent and going back to the pool of water with him. How for once, I didn't feel lonely last night.

I am about to turn around and leave, to sneak out, and see Trent, when his door swings open.

"Melinda! You startled me. I was on my way to the men's room. What are you doing just standing there?"

"I was about to go in."

"Okay. Go ahead. I'll be right back."

Damn!

That's the second time in one day I swear and I think it still counts even when I say it to myself. Oh, well. I think maybe part of the old Melinda is actually making its way back to the surface. That may be a good thing.

But now, I'm stuck. I will have to talk to Alex. Maybe I'll be able to get away early. I guess I will have to play it by ear.

"Well, good morning," Alex walks back in, closing the door. He indicates the chair and says, "When we went to lunch, I mentioned perhaps taking you out again. Dr. Allcott won't agree to a movie, but he said we can have lunch again. How does that sound?"

Honestly, I wanted to say no because secretly I wish it was Trent asking. But that's not fair. Alex is good to me, kind.

"That sounds great. When?"

"Tomorrow perhaps? I'll check with Dr. Allcott."

"Okay. Thank you."

"Now, are you ready for today's session?"

"Yes, but I'm really tired today. Do I have to stay all day?"

"Not if you do not wish to. Why are you so tired? Did you have a bad night?"

"I don't know. Just tired."

"Let's see how much you can stand today and go from there. I believe you left off with speaking to the cops in Idyllwild about Kyle being gone."

"Yes."

I finally sit down in the chair he offered a few minutes ago and mentally prepare myself to recall the ugly truth of what happened. I've been putting off facing this for some time now and it needs to be addressed. I'm not a doctor, but even I know that.

Chapter Forty-Four

"When we got to the police station that day after the cop picked me up from the store in Idyllwild, Detectives Lewis and Brandi Horn were there. I never learned Detective Lewis's first name because after that day, Brandi took over.

"They put me in their break room. There was a couch, a table with chairs, and a counter with a coffee pot, microwave, and other things on it. I sat on the couch and Brandi sat at the table.

"Are you hungry?"

"Why did everyone ask that? No one eats when they're upset. And I was certainly upset. Who wouldn't be after finding out the last person you could count on was missing?

"I left my can of soda back at the lady's shop, so I did ask for a drink. She went over to the corner and put change in the vending machine. She brought me a cold soda then went back and sat down at the table again.

"I thanked her and asked, "Have you found my mom?"

"Not yet. We're looking. It might help if you tell me what you know."

"I already told the other detective."

"Yes. We know your house back home was broken into for some piece of paper with numbers on it and your mother is missing. Now, so is your brother."

"She said this last statement so quietly, I barely heard her. I couldn't help it; tears started forming and spilled over. Brandi came over, sat on the couch next to me, and placed her arm around my shoulders.

"We'll find them," she said. "But right now, I need your help. Do you think you can do that?"

"I don't know," I said and then hiccuped. "I'll try. It's just...you're not going to believe me."

"I drank some soda to get rid of my hiccups.

"Try me."

"I reiterated what Kyle and I knew about the account numbers, that my father had it and after we...found it, we hid it.

"How did you come across this paper?" Brandi asked.

"Well, my dad didn't die in an accident. He was *mur*dered," I stretched out the first part of the word.

"I don't know why I did. I think I wanted to get her attention. It worked.

"Why do you say that? From what our records show, he drowned in a river not far from your house. Going too fast for the weather conditions."

"That's what they want everyone to believe."

"Let's back up a minute, okay? Your dad was an accountant?"

"Yes. You said records. How do you know about my dad's death?"

"When your mother went missing here, we got in contact with the police station in your home town."

"Oh."

"For a minute, my mind went places it probably shouldn't have. I was thinking conspiracy and all kinds of things. Stupid.

"Your father worked in quite a large firm."

"I never went there, but probably. He used to talk about a lot of different people he worked with. I heard him tell Mom about them at dinner."

"So he worked with a lot of paperwork that had numbers on it. How do you and your brother know they were numbers to a bank account?"

"This is where it gets tricky. How do I answer that one?

"It looked like it. Kyle said it was."

"Do you know how he could tell?"

"No, but Kyle wouldn't lie."

"Okay, let's say you're right and they were account numbers. Your father would have things like that in the normal course of his day's work."

"Yeah, but they killed him to get it. They must have made his car go into the river. My dad was a good driver."

"I'm sure he was, but it was raining pretty hard that day, according to the reports. You keep saying 'they.' Who are 'they'?"

"The people who wanted the paper. The ones who killed my father. Who else?"

"I was getting mad again. Why all these questions? Shouldn't the cops be out looking for my mother and brother?

"Why would they kill him over some numbers?"

"I don't know. I'm only thirteen and you're the cop," I snapped.

"So, your brother convinced you of all this?"

"No—yes."

"Which is it?"

"I cried again. God, would I ever stop letting the

tears fall? It wasn't my fault. She was mean. My mother and Kyle were both gone and she wasn't being nice. I sniffle and she gets up, grabs the box of tissue from the counter, and hands it to me. I blow my nose.

"Look, I don't mean to be so hard on you. I'm trying to help. I want to find your mother and brother."

"I know," I said through more sniffles. "Shouldn't you be out doing that and not asking me these damn questions?"

"There are other detectives out looking. I'm trying to gain as much information I can from you to aid them."

"I knew she was trying to do her job, but I'd been through so much already that I couldn't bear much more. And the added thing is her throwing all these questions at me when I just wanted this all to be over. To be back with Mom and Kyle.

"Can we try again?" she asked gently when I didn't respond.

"Okay," I sighed.

"You said you and Kyle hid the paper. Will you tell me where it is? Maybe if we found it, we could use it to find the person who took your mother."

"And Kyle. They have him too. I know they do."

"Yes, and Kyle," she agreed. "Again, do you know who *they* are that you are referring to?"

"No."

"She took my hand in hers and using her other hand, tilted my chin up with her finger.

"I know you're upset and scared. I'm only here to help. You can trust me."

"I didn't know who to trust. I trusted Kyle and he disappeared. I know it wasn't his fault, but still.

"She was wiping the tears from my face with her fingers. It was something Mom would do and it made me miss her more.

"Dad told us," I blurted out before I even knew I was going to.

"What did your father tell you?"

"Everything. About the paper. That his death wasn't an accident. That they were coming after us next."

"Your father confided in you before he died that someone was going to hurt him?"

"No. *After* he died."

"I told her everything, except where Kyle and I hid the paper. I promised Kyle I wouldn't and it was one promise I was going to keep."

"Didn't you say," Dr. Leever interrupts, "that you actually didn't know where Kyle put the paper?"

"Yes, that's true. But I didn't even want her to know the general location."

"I see. Continue."

"It was clear by the look on Brandi's face she didn't believe me. She was looking at me with pity, probably thinking I'm hysterical.

"She asked me again where the paper was and I refused to answer. I kept telling her I didn't know. That damn piece of paper wasn't going to bring Mom and Kyle back no matter what everyone thought. Even if I gave the paper to the people, they'd probably just kill us anyway."

Chapter Forty-Five

"So, this cop didn't believe you about your father?" Alex asks.

"No. She was the first of a long line of people who thought I was lying or insane. That's why I'm here."

I growl my response because I'm still so mad. I stand up, gritting my teeth, and will myself to calm down.

"So what happened after you told her everything?"

****

"Like I said, I didn't tell her where the account numbers were. After I spilled my guts, I asked, "Now what? Will it help to find Mom and Kyle?"

"She excused herself, telling me she would be right back. But I wasn't stupid. After she left the room, I got up and cracked the door open. I heard her talking to Detective Lewis.

"Horn, you know we shouldn't be questioning her. She's a minor."

"I'm just talking to her, trying to calm her down."

"Someone from Social Services is on their way. You've got to stop talking to her. Wait until they're present."

"Fine, but listen, I think she's trying to rationalize things. I can't believe she actually said her father told her."

"The man is dead," Detective Lewis said, shaking

his head.

"So he was listening while I talked to Brandi? I knew I shouldn't have trusted her.

"I know. She's upset. She lost her father and now her mother and Kyle are missing. I think she's traumatized."

"I think she knows more than she's saying. When I talked to her and her brother back at the inn, I felt it then. Something else is going on here. She's protecting someone or herself."

"What are you saying?"

"Wouldn't be the first time we hear about a kid going crazy and killing off their family."

"You think she *killed* them?" Brandi asked.

"I don't know. Maybe. I think we should…"

"They moved further away and I couldn't hear them anymore. I went back and threw myself down on the couch. I knew I shouldn't have told her. They thought I was nuts. To make it worse, they actually thought I killed my own family! I pounded my fists into the cushions, wishing it was that Detective Lewis's face I was hitting.

"How could he think I killed my own family? He didn't know me or my family. I threw my soda can across the room. I didn't care if I got into trouble. Instead of helping, they were making things worse for me.

"I wanted to leave, but didn't have anywhere to go or any idea of where to look for Mom or Kyle. I was trapped.

"When Brandi came back in, I quickly stood up and verbally attacked her because I was angry. I wanted to hit her like I did the pillows, but knew I shouldn't.

"You don't believe me. You think I'm nuts."

"No, I don't."

"You do, too. That other detective heard everything. You let him listen!"

"We're trying to find your family."

"No. I told you the truth and you think I'm lying."

"It's not that we think you're lying," she saw the can on the floor and picked it up. After putting it back on the counter, she said, "You've been through a lot in the last year. It's easy to become confused when you're grieving."

"She pulled some paper towels from the dispenser and wiped up the soda on the floor. It left a trail across the floor and she followed it, cleaning as she went.

"Confused? I'm not confused! You can believe me or not, but Dad told Kyle and me *and* he told Mom. Someone killed him. They wanted the account numbers. Dad *told* us that," I repeated myself. "Now, they have Mom and Kyle and I'm left all alone."

"She tossed the towels into the trash and turned back to me.

"You're not alone. We're here to help you."

"That other cop thinks I killed them or something! That's not helping me! I want to leave now."

"Brandi sighed and sat down at the table. She patted the tabletop and said, "Come here and sit down with me."

"I don't want to sit with you. I want to go home."

"I made a dash for the door, flung it open, and ran through the main room that they led me through earlier. I was almost at the front door when an officer grabbed me.

"No. Let me go!"

"Settle down," the man said.

"I was squirming to get out of the man's grip. Brandi must have walked up because I heard her tell him to let me go. When he did, I bolted for the door again. Only this time Detective Lewis was standing there and I literally ran into him. He stopped me from going any further by holding me back.

"You can't keep me. I didn't do anything wrong," I squirmed to get away from him, but it didn't work.

"I felt everyone in the place staring at me. I was making a spectacle of myself, but I didn't care.

"I didn't kill my family," I screamed at him.

"We don't think you killed anyone," Brandi stood next to my side.

"I was seething. I knew my face was red because I was so mad.

"*He* does." I pointed my finger at Detective Lewis. "I heard him say it. And you're going to put me in a home."

"Calm down, Melinda. We'll get to the bottom of this," Detective Lewis said.

"Please," I could feel the anger slipping away and fear and exhaustion replacing it. I was tired of fighting. "I didn't do anything. I want my mom and Kyle."

"Detective Lewis's thought that I had killed my family apparently wasn't enough to put me in jail. They didn't have any proof. Either that or I was too young to be thrown in with adult murderers. I didn't know which it was and didn't care. They would never find proof that I did something so terrible because I didn't. They'd see.

"I didn't end up leaving until much later and then it was in the company of a social worker. I was told later that because Mom and Kyle disappeared in Idyllwild, it was their case and I was their problem.

"I couldn't fight the fact that I needed adults to take care of me. I was too tired from all the struggling I had been doing up until then. I gave in and I was taken to a nearby foster home. The mother and father seemed nice, but it didn't matter. I knew before I even got there I was going to hate it and that was only because it wasn't *my* family.

"There was only one other kid there at the time. His name was—"

Chapter Forty-Six

"Trent!"

Oh my God. How could it have been Trent?

"Melinda?" Alex asks.

That's not possible. I try to work it out in my head. I was thirteen then. I'm twenty-two now. He's seventeen now. He would have been what…eight?

"Melinda? Are you all right?"

I tremble. I can't answer him.

Trent? *My* Trent?

I feel Alex's hand on my shoulder.

"Who's Trent?"

I close my eyes and try to picture him then. I didn't spend long there. A few weeks maybe. He was shorter than me, but that would be expected since he was younger. Brown hair, scraggly, like now. Skinny like now. I know the physical description means nothing. It could have been any kid. Could it be? I search my memory harder.

"You're scaring me. Answer me, Melinda."

What is his last name? Think, Melinda. Trent…Trent something. I can't remember. I have to know if it was him. How could it be after all this time?

I bolt up from the chair I am sitting in.

"I have to go."

I feel the urgency to go see him. *Now*. I don't have any facts to base it on, but I feel it in my gut that the

Trent from my past is the same Trent in the present.

"What is wrong? Melinda, you answer me before you walk out that door."

His voice is firm and I turn around, hand on the doorknob. My heart is racing. I can't think of anything else but getting to him fast.

"I'm fine. Please, I have to go."

I swing the door open, run down the hall and outside. I run all the way there. In my haste, I don't even take the time to see if anyone is watching where I am going. I am sweating and my entire chest is heaving with the effort of breathing.

"Trent!"

I run into the cottage. He isn't there. I run back out to the tree and rush up the boards as fast as I can.

"Trent," I call again. The tree house is empty.

I race back down and toward the front again. I twirl in one direction then another. Where can he be?

The water. I can't remember how to get there.

"Trent," I yell his name as loud as I can a few times.

I get myself under control. I am afraid to start panicking again as I did back when Kyle went missing. I plop down on the ground, sit Indian-style in the middle of the front yard, and put my head down as far as I can between my legs.

I breathe in and out, as I've had to do many times over the years. Panic attacks are not foreign to me anymore. When my breathing slows, I straighten my head up. I didn't realize before now how hot it is out today. I am sweating, the back of my t-shirt sticky, but I don't know if it's from running or the heat or both. I slowly stand up and walk toward the cottage.

I go inside and sit down on the little sofa. A few hours ago, I slept a couple of feet away from the boy I shared a home with nine years ago. I don't doubt it was him. I don't know how, but am just as sure as I know my own name.

Does he know? Does he realize who I am? Is that why he is here? Is he spying on me for them? But that doesn't make sense because he hasn't asked a thing about money. Or had he? I try to remember all of our conversations. It's useless, I just don't know.

They still haven't found the account numbers, at least that I know of. I can't even remember where they are hidden and Kyle...Kyle is dead and I know he didn't tell.

My amazement at finding out I know Trent turns to fear. He could have killed me in my sleep last night.

My eyes begin to dart around the room. He isn't there. I found this place on my own and I was alone at the time. I *know* I was. Then all of a sudden, he shows up. The book that was missing. I found it in the tree house. I'm sure it was my book.

My fear turns to anger. How dare he! He pretends to be my friend. I bring him food and pillows and blankets. Then it turns out he's using me. He doesn't want to be my friend. He's trying to find out about the account numbers, where they are. I just *feel* it.

I feel the tears coming again. I stiffen my spine and stand up.

"No. I will not cry anymore. I'm tired of being a victim. No one is going to use me again."

I ball my hands into fists then release them. I do this a few times as I stand there.

"I *will* remember where those account numbers are

222

and I *won't* let anyone hurt me again." I am ranting in anger now. "The doctors can go to hell. No more trying to prove myself to them. I can walk right out of here."

But I know that isn't true. I will have to escape and hide. I will be on the run for the rest of my life. I have to get Alex's approval or I will be a Skyview Haven patient for the rest of my miserable life.

But I make a decision: I am done. I am going to live my life, free of doctors. I will convince Alex and I will find out what Trent is up to. I intend on confronting him. That will show him and whoever he's working for that I'm not a fool and I know what they're up to.

It's time I stand up for myself. I *will* be strong.

I'm still standing in the middle of the room, shaking with rage and determination to find the truth.

"Melinda?"

I spin toward the voice. I had left the front door open and Trent stood in doorway.

I'm mad, convinced he knows who I am and is hiding the truth from me. He is working for the people who killed my family.

"You," I yell with accusation thick in my voice, pointing my index finger at him.

"What?" he asks.

I can see the confusion on his face. His eyes get wide and he steps back as I advance on him.

"Get back in here. I need to talk to you."

"Melinda, I… What's going on?"

I grab his arms and pull him into the room.

"You know. You know me. Admit it."

"Know what? We just met a few months ago. You know that."

"No. You knew me nine years ago. Are you here

for the money?"

"What money?"

"Who do you work for, Trent?"

"What are you talking about?"

"Admit you know me! You remember who I am."

He doesn't respond.

"That home in Idyllwild. I was there for a few weeks. You were there."

"How do you know I was at a place there?" he asks.

"Because I was there. You know that."

"No. I don't."

"Don't lie to me anymore. I know everything."

"I was at a place there for a while before they moved me to another home that's only a little ways from here, where I stayed for a year. That's how I got here. I ran away. I told you that."

I grab him again and this time I'm shaking him, when I say, "I know what you said. But it's not the truth, is it? I remember."

"It is true. What are you talking about? Why are you so mad?"

He rips my hands off of his arms and moves away from me.

"What's your last name?"

"Miller."

"It is you. I remember now. I was thirteen. You were eight."

He looks like he is trying to recall that time.

"It was a long time ago. I was young. I remember a girl coming, but she didn't stay long. That was you?"

"Yes. Melinda James."

"You didn't talk much. You were always crying

and off by yourself."

"How did you find me? Who hired you?"

"What? Melinda, I don't know what you're talking about. Honest."

"You want the money, right? Or they do."

"You said money twice now. What *money*?" he seems frustrated, his face turns red and he looks like he's going to cry.

"You know."

"No, I don't," he moves further away from me and stands near the entry to the small kitchen. "I've never asked you anything. If I was trying to find out something, wouldn't I have been asking by now?" Trent asks. "Especially if someone hired me to get your money?"

He has a point. Can I be wrong about him? Can it be a coincidence that nine years later I see the boy again I shared a house with for two weeks? That never happens. Does it? Then again, how often do the dead speak to the living and vice versa?

I start to calm down a little. I sit down on the sofa. I have to think.

"Melinda, I'm not lying to you. Promise."

I look up at him and he looks guilty. His eyes are darting from me to the floor and back again. He knows something.

"What Trent? What are you keeping from me?"

"Nothing."

He moves to the doorway. I quickly get up and grab his arm again.

"Oh, no! You're not going anywhere."

My anger quickly blazes back.

"Melinda, I swear. I don't know anything about

any money."

He's looking straight into my eyes as he says this.

"Promise! Promise me. And if I find out you're lying, I'll never forgive you!"

This time when he removes my hand from his arm it's to take my hand in his.

"I promise I know nothing about any money. I'm not working for anyone. I would never hurt you."

I stare into his eyes for a few minutes, then take a deep breath.

"Okay. I believe you. I think."

"So, are we okay?"

"I don't know. I'm so confused."

"I'm not sure what's going on, Melinda, but I'm not lying. I swear I didn't remember it was you at the place in Idyllwild and I'm not after any money."

"Okay. All *right*."

Everything is such a mess and I don't know why. For some reason, finding out that he is the one and same Trent is important. I'm just not sure why.

He comes over and sits down next to me. I didn't pay attention before, but now that I've stopped being so mad at him, I can see he is damp.

"Were you at the water?" I ask.

"Yeah. Are you all right?"

"I wish people would stop asking me that. Yes, I'm fine or I will be. I…well, when I realized who you were, all sorts of things ran through my mind. I'm sorry I was bitchy."

"It's okay. Do you want to talk about it?"

"That's all I do. With Alex. Talk about my past."

"How about the home we were both in then."

"I don't know. I'm so confused. I was talking to

Alex about things and that's when I remembered you and the place in Idyllwild. I was convinced…never mind."

"How old were you when you arrived there?"

"Thirteen. They put me in here right after I turned fourteen."

"Won't they let you out?"

"Yeah, if I can get a doctor to say I'm not mentally unstable. That's why I'm talking to Alex."

"But why do they think you are? Why did they put you there in the first place and not a foster home like they did me?"

I don't want to answer that question, but I feel like I owe him, especially after accusing him of trying to find the account numbers.

"I'll tell you everything. Tonight. I'll come back. I just can't deal with that issue right now. I had better go. I sort of ran out on Alex."

I walk to the front door and onto the porch.

"Melinda James!"

Looking, I see Nurse Hamilton and two security guards standing on the front lawn. She has her hands on her hips, her face is red and I can tell she's angry. I know I'm in trouble. How will I get out of this one?

"What are you doing here? And who are you speaking with?"

"Shit," I murmur to myself.

I look back and Trent is gone. Where did he go? Did he hide in the bathroom or bedroom? This place isn't that big and if they look, they are sure to find him. For some reason, I'm protective of Trent.

"Well? Answer me."

She had walked up to me on the porch while my

head was turned. She grabs my arm.

"How did you find this place?"

"I don't know. I just came up on it," I say.

"How long have you been coming here?"

"I just found it," I lie.

I don't want to let them know how long I've been coming here. As it is, I'm sure they won't let me anymore.

"You are not allowed past the garden. You know that."

"I'm sorry."

I want to cry and she must see this because her face softens when she says, "It's not safe for you to go off by yourself, especially back here in these woods."

"I'm sorry," I repeat.

"Well, you have to answer for this. They may take some of your privileges away." She turns my head to face hers and says, "I have to tell. The security guards know. Be honest and they'll go easy on you. Okay?"

I nod my head.

"Who were you speaking with?" she repeats her earlier question.

"No one. Myself, I guess."

"Let's go."

"Nurse Hamilton? I'm not hurting anything being here. Can't I stay?"

She frowns and shakes her head, "That's not possible. You can get hurt out here by yourself."

I sigh and look longingly back into the cottage, knowing I won't be back, at least anytime soon.

"Melinda, if it was up to me, you wouldn't even be in Skyview, but it's not. I have a job to do and one of them is to look out for the patients. You are the last person I want to see anything happen to. Do you understand?"

"Yes."

I'm not sure what's going to happen now. What will Trent do? Who's going to bring him food? There is only one answer. I made a vow to myself in this cottage. No one is going to use me again. I will convince Alex I'm not crazy and will get out of Skyview Haven, just as I promised myself earlier. I may even make this my home, if I can. Then again, I don't know who owns it or if they will let me live on their land. I sigh again as Nurse Hamilton gently pulls on my arm. It's time to go and face the music.

She leads me down off the porch, but I pull my arm free and go back to the doorway.

"Trent," I whisper, "I'll try to come back. I promise."

"Melinda, we need to go."

Feeling defeated, I follow them back toward my boring, unfulfilled life, knowing they'll probably lock me up after this…for good.

Once we get at the entrance to the garden, I see nurses and patients scattered everywhere. Nurse Hamilton stops and I catch up with her and the guards are still behind me.

"What are you hiding? Out with it," Nurse Hamilton says as we walk across the lawn.

"I'm not hiding anything."

I wonder how I got so good at lying. It isn't something I normally did, even before I was thrown into this place. Now, it seems to flow out of me. Lie after lie.

"You will be spending the rest of your day inside."

She grabs me by the hand. "Let's go."

I walk next to her silently.

"You have to explain yourself to Dr. Leever. He's worried sick. Why did you run out?"

"I got upset and wanted to be alone."

"You can tell him that after you speak with Dr. Allcott."

I rarely see him. No one usually does unless they get into trouble. I guess I am in that now.

I am escorted to Dr. Allcott's office. Nurse Hamilton goes in with me.

"Have a seat, Melinda," Dr. Allcott says, already sitting at his desk.

He smiles, but that does not reassure me as I believe the smile is for Nurse Hamilton, not me. I'm nervous, worried about what he's going to do to me for disobeying the house's rules.

I sit while Nurse Hamilton stands next to me. She explains to the director where I was and how she has no idea how I found the place.

"What do you have to say for yourself, Melinda?"

I look up at Nurse Hamilton, but she ignores me and instead, stares straight at Dr. Allcott.

I remain silent.

"Melinda, what were you thinking? You've been doing so well. As far as I'm aware, you always behave and have never broken rules. Until now. Can you explain yourself?"

"I found the place by accident. I didn't mean to leave the garden. I was out thinking and walking and didn't realize I'd left the garden until it was too late."

That part is true. I just omit the fact that it was a long while ago I actually found the cottage.

I am admonished for worrying the staff and told to never run out like that again. They also forbid me to return to the cottage. As punishment, I must go directly to see Dr. Leever then proceed to my room, where I am to eat by myself.

To make matters worse, Dr. Allcott warns me that I will be under surveillance for a while to be sure I don't leave the premises until I'm given the permission to do so.

"And that could be a very long time, Melinda, if you don't abide by the rules. I'm also forbidding you to take lunch off these premises again or anything else with Dr. Leever until I feel you can be trusted. You have been here a long time and there is no excuse."

I cast my eyes to the floor, hopefully appearing remorseful.

"Now, let's talk about another subject." He doesn't speak again right away, so I look up at him. "Dr. Leever told me you've already vetoed the idea, but I think you should reconsider hypnosis."

Where did that come from? The thought still scares me and I tell him this.

"I don't want to do it. It's too scary to me and I doubt I'll change my mind on the subject."

"Very well. It is your decision, after all. Although I do think you're making the wrong one."

He nods to Nurse Hamilton as if to signal that he is done with our talk.

Back in the hall, Nurse Hamilton says, "You're a good kid, Melinda. I know you want to get out of here. You could ruin your chances if you keep running off like you did."

"I know."

She stops me and faces me. "I don't know what that place is or why you go there, but I don't think it's the first time you've been there. Am I right?"

"Yes," I admit.

"Is there someone that lives there who you visit?"

She is being so nice, I feel bad not telling her the truth, but I can't. Not about Trent.

"No. No one lives there. I go there to be alone."

"If I were you, I'd stay away."

"But…"

"No buts. I understand that sometimes you need to get away. I can't condone your behavior, but I can't say I'm surprised. I also know how bad you want to start your own life. Be careful, Melinda. The world is full of people who can hurt you."

I appreciate her caring, but I can't allow anyone to change my mind. I made promises to myself at that cottage and I'm not going to stray from them.

"I am careful. I won't let anyone hurt me anymore."

"It's not always that simple. Now, off to Dr. Leever's office. You still have to explain to him."

This isn't going to be easy. He will want to know who Trent is. There is no way I can tell him.

"Remember, you are to go directly to your room when you are done here. Is that clear?"

"Yes, Nurse Hamilton."

She really isn't mean, even though she sounds like it sometimes. She can be stern, but most times, it is out of concern for her patients. Over the years, I haven't made it easy for her. I don't blame her now for being hard on me. I deserve it. Secretly, I think she likes me. She could have reported me half a dozen times and didn't. She caught me with books, food in my room late at night, and being out in the dark in the garden. They don't allow the patients to be outside after sunset.

I walk into Alex's office and quietly close the door behind me. He is seated at his desk with his back turned to the door.

"I understand. I don't think she's ready for that. Uh, huh. No, you look. I can't take the chance of…" He turns his chair around and sees me. He motions with his finger for me to wait a minute. "I have to go. I have a patient." He says goodbye, hangs up the phone, then says, "Melinda, I'm glad you came back. Please sit," he points to the chair in front of his desk.

I sit down and try to think what I will tell him. I got it. I *will* tell him about Trent.

"First, are you okay?"

"Yeah. I'm better."

"Do you want to tell me what got you so upset?"

"When we were talking, I remembered when they put me in that home in Idyllwild. I met a boy there named Trent. It made me sad, thinking of him."

Alex looks at me as if he doesn't believe me. He frowns, creating wrinkles in his forehead.

"Is that it? You seemed more anxious and upset than sad."

"Well, a little upset, I guess."

"Why is that?"

I stay silent. I don't want to answer.

"Why did you feel the need to leave so abruptly?" Alex asks.

"It's just all of the past I'm remembering. It's getting to me," I say.

"I guess you will tell me when you're ready," he

obviously doesn't believe me. "Life has been hard on you and frankly, you've been a bit mystifying to me lately. You need to seriously consider being truthful with me, Melinda."

"I have been."

"With some things, yes. But others…you choose to keep them to yourself. That is not going to help you."

"I know."

"I hope so, Melinda, for your own good. Now, we'll resume tomorrow. I suggest you think hard about what you want. If you really desire to leave Skyview, you won't do it by lying to me or yourself."

I go back to my room and sulk for the rest of the day. Everyone deserves to have a little self-pity at times. Today is my time.

Chapter Forty-Seven

I eat my supper in my room, as I was ordered to. I play solitaire for a while then try to read a book. It's juvenile. Don't they understand I am twenty-two years old? Actually, I will be twenty-three in two months. This nonsense needs to stop.

The nightmares come back. It's the same as always. I'm running next to the river and I see my dad's car. I try to save him, but then my Dad turns into Beth. Then they're both gone and I'm laying on the rocks half in and half out of the water, crying.

I wake up screaming, but no one comes in. The dream never makes total sense. I guess I just wanted so bad to save my dad and Beth and my rational mind knows I couldn't, but my dreaming mind still thinks it's possible. It's not and it never was. I think sometimes that if I could have saved Dad and Beth, then none of this would have happened. I'd be home safe and sound in my bed with Kyle down the hall, my parents in their room, and Beth across our backyard.

I lay in bed the rest of the night, staring out into the blackness. The window doesn't provide any light. It's like the moon is on hiatus.

While lying there, I remember my earlier resolve. I am going to be strong. I will not cry anymore. I will convince Alex I'm not crazy. Repeat. Repeat. If I say it enough and keep expressing my desire to get out of here, then someday it will come true. Right?

After a few hours, I finally fall back to sleep and wake up late. I get dressed and go into the dining hall. It is already full of people. I take my usual seat next to the window overlooking the garden. I look toward the area where I usually sneak out of the garden and think of Trent.

He didn't have any dinner last night. Thinking back, I realize he hasn't eaten since the day before yesterday. It was only yesterday morning I left after sleeping over and then yesterday afternoon when I foolishly ran out of here to go see him. He must be hungry. I have to find a way to get food to him.

I think I see a shadow near the fence line. I squint, but it doesn't help. There it is again. It's Trent, it must be. He's probably going to the kitchen door. I get up and walk toward the kitchen. Nurse Hamilton stops me.

"Where are you going?"

"To see if Manuel needs help."

"He doesn't. Take your seat. The buffet will be out in seconds."

"I can help bring it out."

She hesitates like she's thinking about it.

"Very well, go ahead."

I go into the kitchen and see Paul, another patient, putting food into the warming tins used to hold the food. I walk over to Manuel.

"Is there any extra food?" I quietly ask.

"Breakfast is being served. Why are you asking?"

I need to take him into my confidence. There is no other way.

"It's not for me. Can you put a plate of something outside this back door? Please, it's for my friend."

He studies me before answering.

"So is that why you were caught running off to some shack in the woods yesterday?"

"How do you know about that?"

"I hear things. Not hard to in this place."

"Are you going to tell that I have a friend there?"

"No. I'll take care of it, don't you worry. Just go eat breakfast."

"I don't know when I can go back there to bring him anything."

"And I told you I will take care of it. Your friend won't go hungry. Now go."

"I told Nurse Hamilton I would help carry the food into the dining room."

"Then get to it. Don't worry," he repeats then nods his head toward the tins.

"Thank you, Manuel."

I help Paul with the tins then make my plate and sit down to eat. I feel better knowing Trent will have food.

After breakfast, I walk to Alex's office. He'll probably ask me again about yesterday, but one thing I won't do is give up Trent. Despite the fact that I still have unanswered questions about him, no matter what, I will not desert him.

Alex greets me when I walk in.

"Can I have a cup of coffee?" I ask after noticing he has some on the tray.

I'm tired and the extra caffeine will help.

"Of course."

I pour sugar from two packets into a cup, add some non-dairy creamer, and then the coffee. I found out a while ago I don't like black coffee.

"I won't ask you anymore about the little cabin you

were found at yesterday and why it's so important to you. I believe you will tell me in your own time, much like you've told me everything else."

"Thank you and I'm sorry about running out yesterday."

"I know you are. And it cannot happen again. It reflects poorly on your progress. Now," he adds as he stands up. He walks over to his window and looks down over the lawn like I enjoy doing. "Before we begin today, I want to discuss an idea with you. I've been giving your situation a lot of thought. Most times, I find patients heal in a more complete manner if they are able to visit locations that have been most problematic. I think your neighborhood where you grew up with Kyle, your parents, and Beth is just that."

"What are you saying?"

"I'm suggesting we do a sort of field trip. I'd like to take you back to your old house, the river where your father died, and the fort where you visited with Beth. How do you feel about that?"

I am speechless. I didn't see this coming. I sit down in the chair.

"I'm not sure. Dr. Allcott said I can't leave the premises, not even to have lunch with you."

Even if Dr. Allcott agrees, how can I face it? All of it? Knowing it can never be the same as it was back then?

"I know, he told me the same. I will discuss this with him. And I'm not proposing we do this today but soon, maybe in a few days. Why don't you think about it and get back to me tomorrow?"

"All right."

"Today, let's continue on. At this point in your

story, I know that your father is dead, but you still had communications with him, you were attacked in your home, and your mother went missing, and then Kyle. During all of this, did you see or talk with your father or Beth?"

"Around that time, the last I spoke to Dad is when he told us Mom was gone. As to Beth, I saw her after I ran away from that home in Idyllwild."

"Tell me about that."

Chapter Forty-Eight

"It was almost the end of September in 2005. I had been at that home for a few weeks. I couldn't stand it anymore. The people were okay and this other kid…well…anyway I missed my family. No one was giving me any answers. The cops showed up a few times to question me. I still wouldn't tell them where the account numbers were.

"The night before I ran away, I had a dream. I didn't know if it was just a *dream* or if he was actually talking to me. For argument's sake, we'll call it a dream. That's when my nightmares began. The ones where I wake up screaming. Anyway, Kyle told me he was safe, that he was…he was with Dad and Mom. Even in the back of my mind, I knew what that meant. They were all gone and I was alone. An orphan. Yes, there was Uncle L and Aunt Bet, but they were far away in New York somewhere. And they didn't want me.

"I asked Kyle where he was. He said not to worry. He told me to leave the town if I could because they were looking for me. If he was with Mom and Dad then they all must know who 'they' were. I asked him. He told me a name, just one name, but I can't recall it. I must have blocked that out the same as I have the location of that paper."

****

"He told you who it was?"

"Yes," I answer.

"And you can't remember the name now?"

"No."

"Why didn't you take that name to the police at the time?"

"I didn't have much faith in them. All they did was ask stupid questions. Besides, they kept insinuating that I killed my family. They didn't believe a word I said. They sure wouldn't believe that my dead brother, who they think is just missing, told me the killer's name."

"I understand how you must have believed that. Okay, go on," Alex says.

****

"In the dream, he told me that Mom was okay, too. I asked if that meant they all died and he said yes. I cried then. He said it would be okay, he and Mom and Dad would come and visit when they could. He said in the meantime, I had a friend here in our world that I would meet again, and would be able to trust. I had no idea what he was talking about."

"Have you met this person?" Alex asks.

I shrug my shoulders and say, "No. Anyway, Kyle cautioned me not to tell where the account numbers were. I was scared. If they wanted the numbers, I should just give them the paper and they'd leave me alone. Kyle said no because now I knew the name of the man who killed my family and who was after me. And even if I didn't know his name, they'd kill me anyway. I guess that's why Kyle figured it wouldn't hurt to tell me the person's name.

"The person never found me at the Idyllwild home. After Kyle visited me in the dream, I ran. I waited until the foster dad left for work and the woman was busy pruning her flowers out back. I felt bad about doing it, but I took cash from the woman's purse. There was forty dollars. I figured that should get me back home.

"I quickly packed my bag—the same one I came with—including a flashlight I took from the closet, and left by way of the front door. The other boy saw me, but obviously didn't tell. Otherwise, I'd have been back there in a blink of an eye.

"I sort of knew the way back to our family home. I knew where the road was, so I figured I would walk there. I remembered the road being quite a ways down the mountain.

"I finally came up with some sort of plan and it felt good. Action was better than sitting around waiting. I would have to walk, there was no other choice. In town, I avoided the store I went to for help. Instead, I went into a convenience market. There I bought some water, crackers, beef jerky, and a whole chicken that was already cooked and warm. It would have to last me.

"I began walking, staying off the road, going parallel to it just behind the trees. At first, I would stop for a few minutes to nibble on a piece of chicken or get a drink of water, but I was stopping too often. I forced myself not to take so many breaks.

"I knew it was going to take me a while, but when it started getting dark and I was still not at the bottom of the mountain, I got worried. I would have to spend the night in these woods with God knew what kind of animals.

"Night fell and I was scared, downright petrified. I was tired of walking, exhausted really. All I had to do was get through the night and I would be okay. I kept telling myself that tomorrow, I would be close to home and out of the mountain.

"I found a spot near the road, behind the tree line. There was a bunch of bushes that I figured would at least half cover me from view. I laid down and cried from fear. Then I felt like someone put their hand on the back of my head. I was startled and jumped up into a sitting position. It was Beth. She was smiling at me.

"You're not alone. I'm here with you."

"It was reassuring. I was happy to see someone and I'm glad that someone was Beth, even if she was dead."

"That must have been comforting for you."

"It was."

I stand and pace for a few minutes before sitting back down again.

"Despite her being there—probably because she wasn't *really* there—I was scared to fall asleep. Owls hooted and far off, I heard the cries of what could have been wolves. I had no idea what animals were up there. Sounds of the night were all around me, but something seemed particularly near me. I had no weapon and figured I'd just have to fight off whatever it was with my bare hands. I doubted a ghostly apparition that was Beth would be able to do anything."

I hesitate again. I feel like I'm back there, in that forest alone, in the dark. I remember that's in the past and I'm safe now.

"I remember bringing my knees up to my chest and hugging my legs with my arms. The wind started picking up. There was nothing I could do but wait out the night. Shivering, terrified and alone, I finally fell asleep. Once, I woke in the middle of the night. I was warm and had the sense I wasn't alone. Opening my eyes, I see Beth lying next to me. She was facing me so I could see her looking at me.

"It's okay," she whispered.

"I fell back to sleep easily and woke up to birds chirping and the sun streaming through the trees. I made it. I survived the night. Thanks to Beth, who was now gone.

"I shoved the flashlight into my bag, drank some water, and took a bite of the beef jerky. It was disgusting, but it was food. I still had the crackers and some chicken left for later and I figured I would be back to my house by dinnertime, so I finished off the jerky without worrying. However, unfortunately, no one would be home making dinner when I arrived. It would be just me. I swallowed the lonely images along with the ball in my throat and tried to concentrate on making it through the day.

"I didn't want to waste any more time and began walking again. I began to get warm so I stopped and took off my jacket. It seemed like I'd never make it down the mountain. I rested when I needed to, but never for long. I was worried I wouldn't get going again.

"After what must have been hours, I was completely exhausted again, but I came out into a clearing. The road was still to my right and I could hear cars coming. I backed up into the trees. Looking in front of me, I saw a huge field then a building. It looked like a storage building.

"After the cars passed and were a safe distance down the road, I walked into the clearing again. To the right beyond the road, was more field. I knew this was the road Mom drove up because I'd stayed parallel to it, but it didn't look familiar. I guess I wasn't paying enough attention in the car. That was typical for me though. And in my defense, I was scared that day because of the guy with the gun.

"I could see houses up ahead to the left of the big building and on the other side of the road. The trees weren't sheltering the sun anymore and it was hot. I started walking, rolling my shirtsleeves further up my arm. I figured if anyone saw me, I could just say I lived in one of the houses.

"When I got closer to town, I had to walk over the tracks. I was still avoiding the road. I was at the big building I saw earlier and realized I was right. It was some kind of storage facility.

"I stopped and drank some water as I leaned up against the structure. I thought I recalled Mom turning right onto this road. That would mean I had to go left. I hoped I remembered correctly. I didn't want to get lost. If I had to ask for directions, they would probably turn me into the cops. That's all I needed. Up to this point, I already had enough of them, thank you.

"I headed left and came into the main part of the city of Banning. Mom had taken the freeway, but we weren't on it long, just a couple of exits. I had no idea how far it was to Beaumont and really, how long it was going to take me. It couldn't be that long.

"I saw an area where people sit and wait for buses. There were a few people there. The thought occurred to me that I could take a bus, but where would I buy my ticket? And how much would it cost? I decided to ask one of the people sitting there.

"I walked up to a man who looked to be my dad's age. He was reading a paper.

"Excuse me. We just moved here and I'm not familiar with the town yet. Could you tell me where I go to buy a ticket?"

"Up the street a few blocks. On your left. You can't miss it."

"He went back to reading his paper, dismissing me in the process. I walked in the direction he indicated. I found the place without a problem. I walked in and found the ticket counter. I waited in line, which didn't seem like it was ever going to move.

"When it was finally my turn, I walked up and told the lady I needed to get to Beaumont and asked how much the ticket was.

"How old are you?"

"Uh, sixteen," I lied.

"I rarely lied, but did it anyway. I had to do what was necessary.

"One way or round trip?"

"The lady didn't seem to care who I was or how young I was. She just kept looking at her screen.

"One way, please."

"Well, for minors it's four dollars."

"Whew. I had that. I was worried I wouldn't have enough. I paid her and she gave me a ticket. I asked her where I picked up the bus and how I knew which one was going in my direction.

"Blue bus, not the red one. You can wait outside. Another's comin' along in about half an hour."

"Thank you."

"I stayed close to the side of the building in the shade, instead of sitting on the concrete seats they provided next to the road. It was closer to an hour before the bus arrived. It didn't matter to me as long as

I didn't run into any cops.

"The ride was very short. I was right that it had only been a few exits. Once the bus took that exit, I knew exactly where I was. Kyle and I used to walk around Beaumont all the time. It wasn't a large town—at least then, I have no idea about its size now. We knew it like the back of our hands because we grew up there.

"Mom used to yell at me if I went traipsing off by myself. The thought of Mom made me begin to cry. But I stifled my tears and told myself I could cry later. Right then, I had to get home. Maybe Mom and Kyle were there. But I knew they wouldn't be, especially after the dream."

Chapter Forty-Nine

"So, you made it back home and then what? Was anyone there?" Alex asks.

"No. I knew there wouldn't be. But at least I was safe. The house was locked and I didn't have a key. It was hard to do, but I ended up taking the screen off the office window at the back of the house and crawling through. Thank God, the window itself wasn't locked. By this time, I was so tired that I just went up to my room and crawled into bed. I didn't wake up until the next morning."

"I imagine you were worn-out, especially after almost two days of walking. I admire your courage. You were so young. You had to grow up too fast."

"There was nothing else I could do."

"What did you do the next day?"

"I stayed in the house for a few days, afraid to go anywhere. I didn't want the cops to find me and send me back to that home, or any home for that matter. Fortunately, there was enough food and the rest of my clothes were there. I couldn't really cook, but I made do."

"You must have been so lonely."

"I was. The house was so quiet. It had been empty for almost three weeks. At night, I kept the lights off so people would think no one was there. Especially the people who were after me." I am tired of talking and I need some time alone. "Can we take a break? I want to get some air before lunchtime."

"Sure. How about we resume this afternoon around two? Sound good?"

"Okay."

****

After leaving his office, I go into the garden and sit on a bench. There is no way I can try to sneak back to the cottage. If they can't find me, that's the first place they'll look. I don't know what I'm going to do. I want to see Trent again though.

Remembering my determination, I decide to sneak out after everyone goes to bed. I will have to be careful. I know Nurse Hamilton's shift ends at five. The evening nurses never pay close attention and I've seen one of them sleep at night. So, I plan on trying. That night.

After I eat lunch, I go back to Alex's office. I am ten minutes early, but I doubt he'll mind. If he's there. As I'm walking down the hallway, I see Alex speaking to another man. He looks familiar, but I can't place him. He's tall with blonde hair and a mustache. Alex has his back to me, but turns when the man nods his head in my direction and says something.

"I'll speak with you later, then," Alex tells the man. "It was nice seeing you."

"Yeah, you, too," the man replies and walks off.

"Hello, Melinda. You're a bit early," Alex says to me.

For some reason, I'm anxious. I'm not sure why, but I'm nervous. Something is wrong. I have to tell myself to calm down. Breathe, Melinda, breathe.

"Yes," I manage to say.

"Well, come on in. We can get started."

I walk into his office. My head is swirling, the feeling of anxiety is worsening. What is wrong with me? Why did seeing that man have such an impact on me?

"Are you okay? You look a little peaked."

"I'm fine," I say.

Why am I not saying anything? I should tell Alex what I'm feeling.

"Have some water," he suggests.

"Okay, but I'm fine."

"Good. This morning I proposed an idea of taking you back to your neighborhood. I realize I told you to think on it, but after hearing your story this morning, I feel it will be extremely helpful for you to go back there sooner rather than later. That way, I can gauge your reaction. See how you respond to being outside of these walls and the only grounds you've known for so many years."

"When do you want to do this?"

"Tomorrow, if you're feeling up to it. I was just speaking to Dr. Allcott's new aide in the hallway about it. I've managed to gain permission for this trip. How do you feel about all of this?"

I can feel my heart beating faster. Do I want to do this? I haven't had a chance to think about it. Alex is right. I need to see how I do away from this place and it's best I do it before I actually move out.

"I guess it will be okay. You'll be there, so I know I'll be safe. Besides, I have to confront it. After getting out of here, it is one of the first things I planned on doing anyway."

"Are you sure you feel comfortable?"

"Not comfortable, no. But honestly, I would rather do it with you there."

"Then we're all set. We'll leave here after breakfast tomorrow. I will drive us. The man you saw will be coming with us. Dr. Allcott insisted."

I am nervous. For some reason, I don't want him to go.

"Why does he have to come? Can't it just be you and me?"

"No, I'm afraid not. Dr. Allcott said the home is liable for you and frankly, your recent excursion made things a little difficult. If something happens, it wouldn't be good. I'm not an actual employee of Skyview as I explained to you when you first started seeing me. They have to have someone who works here accompany us."

"Then how about Nurse Hamilton?"

"Are you anxious because you haven't met him yet?"

That must be it.

"I guess so."

"It will be okay. His name is Parson Smith. He's a nice man."

My head starts to ache and the anxiety isn't going away. It feels like butterflies are doing cartwheels in my stomach. What is making me feel this way? It must be my nerves at the anticipation of facing a place I haven't been to in years.

"All right," I agree hesitantly.

"I think you should have the rest of the day to have some fun. Try not to think about tomorrow, but even I know it's easier said than done."

"I'll try."

"Good. I'll see you back here tomorrow morning."

I leave and walk back to my room. Sitting on the edge of my bed, I start to think about Parson Smith. Alex seems to trust him, so I should, too. More than that, I'm worried about how I'll react tomorrow. I haven't been there in about eight years, so it's going to be hard. That's probably what my anxiety is all about. Nerves, just like I thought.

After dinner, I bide my time and wait until it's almost ten p.m. I don a sweater and quietly as possible, I open my door and cautiously peek out into the hallway. I don't see anyone and it's silent. I shut my bedroom light off so they think I'm sleeping then go all the way into the hallway and close my door. After creeping down the hall, I inch past the nurse's desk near the stairs. Once past, I dash to the door. When I open it, it squeaks. Damn it. This one needs oil or something. I hold my breath, thinking someone will hear me breathe. I look and find no one is around. I enter the stairwell and shut the door. It squeaks again, so I hurry down the steps.

As I'm rushing toward the cottage, I keep thinking about how ridiculous this is to be sneaking around.

Tomorrow may be a pivotal point for me. If Alex thinks I can handle going to my old neighborhood, I could be free by my next birthday.

The thought elates me.

As I duck under the overhanging branches to make my way toward the burned out house and back to the cottage, I hit a wall.

"Uh!" I say aloud. "What?"

"You must go back."

"What?" I repeat my question of confusion.

A shadow suddenly materializes into the form I know so well.

"Dad?"

I haven't seen or heard from him in years. Why now?

"Yes, it's me."

I jump into his arms and melt into his chest. It has been so long that I've felt any human contact like this. I miss my family more than I can say. Tears drip down my cheeks from joy.

"I've missed you all so much."

"And we have missed you." He pulls back from the embrace. "But we don't have the time to reminisce right now. I'm sorry. Melinda, go back. It's too dangerous. There is someone waiting up ahead for you who wants to hurt you."

"Who? Not Trent. He wouldn't hurt me. He's my friend."

"Not Trent, no. It's him. After all these years, he's finally been able to get close to you. Please, go back to Skyview where you're safe."

"Dad, who wants to hurt me? Why after all this time?"

My head is swimming with questions and I feel an urgency to get answers. And for some reason, I know I need them now.

"The account numbers are still hidden. You are the only one left who knows where they are. There is a great deal at stake. Millions of dollars."

"I don't remember!" I'm frustrated. "Why can't I remember where Kyle and I hid them?"

"You will and soon. When you do, you must give them to the police. Instantly. Don't hesitate and don't give them to anyone else. Understand?"

"Yes. Dad, I can't remember the name Kyle told me. The guy who's after me."

"I have to go." He starts disappearing. "Go back." He nudges me back the way I came. "You can't come back here. Not for a while."

"But what about Trent? He's my friend. I want to see him."

"Trent will be fine. I promise. You will see him again, just not now."

"But, Dad, please. Don't go yet," I say as I start to see him revert to full shadow form. "What about Mom and Kyle? Where are they? Are they okay?"

"You will have all of your answers soon. Right now, you need to leave."

He is gone. That's it. Two short minutes with my father whom I haven't spoken to or seen in years. I feel disappointed and cheated, but I'm scared, too. Dad has never steered me wrong, so I heed his words and run back to the safety of the garden.

I immediately feel better. I'm not sure who Dad saved me from tonight, but I am grateful. I know, even though I can't tell you how I know, that this is it. Tomorrow is going to be important.

Chapter Fifty

The time is at hand.

It is the first thought that enters my head even before my eyes open this morning. Last night, there were no nightmares, no waking up screaming and sweating. I feel almost calm now. I say almost because I was frightened last night after hearing Dad's words, but by the time I lay my head on my pillow, the fear was replaced with joy and serenity. Still, a small piece of my mind aches, like a memory is trying to come through. I dismiss it.

Whatever happens today, I'll have to deal with it. The events could create the ending of this chapter in my life allowing me to move forward to a new one.

I get dressed and go to breakfast. Although I was mostly calm a few moments ago, I'm now a little nervous. I think that's normal though. Today is already set in motion and there's nothing I can do to stop it. There is nothing specific I can think of, but it's something I feel…deep inside of me. I don't question it.

I go to Alex's office and he is there waiting for me. The man from yesterday—Parson Smith—is there with him. My palms become sweaty and my heart starts to beat rapidly. I don't know why. It must be my nerves again.

"Good morning, Melinda. You remember Mr. Smith?"

"Yes. Hi."

"Hi, Melinda," Parson responds.

"Are you ready?" Alex asks. "I have a feeling today is going to be the start of something wonderful for you. It will help determine how ready you are to be back in this world and this time, on your own."

No matter how much of the story I tell him, he can't understand how 'alone' I was so much of the time right before I came here.

I say nothing, except agree, "Yes."

Out in the parking lot, Alex unlocks his SUV. He opens the rear door for me and I climb in. Parson sits in the front and Alex gets behind the wheel.

"You're going to be fine, kitten."

I hear a voice in my head and know it's Dad.

I can't answer him out loud because I don't want Alex and Parson to question who I'm talking to. I silently thank him for being with me.

Alex turns on classical music and it plays softly in the car. I hear Alex and Parson murmuring to each other up front, but turn my attention to my surroundings, not caring what they're talking about.

****

We get on the I-10 going west. It takes only about ten minutes or less before we are turning off the freeway to Beaumont. I remember this off-ramp. It is the same one the bus took all those years ago after I walked down the mountain. I didn't realize I was living *this* close to my old home. I mean, I knew it wasn't that far, but I really didn't think about it. I guess I never asked or cared enough. Until now.

Now it is important.

We pull up in front of my old house. My palms are

sweating and I feel like I'm going to jump out of my own skin. My insides are quivering. I'm not sure I can do this. I look at our house and my gaze roams upward toward the second floor. I see the curtain move.

"Who lives here now?"

"Another family," Alex answers. "It's okay. No one is home and we're not going inside. I don't think the new owners would appreciate it. They know we're coming and are aware we may be on their property."

"Is it too late to change my mind?"

I hear my own voice shake as I speak. Images of our once happy family keep jumping around in my head. Dad. Mom. Kyle. Even the times Kyle was mean to me when we were growing up. I'd take whatever he wanted to dish out again if I could have them all back.

Then I recall what happened after I took that bus home that day.

"It's all part of healing, Melinda," Alex turns in his seat and looks at me. "You can do this."

He and Parson get out of the car, but I remain seated, remembering...

****

After a few days hidden in our house, I finally ventured outside. I headed back to the fort, hoping to see Beth. She didn't show up. I sat there for a little bit and waited, hoping. After a while, I got back up and headed back to my house.

But Krissy saw me. She was in her backyard. I guess she heard someone walking and looked up. She came running to me and hugged me.

"Are you okay? Where are your mother and Kyle?"

"I'm okay, I guess."

I avoided responding to her other question and

tried to leave.

"I haven't seen you guys since the cops were there a few weeks or so ago. Is everything okay?"

"No." I couldn't help myself and I looked at her with pleading eyes.

Part of me was begging, I wanted her to be Mom. I needed consoling, reassurance. But I wanted it from my mom not Krissy.

"Come on over to my house. I'll pour you a glass of iced tea."

She steered me into her kitchen. The last time I was there was after the man broke into our house. Then Mom and Kyle were home. Now…

"I tried calling your mother. I can't reach her," Krissy said as she poured tea into two glasses.

"You won't," I said.

I was tired of being alone. Maybe Krissy could take me in. I could live with her. Then if Beth came to visit, she could see her mother, too. I was kidding myself, but I didn't know what else to do. I had made it home and…and what? I had no next course of action.

I told her about Mom and Kyle's disappearances.

"Have you been all alone this whole time?"

I explained about how I ran away from the foster home. I didn't want to be there. I only wanted to come home.

"I can live with you though. I'll help around the house. I won't be a problem. I promise. Just until Mom and Kyle come home."

I knew they weren't coming home, but if I could get her to agree, then I was pretty sure she wouldn't kick me out once she found out they were both dead, right along with Dad.

She looked at me with such sadness, I knew my answer.

"I would, but since we don't have Beth here with us anymore," she dropped her head and stared at the floor, "Howard and I have decided to sell this big house and move to a small condo. Out of state." With the last three words, she looked back up at me again. "I'm so sorry, Melinda. I doubt they will let me take you."

My last chance at happiness. *Gone*. She had no choice but to call the social workers. She explained that she couldn't let me live alone like that. It wasn't good. I needed looking after. I knew it wasn't her fault and I didn't blame her.

After that, I wouldn't change my story. The cops decided I either killed my family or I was nuts. That's how I got to Skyview Haven. I was just a kid, and did what my parents brought me up to do: I told the truth.

I'm an adult now. I'm not that kid anymore. I'm stronger. I try to think all positive thoughts, but the negative keeps creeping in. I'm alone, an orphan with no family. I live in a mental institution. I have no friends…wait, that's not true. I have Trent and Alex.

Chapter Fifty-One

I look up at Alex. He's talking to Parson at the front of the car. Okay, it's time. I have to remember my resolve. I take a deep breath, unbuckle my seat belt, and get out of the car.

Alex walks over to me and asks, "How do you feel at this moment?"

"Nervous, but I'll be fine." I stand up as straight as I can. "I'm ready. What do we do first?"

"That's the spirit. Let's take it slow. We can walk the street. Are there any friends you had in the neighborhood you'd like to see?"

"Beth, but she's dead. Remember?"

"I'm sorry. Did you want to see her family? You were close with her mother."

"They moved."

I frown from the sadness that is enveloping me.

I begin walking down the street with Alex and Parson behind me. I look around. The neighborhood hasn't changed that much. The sidewalk has been repaired though. I used to trip over the cracks caused by tree roots just past our house. The sensation is so surreal, especially knowing I don't live here anymore. I feel like the visitor I am.

I pause a few houses away from the start of the woods at the end of the street. The last time I went this way was to give Kyle baggies to wrap the paper in before we hid it.

"What is it, Melinda?" Alex asks.

"There are things I don't remember. You know that. They seem to be there, right on the edge of my mind, but I can't grab them. It's so frustrating. If I could remember, I could tell you. Prove I'm not crazy."

"Are you talking about the account numbers?"

I turn when Alex asks this and see Parson is staring at me intently.

"That and…there's something else. Maybe someone else. I don't know."

Parson now glances at Alex and then back at me.

"Let's walk a little further. That may help," Alex suggests.

I turn my back on them and walk to the end of the road. I'm at the precipice between street and woods. I'm beginning to hate clusters of trees. I know what's up the hill beyond them.

"Dad died in the river up there," I point upward. "That's where he drowned. Beth drowned there, too."

"You have never shared how Beth died, besides drowning. Was she swimming?"

"I can't remember. Why can't I remember? She was my best friend."

I feel Alex's hand on my shoulder. "It will come back. Maybe it will help if you walk up the hill, to the river."

I hesitate. I'm not sure I want to do that. Actually, not sure I can.

"Not yet," I answer.

"I understand. You said you and Beth used to go to this fort in the woods. How about you start there? You may remember more about Beth's death."

"I doubt the fort will still be there, but we can try," I say.

I backtrack heading to my...old house.

"You said we can walk on the property?" I confirm with Alex.

"Yes."

I walk around the side of the house and into the backyard. I notice there are swings and a slide. They must have small children. I look up at my old bedroom window. There it is again, a curtain moving. I dismissed it earlier, but now it happens again.

"Didn't you say that no one is home?"

"That's right."

"I saw a curtain move at my bedroom window. And I saw it in the front, too, where Kyle's bedroom was."

"Maybe one of the children is home from school sick or something. Let's continue."

I walk across the yard and to the path where Beth and I met all the time. It's overgrown, but I can still see part of it. No matter, I know where I'm going. I head left and down the other path toward where we had our fort. When I get to the place, it's gone just as I suspected it would be.

"It was here," I motion to the tree.

I sit down at the base of the tree. I miss Beth. I lower my head into my hands and sigh. What did I expect coming here? Did I think everything is going to be as I left it? New people in my old home, our fort gone. No, I must not be weak. It will not be good for Alex to see me break down.

I raise my head and look at the two men, both in dress slacks, collared shirts, and loafers, as if they're going to a barbecue, or out to dinner or something. They look odd standing in the forest with me in jeans sitting on the dirty ground next to a tree.

For some reason, I find this hilarious. I start laughing. Really, I think it's from nerves and having to force myself to appear just fine while at the same time not knowing how to react to being back here again, but I can't stop laughing. Tears are rolling down my face. Both Alex and Parson are looking at me as if I've lost my mind. Maybe I have.

"Are you okay?" Parson asks.

I'm surprised. Why would he care? Oh yes, he's the responsible party. The one who has to be sure I'll be okay so Skyview won't be liable if something happens to me. I find his question funny, too, and start laughing harder. It's a few minutes before I am able to collect myself. The entire time, both men look down at me. Obviously uncomfortable and probably not knowing what to do with me.

I take pity on their uneasiness and wipe my eyes. I stop laughing but am still smiling as I stand up.

"Are you all right?" Alex asks since I didn't answer Parson.

"Yes."

"What is so funny?" Parson asks.

"Well, the two of you. If you could see yourselves," this starts me giggling again. I get myself under control and say, "You look funny being in the woods dressed like that. I don't know. It made me laugh."

"Laughter is good for the soul," Alex in all his wisdom states. "So this is where the fort used to be?"

"Yes," I look at the tree. "It really wasn't much of

one, but it was mine and Beth's. Something only she and I shared."

"Not Kyle?"

"Sometimes he came here. Mainly to see Beth after she died."

I see Parson looking quizzically at Alex, but he doesn't acknowledge Parson. I realize I'm revealing things I've only told Alex.

"I mean, Kyle and I came here after Beth died to talk about her."

Parson's facial muscles relax a little. Good. I don't want him knowing anything.

"Shall we continue on? I think it may be a good idea for you to face the river where they both drowned."

My insides are shaking again. I know he's right, but it's not easy.

"Okay," I agree. "I might as well do it now. It has to be done."

"You've come a long way, Melinda. I'm proud of you."

"Thank you, Alex."

We leave the woods from the other side, coming out near the end of the street where the hill begins toward the river. I start the climb with Alex and Parson on my heels. I get to the middle of the hill and stop. I grab my head. All of a sudden, I get an intense headache. I drop to my knees and hold my head in my hands. It hurts beyond anything I've ever experienced. I groan and rock back and forth.

"Melinda?" Alex asks as he bends over me.

A road. Two cars. Dad's car and another. The other one crashes into Dad's driver's side. He veers.

Pain, blinding pain.

Dad's car is flying through the air.

"No," I scream.

I have to stop it. Dad can't drown. I'm powerless. I watch as his car nosedives into the river. Dad is slumped over the steering wheel. Blood is running down the side of his face.

Suddenly, I'm in the car, shaking Dad.

"Wake up! Dad!"

I'm back on the ground. I blink my eyes and focus. I see Alex on his knees next to me and Parson standing over us looking concerned.

"Melinda?"

****

The Other Side

"Kyle, we have to get ready. Melinda needs our help."

"I'll come, too," Meredith says.

"No. Stay here. We'll be back, I promise."

Kyle and I make our way to the portal we need, the one closest to the spot at the river where I died. I haven't been through this one since I went through after passing.

I take my son's hand and we pause at the doorway, waiting until the very last second so we don't waste our time on Earth. I will try to speak to her from the opening of the portal, as I've done on so many other occasions.

****

I try to get up off my knees, but find that I feel dizzy. Alex grabs my arm and helps me up. The headache is gone, but I feel like a wrung-out dishrag. I don't know why I saw what I did, but I've come to understand that nothing is as it seems. What I witnessed is important. I'm not sure how, but I know deep down it is.

"I'm okay. I just got a headache all of a sudden."

"Do you want to continue? Or shall we go back?" Alex asks.

I see Parson grab Alex's arm and nod his head in the opposite direction, telling him he needs to speak with him.

"I'll be right over here. You sure you're okay?"

"Yes."

As they walk away, I wonder what Parson needs to speak to him about. I find it curious. I dismiss it and look around.

I can hear it again. The rushing of the water. It's fast. I know because I can hear it from here. Just like the last time Kyle and I were here. The last time the water ran that fast, Dad was around. It calmed down when he went back to wherever it was he came from. Dad must be here.

"I am. You need to go back. You're in danger."

He is in my head again, instead of in person.

"I don't want them to see me, honey. Just think it. I'll hear it. The same as before."

"Why am I in danger?" I think.

"I can't explain everything right now. Don't trust…"

"Dad? Don't trust what? Don't trust who?"

It's almost like losing a radio station. He's clear, then it's nothing but static.

"Them. Go back. I tried to warn you at the—It was me you—in the windows."

"Don't trust Alex? He's been helping me. He's my friend."

"Go back and find Trent. It's important. He'll tell…everything."

He's gone again. I hate when that happens. It's time to make some decisions on my own. Dad said to go back and find Trent, so I will. I walk over to Alex and Parson.

"I want to go back to Skyview now."

Alex looks at Parson before speaking.

"I think it best we continue. You need to confront this."

"Can we do it another day?"

"You told me you want out of Skyview Haven, that it is the most important thing to you. If you can't face your fears, I can't recommend that you be released."

"What?"

That can't be. I *have* to get out. It's become my mantra. I say it over and over and that's not going to change.

"It's vital to your well-being that you come to terms with everything that happened in your past. Once you do that, healing can take place. If you don't face this here and now, you may never be able to."

He is right. I do have to face this. I don't know what Dad was referring to, but I'm not in danger as long as Alex is here.

"All right," I decide. "I'll do this."

I turn and walk up the hill toward the river. At the top, I look out over the water. It's calm now and flowing peacefully toward the bridge. That worries me. Does it mean Dad isn't here any longer? I climb down the incline and over the rocks and stand at the water's edge.

"What are you thinking?" Alex asks from above the rocks.

"That I miss my family. The last time I was here was with Kyle."

"Isn't that the day you hid the paper with the account numbers?"

It was. I recall my last memory before hiding the paper. I was on the hill coming here. I got baggies from the house.

Rocks. Kyle was there. He's talking to me, but I can't hear him. I don't know if this is the present or something that happened in the past. Bits and pieces of pictures are forming in my head. I have a raging headache again.

"—bury this."

"What?" I ask aloud.

"Melinda?" Alex is asking.

I ignore him, concentrating instead on Kyle, realizing now I'm remembering. He has the baggie and I can see the paper in it. He wrapped it again with another baggie.

"—right here. What do you think?"

Almost as if it's happening now, I can see him. He's standing up top, near the bridge's underpass. There are concrete blocks. I see an opening.

"Is she okay?" I barely hear Parson asking.

"I don't know. Melinda?"

I'm back to the present again. I look at Alex. I focus on his face, then I look up at the place I saw Kyle last. There is no opening where I thought I saw one. Only rocks and concrete blocks. Wait…is that it?

I close my eyes, willing myself to go back. To

overcome the searing headache and *remember...*

****

"Is that really going to last there?" I asked Kyle.

"I hope so. It's the only place I can think of right now. It has to be hidden."

Kyle took the baggie-wrapped sheet and stuffed it in a crack between two concrete blocks.

"I'll come back. Dad has a leftover bag of concrete mix from the back patio. I saw how he mixed it up. I'll do the same and fill this crack in."

"Let's do it now. I'll help."

"No. Later, when it's dark. I don't want anyone seeing me."

"No one will if you go through the woods instead of down the street."

"Good idea. Okay, let's go get the mix."

We headed down the hill and...

****

And nothing. I don't remember what happened after that. I look up the hill again. No cracks. Kyle must have come back.

"Melinda? Damn it, answer me!"

Alex was practically shaking me. I look at him, then back to the concrete blocks. Then I see Parson. He is watching me.

"Alex," Parson says.

Parson lays his hand on Alex's arm and nods his head in the direction of the concrete blocks. That's when I see it. A tattoo of a homemade cross between the thumb and index finger of the man's hand. I freeze in fear.

Is it him? After all these years. How did he finally find me? Is he going to kidnap me and kill me, too?

Like he did Mom and Kyle back in Idyllwild? Parson Smith? He must be the one. My heart is beating wildly. Oh my God. What do I do? I have to think.

I try to calm myself down as Alex turns to me. I can't let him know. Or maybe I should? If that man is here to hurt me, Alex will help, I know it. I don't remember him having a mustache, but he could have grown one. Maybe a lot of people had those tattoos. Maybe it was part of some gang. It can't be the same man. Can it? Maybe the man doesn't even realize it's me. But he must, he knows about the account numbers. He knows I remembered.

"It's you," I accuse, pointing my finger at Parson.

He laughs at me, "Yes, little delusional, crazy girl. It's me and I came to finish what I started."

I can almost feel my face drain of color. That's what Dad meant. Parson is the danger. Parson Smith was the name all along that I couldn't remember. But Alex is here, he'll help me.

I know this is my chance. Tell him, Melinda! But, maybe I'm overreacting. It's been eight years. I'm probably getting what the man who tried to kill us in our house looks like mixed up with other people I've seen over the years. Maybe I really haven't been in my right mind. I must be wrong. Before I can think anything else, things go from terrible to worse.

Alex turns to Parson and says, "Check it out."

Check it out? What?

"What did you say? Check what out?"

"Did you remember? Is that where's it hidden?"

"Alex?" I question.

Now I'm frightened. He's scaring me. It's not so much what he asks, but how he is looking at me.

I back up.

"Dad?" I yell out.

I need him more now than I ever have. I'm terrified. I should have listened to my intuition when I first saw Parson and Alex talking.

"Melinda, do you remember?" Alex asks more insistently than he should.

"Yes," I yell back at him.

I may have been sheltered for the last eight years of my life, but I'm not stupid. Something is very wrong here. The hairs on the back of my neck are standing up. Alex looks and acts anxious.

Parson walks back to us. He grabs my arm and I scream in pain. His hold is firm and he's pressing his fingers into my arm.

"Where?" he angrily asks. "Tell me where it is!"

"I don't remember," I try and recant my statement. I pull my arm free and rub it. "All I know is it's around here somewhere."

I hope Parson believes my lies. I look to Alex for help since Dad hasn't answered my cry.

"Tell us where the paper is," Alex says.

"It's probably disintegrated by now being in the weather all of these years," I insist. "So what does it matter?"

"Five million dollars matters," Parson roars. "If your greedy father didn't steal what was ours…"

"Shut up!" Alex yells at him.

"Ours?" I question.

I look from Alex to Parson.

"Melinda, it's not what you're thinking. I'm here to help you, remember?"

I want to believe him. He's my friend, after all.

"You're not helping me now. He hurt me," I hold my arm up, "and you let him."

"Parson, leave us alone."

"No way. That's half of my money."

"Damn it, I said go!"

Parson walks away, but not very far.

Alex turns to me and says, "Melinda, listen to me, that man is going to hurt you, hurt both of us, if he doesn't get what he wants."

"What is going on? Are you working with him? Is that your paper?"

"This is important. Trust me and tell me where the account numbers are."

"Trust you? I'm not saying anything."

"You must. Your life is at stake. I've come to really like you, Melinda and I'm sorry, but you need to turn over the paper or—"

"Or what? You'll let him hurt me? Or you'll do it? Are you the one who killed my family? Or was it him?"

I'm yelling at this point. I don't care if Parson hears. I'm furious and my anger is outweighing my fear.

"It was both of us. Don't let your doctor *friend* fool you. He doesn't care about you," Parson says as he walks back over. "Ask him about Beth. Go ahead," he says when I look confused.

I look at Alex. My eyes widen as the truth sinks in. I'm in shock. All this time, I've been pouring my heart out to him and he is the one who wants the money. He killed my family *and* Beth?

"What does Beth have to do with this?"

"Tell her, *Dr. Leever*."

"Leave us, Smith. I will take care of this."

"What did you do?" I ask Alex.

My insides are churning, my stomach is upset. I've never been so scared.

"You looked up toward the bridge. Is that where it's at?" Alex asks, ignoring my question.

"I told you, I don't remember."

"You do. Tell me."

Alex's face is red. He looks extremely angry and his wrath seems to be growing. I see sweat beads dripping down his temples and his nose is actually flaring.

"No."

I'm still near the water's edge. Alex grabs me and throws me into the water. I go down and fortunately, the water where I'm at is shallow and I find my footing. I'm drenched and sputtering water. As I stand back up, he grabs me again. I think he's going to throw me back in, but instead he wrenches my arm behind my back and pushes me up the short incline.

"Show me, now," Alex demands.

"Go to hell."

"Feisty for someone who's been in seclusion for the last eight years. Swearing and everything. Look at you," he says sarcastically.

"Tell me what you did to Beth," I insist.

"He drowned her. She saw him force your father off the bridge that night."

"She couldn't very well be left alive to testify, now could she?" Alex asks.

I look at Alex and suddenly the images I had earlier all came together. My father crashing into the water. It wasn't me in that car, it was Beth. Somehow, I know that for sure. Now, I remember Beth calling me when she was on her way home. My dad was going to pick her up on his way home from work. She was at a piano lesson and her Mom couldn't get her. She was in the car with Dad!

"Beth tried to save him. She was in the car that night."

"Yes, she survived the accident long enough to see my face. Too bad for her," Alex sneers. "She died before your father. He didn't make it much longer than his ride to the hospital."

I lash out and hit Alex, my blows landing on his face and chest. He easily subdues me, pinning my arms behind me.

"Let me go!"

I struggle and manage to free myself.

"I can't get rid of you yet. You need to get me that paper first," Alex says.

"I won't."

I try to run down the hill toward the wooded area, but Parson catches up to me.

"It was you," I say to him, "who held my mother at gun point. Your tattoo," I point to his hand, "I recognize it."

"You're not as stupid as Alex made you out to be after all. Get me that paper and maybe I'll let you live."

Parson draws out a gun from behind his coat and I'm scared and angry.

"Let's go," he waves the gun back in the direction of the bridge.

At this point, my face must be stark white. I feel all the blood rushing out of it. I don't know what to do. I somehow know that if I tell him where the account numbers are hidden, he's going to kill me anyway.

When I don't move, he nudges me forward. I trip and fall into the dirt, scraping my knees. I put one leg up, foot on the ground, look, and see my jeans are torn. I wipe at the spot and fortunately, there's no blood. My wet clothes are now muddy. I don't know why I even care.

"Get up," Parson tells me.

"Don't make this any harder than it has to be," Alex warns me.

I get up and I'm shoved forward again. I'm not sure if it was Alex or Parson doing the pushing, but it doesn't matter.

What am I going to do? Think, Melinda. I'm shaking from either my wet clothes or from fear. Probably both. I look around frantically for some kind of weapon. There are only rocks, most of which are too heavy to pick up. I have no choice but to walk to the bridge, to the spot I know holds the paper they want.

"I told you, I don't really know where it is. Somewhere around here," I lie.

"Then I suggest you get to finding it," Parson says.

I go the furthest point at the top of the bridge. I look up. If I can make it the rest of the way up the incline, I can get on the bridge and start running. Maybe a car will come and save me. I look back at them and unfortunately, they're watching me. I need to divert their attention somehow.

I pretend to dig around in the rocks, pushing them aside. Rocks are all I have. I try to pick up one that looks like it can be used as a weapon. Too heavy. I try another and I can lift it, but it's awkward. I will have to hold it in two hands. Possibly doable, but I won't be able to even throw it at them before they shoot me.

I hear the river, it's getting louder. Does that mean Dad's here? I hope so. I'm running out of options and time. I look back and see that the water is turbulent.

"What are you looking at? Get to work," Parson orders.

Before I can answer, Dad appears. He stands behind Alex and Parson. He's in full form and he looks angry.

"You will not hurt my daughter."

I'm so happy he's here and at the same time, Dad standing here in solid form, here to protect me, is…surreal.

They are obviously startled because Parson slips when he turns around. Alex's face pales before he moves to face the voice. I'm sure it's whiter than what mine looked like when Parson took out the gun a few minutes ago. I can only imagine what must be going through their minds at this point.

"Melinda, leave. Run."

"She's not going anywhere," Parson speaks up and aims his gun at me. "I'll kill her."

"What's happening?" Alex asks.

"You should know. I've been telling you for months," I say. "You must not have believed me after all."

I'm feeling more confident knowing Dad is here with me.

"Do what Dad says, Melinda. Go."

Kyle is standing next to me now. Alex and Parson swivel again and see Kyle.

"That's right, Parson. You killed me and our mother. You're not going to get away with hurting Melinda."

My heart is beating erratically. This can't be happening. I look at the two men. Alex looks like he's going to faint and Parson doesn't look much better.

There's no way I'm going to miss Dad and Kyle, who are dead, protect me from two men, still alive, and one toting a gun. But I do get out of the way. I crawl up the rest of the slope and stand at the beginning of the bridge. I look down on them and can't believe my eyes.

"It's bad enough you kill me and Beth and then harass my family, but when you murdered Meredith and then my son, you went too far."

My dad is really pissed.

Can ghosts look mad? Apparently, they can. Both Dad and Kyle's faces are red with anger. Kyle is balling his hands into fists, just as he did when he was alive.

"Give us what we want and we won't hurt her," Alex says.

Dad looks up at me and says, "Leave, Melinda. Get to a phone and call the cops."

I can't, I'm rooted to the spot. It's not every day I get to see two dead people fight living, breathing humans.

Parson aims his gun at me. Honestly, I hear the trigger being pulled. I know that's not really possible, so maybe it's in my mind. All I know for sure is Kyle steps in front of the gun. I never see a bullet leave him. This is so weird. No one is going to believe any of this.

"You can't kill a dead person," Kyle tells him.

"And you are powerless because you're dead," Alex quips.

"Are we?" Dad asks.

In an instant, he's in front of Alex. He grabs the front of his shirt and—I feel like I'm watching a bad movie—picks him up and throws him down the incline. He stops right before the rocky slope going down to the water.

I feel my mouth hanging open again and my eyes must be as big as saucers.

Parson shoots at Dad. Sheesh, didn't he get it the first time when it did nothing to Kyle? In an instant, Dad is on Parson and starts grappling with him. Kyle is at my side just as fast.

I throw my arms around him.

"I miss you. I never got the chance to say how sorry I was for our argument that last night I saw you."

"We can talk about all of this later. Right now, you need to go. Call the cops. By the time they get here, those two will no longer be threats. Just go."

"But…"

"Please, Melinda. They're dangerous."

"Where have you been all this time?"

"We'll answer all your questions later. Now go!"

He is back down with Dad and the other men now. For once, I heed his instruction and start running across the bridge. On foot, it's the slowest way to our house, but I don't want to run down the incline and past them. Alex or Parson may grab me or shoot me.

What am I thinking? Our house? It's not our house anymore. It's almost like I'm thirteen again, at least that is the way I am thinking. Stop it, Melinda. You're an adult now.

My wet clothes are weighing me down, but I do the best I can and run to the first house I come to. I bang on their door. No one answers no matter how hard I knock. I leave and go to the next one.

"Help!" I scream as I try that door.

A man opens the door. He looks to be my Dad's age, well the age he was when he died anyway. He's unshaven and his t-shirt is stained with his belly protruding out, exposing his skin. Yuck. I didn't have time to care right now.

"I have to use your phone to call the police!"

"What's happening, girl?"

"Can I use your phone?"

I'm practically through his front door now and he stops me.

"Whoa! I don't wanna get mixed up with nothin'," he says and pushes me back.

"Please. Two guys are trying to *kill* me. I want to call the cops."

"Fine," he relents, "but my name better not get mixed up into anythin'." He allows me to enter and points to the living room on the left. "Phone's on the table in the corner."

I dial nine-one-one and as soon as the operator answers, everything—well, almost everything—rushes out.

"You have to send the cops. Two men down at the river, under the bridge. They're trying to kill me. Hurry!"

The operator tries to get information from me.

"What's your name?"

"Never mind that. Please just send the cops."

"Can you tell me where you are?"

I give her the general location.

"Okay, I'm dispatching a unit right now. Now, try and calm down and tell me what's going on."

How do I explain this?

"Two men are trying to kill me. They want the

account numbers. Please, send the cops," I'm near tears.

No. No crying. I think I'm overwhelmed by what's happening. A man I trusted with my innermost thoughts is using me and has been the whole time. He doesn't care about me, never has. He just wants the money.

I think the operator is asking me another question, but I don't hear her. My mind is on what's happening at the bridge.

"I have to go."

I slam the phone down and run out of the house.

"Hey," the man is yelling after me. "You better not get me involved."

That's all he cares about. But what can I expect? He doesn't know the situation or me.

I race back to the bridge. The first thing I hear before even getting there is the water. It's still running rapidly. That means Dad and Kyle are still there. As soon as I hit the bridge, I look over the railing. I don't see anyone.

What's going on?

I go to the other side and start down the incline. I see both Alex and Parson unconscious under the bridge's overpass. Alex is slumped over large boulders near the top while Parson is out cold at the water's edge, his hand floating up and down as the current moves. If he didn't weigh so much, he'd have been floating down the river. Too bad.

I stand and stare at them, wondering what happened in my absence. I wasn't gone that long.

"Mel, wait here for the police. When they get here, tell them what they were after," Kyle appears next to me.

"What do I tell them that happened to them?"

Dad appears next to Kyle.

"They'll never believe you, kitten, if you tell them the truth and I don't condone lying, but in this case you must. Tell them they were fighting between themselves over the money and while they were distracted, you managed to escape to call the cops," Dad says.

"Okay. What did happen?"

Kyle smiles and says, "They didn't expect two dead guys to beat their asses."

"Watch your language, son," Dad says, but he's smiling, too.

I can't be happy like they are. I keep thinking about Alex and how he deceived me for all these months.

"You're okay now, Melinda. Why do you look so sad?" Dad asks.

"I thought he was my doctor. I thought he was my friend. I trusted him. To find out he is one of the bad guys feels awful. I told him a lot of personal things."

"I know you did. It's okay to trust, don't let people like him stop you. You are going to be fine now."

"How do you know that, Dad? They may never let me leave Skyview Haven now. Not after what's happened here."

Instead of answering me, Dad turns to Kyle and says, "We have to go. That's our summons."

Kyle takes my hand in his and says, "Trust *us*. You will be leaving there soon. Not today, but very soon. And you will be happy."

"We need you to go see Trent as soon as you can. There are some things he needs to tell you," Dad says.

"How do you know about Trent? I don't even know if I can trust him. After all, I thought Alex was my friend and he's obviously not. How do I know Trent really is?"

"He is," Kyle says. "Just go to him," he pauses when we all hear sirens. "The cops are coming and we have to go. Everything is going to be fine."

"But I don't want you to go. I need you."

Dad hugs me to him.

"Kitten, I love you and so does your mother. We are never far from you."

With that, they are gone.

I sit down and cry. I'm glad I'm not dead and I'm here, but everything that happened is overwhelming to me. It's okay to have a minute of self-pity. Okay, yes. Self-pity again.

And a minute is all I am able to have because I hear tires screeching to a halt on the bridge above me. Police radios are squawking and there is movement near me. I don't move. I let them find me sitting on a large rock, staring out into the now calm river.

In my haze, I barely hear them asking me if I'm all right. I don't answer them. They must have noticed my wet clothes because I feel a blanket being put around my shoulders. I hear handcuffs being snapped onto what I assume are Alex and Parson's wrists, but still I sit there quietly.

I need a few more minutes. I need to collect myself and calm the ache in my heart. I miss my family more now than I ever have. Seeing Kyle and Dad coming to my rescue made me happy and now they're gone. I'm on my own again the same as I was all those years ago when they put me in Skyview Haven. I'm not sure I can handle this happening again.

I latch on to Kyle and Dad's words that everything is going to be fine and that they are never far from me.

It makes me feel a little better, so I shake my head to clear my thoughts and stand up.

A police officer is standing there, for how long, I don't know.

He is asking me, "Are you all right? Do you need medical attention?"

"No. I'm fine."

"I'm officer Dunnigan. Can you tell me what happened here?"

I see another cop putting Alex in the back of the police car. I don't see Parson, but assume he's already in there or in another car. My anger returns and I dart over to him before he disappears into the back seat.

"You bastard! How dare you."

"Stop it, you little bitch," Alex yells out.

I kick at his legs before he pulls them into the car. I lean down and try to hit him, but the cop grabs me.

"Hey, hey," he says.

Officer Dunnigan comes over and puts his hand on my arm. I quickly jerk it away.

"That bastard tried to kill me."

I try to go after him again, but the cop quickly shuts the door. I bang on the window and start yelling at Alex.

"I hope you rot in jail. You were supposed to be my friend, my *doctor*!"

"Miss, please, calm down," Officer Dunnigan says, trying to pull me away from the car.

I look at him and say, "He and Parson tried to kill me."

"Okay, calm down. Let's get your story."

I look back at Alex. Through the window, he is smiling. It makes me angrier and I run over to the window again and bang my fist on it. I'm pulled back again by someone, but I don't see who. All I can see right now is red.

"Miss, this is not doing you any good," Officer Dunnigan is saying.

I'm shaking with rage. My legs don't want to hold me up anymore. The adrenaline is quickly leaving me. I drop to the ground, right where I am as the cop car pulls out, carrying Alex with him. I see another one pull behind it and I see Parson looking out the back window. He's not smiling.

Good. He knows he's done.

"Do you need medical attention?" Officer Dunnigan asks again.

"No. I'll be fine."

I close my eyes and breathe in and out. When I don't feel as jittery, I stand back up.

"Can you tell me now what happened here?"

"They tried to kill me."

I remember the rest of the story Dad told me to say and I repeat it.

"So, you come back here and find them both lying on the ground?"

"Yes."

"Uh, huh."

He clearly doesn't believe me.

"I find that a bit odd. They fight amongst themselves and what? Just forget you're here?"

"They must have."

"Uh huh. So, why did you come back? If they were trying to hurt you, why not run?"

I'm stumped. I'm not sure how to answer that one. It takes me a minute to come up with something.

"I'm not sure," I say. "They are the ones who brought me here and I guess I hoped Alex—that's Dr. Alex Leever, at least I think he's a doctor—was not trying to hurt me and could take me back."

That doesn't even make sense to me, but I go with it.

"You'll have to explain why you said you think he's a doctor."

So I tell him about Skyview Haven and how Alex had been my doctor there for quite some time and about Parson Smith and that they are actually working together and I didn't know it until today. I told him the entire ugly truth, except for my dead family saving me that is. How Alex killed my best friend and admitted to it. And that they killed my family and came after me for the account numbers.

"And where is this piece of paper you supposedly hid all those years ago?"

I walk over and show him where Kyle and I sealed it up.

"Wait here."

The officer goes over and speaks with a few others, then comes back.

"You need to stay here until we look in there. To see if you're telling the truth," Officer Dunnigan tells me.

I am. They will find the account numbers and hopefully find out why Dad died for them.

While we wait, he calls in and verifies I'm indeed a patient at Skyview. I know he thinks I'm a nutcase, given where I live, but he'll see.

It doesn't take long for them to chip away at the concrete Kyle and I used. They find the opening, just as

I told them they would. An officer put his hand in the crack.

"My hand won't fit. Domingo!" the officer yells. "Come over here."

Domingo is a female cop. I guess they're hoping that her hand is smaller and can fit. It works.

She brings out the baggies. They are damp and the outside is green with mold. I hope the inside is okay.

Dunnigan takes them and opens the first baggie. He pulls out the second one and opens that one to find the slip of paper. He carefully takes it out. It's not in that bad of shape. I'm surprised. I look along with the officers and see that oddly enough, the numbers are still readable.

He hands the paper carefully back to Domingo and tells her to mark it as evidence. He turns to me.

"We'll run these. If we find out you're lying at all, you'll be in a lot of trouble. Is there anything else you want to tell me?"

"No, sir."

Nothing at all I *want* to tell him. Should I have? Maybe. Maybe not.

Dunnigan escorts me back to Skyview and after I tell him who's in charge, he speaks with Dr. Allcott. They have me wait in the hallway while they go into the director's office. After about a half an hour, they finally come out. Dunnigan says he will be in touch if he has more questions, but I doubt he will. Once he found out where I *resided*, his facial expression said it all. He thinks I'm loony. The rolling of his eyes when I told him they must have fought themselves and knocked each other out, gave it away and in his mind, I am not quite all there.

Dr. Allcott ushers me into his office next. I'm exhausted after my...let's call it a practice test run of confronting my past, and I honestly just want to go rest. But I have to repeat my story to him. I do, but again omitting the part about my dead family coming to my aid.

He has no idea who Parson Smith is and is shocked to hear about Dr. Leever and expresses sympathy for what I've been through. I don't want his pity, just an answer to whether or not I can be released now that he knows the whole story. He says he wants to consult with a few psychologists and review my file.

I don't care what that cop Dunnigan thinks, but I do care about Dr. Allcott's reaction. Kyle did say I'd be getting out of there very soon, but I hope I'm not trading one prison for another. I was also told to go see Trent because there are things he needs to tell me. What can they be? I'm not sure much can surprise me after today.

I am wrong.

Chapter Fifty-Two

I wake up and the first thought in my head is Alex. To say I'm angry about his deceit is an understatement. It's something I will have to work through on my own. I'm hoping that my ramblings to him aren't on tape or in a folder in his office somewhere. He had a tape recorder, I saw it. He may have used it in my case. I recall his words. He said he used it for some patients, but when I first started seeing him, he said I was his only patient at Skyview. That means, God help me, he probably *was* recording me. If anyone finds out that I still believe in the Other Side, it won't bode well for me. I have to find out.

Since I have no sessions—thank God—I have no plans for today. Alex is a weasel and in jail where he belongs, so no one will be in his office. Do I dare try to get in there? Should I wait until tonight? No. They could come and go through his office before then. I must do it now. What if I'm caught? I feel it's a chance I'll have to take.

I sneak up to Alex's office. No one is in the hallway. I cautiously approach his door and put my hand on the knob, but stop when I hear someone inside. Shit! Are they already searching his office? I run down the hall and around the corner. I'm breathing heavy and my heart is pounding. I'll be doomed if he did make recordings of our sessions and they find them. Dr.

Allcott will keep me here forever! I peek around the corner. I don't see anyone. I didn't hear anyone coming out of the office, but that doesn't mean they didn't.

What do I do? I decide to listen at the office door. Just as I walk back around the corner, Dr. Allcott is at the top of the back stairs. It's the staircase that I rarely use. It is closest to Dr. Allcott's office on the first floor, so it makes sense he would use that one.

He sees me and walks my way. I stop. Two men in uniform are behind him. *No, no,* I'm silently screaming, *I'm too late.*

"Melinda, what are you doing up here?"

I shuffle from one foot to the other. Okay, Melinda, it's time for another lie. Think.

"I wanted...I guess I'm still upset over what Dr. Leever did. I wanted to see for myself that he was really gone from here."

He looks like he believes me as his face softens and he smiles with what looks like pity.

"You don't have to worry anymore, Melinda. He's gone. You're safe."

Safe? I doubt it. I don't feel like I'll ever be safe again. I know they arrested the criminals, but I guess everything is just too fresh. It will take some time before I feel secure again.

"Thank you," is all I can say.

"You really shouldn't be up here anymore. Go down to the common area and relax. Or go outside to the garden," Dr. Allcott suggests.

He turns back around and leads the officers to Alex's office. He uses a key and unlocks it. They walk in and leave me standing in the hallway.

There's no way I can relax. If Alex recorded me, it

won't look good for me. I have to do something. But what? Another thought hits me. If it wasn't Dr. Allcott and the police officers in Alex's office, who was? I didn't see anyone come out before they went in.

I tiptoe back to the door and listen. I don't hear anyone arguing or anything. If someone broke in there, surely they would have noticed. The only other person who belongs—or used to belong—in that office is Alex.

I hear drawers being opened and closed and muted talking. That's it. They're looking for something. What? Evidence to keep him in jail? I don't care, so long as it isn't my ramblings on tape.

I decide to go back to the top of the main stairway and wait for them to exit the room. When they leave, they'll probably use the back staircase again, so I should be safe.

Every couple of minutes, I peer down the hall. I'm sure I'll hear them, but I want to make absolutely sure I don't miss them. It feels like they're in the office forever, but it's probably only about a half an hour.

I finally hear them leave and after a few seconds, I peer around the corner. I see their backs and they're almost at the staircase. I wait a good five minutes to make sure they're not coming back before I go to the office. Locked. Damn it. I should have known. Swearing again. Oh, to hell with it. Swearing, not swearing. It won't matter soon anyway. They probably swear a lot in prison, my next 'home.' So, screw it.

I have to find out if there are any recordings and if they found them. I'm in a quandary. I don't know how to pick locks. I shake my head with frustration. I decide to go outside and think. I'm sure Dr. Allcott will be calling me into his office soon or the cops will take me away. Either way, I'm screwed.

I walk back down the stairs, thinking I should try to see Trent for the last time before they either lock me up in a padded cell or haul me out of here in handcuffs. I know I'm thinking negatively, but what else can I do? My future looks bleak at best.

I am still forbidden to go to Mel's Place, that hasn't changed, but I need to see Trent. Dad and Kyle told me to and this may be my only opportunity. I walk through the common area, head to the door, and run smack into Nurse Hamilton. Literally. I wasn't watching where I was going.

"Melinda! Is your head in the clouds again?"

"I'm sorry. I guess it was."

"Where are you off to?"

"I'm just going to the garden," I tell her.

"That's fine. How are you?"

I decide to be honest. "Not so good."

"I understand that. I'm sorry to hear about yesterday's fiasco. No one knew Leever was so despicable."

"Was he even a real doctor?" I ask.

"Yes, if you can believe it."

"I can. Even though he ended up trying to kill me, he really did help me a lot."

"Good. And it's good to hear you spin the whole unfortunate mess into something positive. You really have grown."

"If you can tell Dr. Allcott that, it might help me."

"I already did," she smiles at me. "Despite you intentionally disobeying orders at times, you are no threat to yourself or anyone."

I'm so excited. If the medical director and others

can see the same thing, maybe things will go better for me.

"Thank you, Nurse Hamilton."

"What are you doing for the day?" she asks. "The garden is not that full if you want to take a stroll."

She winks at me and walks away.

Does that mean what I think it means? Is she saying it's okay for me to go to the small cottage? She's always been somewhat nice to me and I always got the impression she liked me, but this...this means she's breaking the rules. I'll have to sneak out like before and not stay long. I don't want her to get into trouble for me.

Before she changes her mind, or I lose my nerve, I sneak through the garden and quickly run back to my familiar quiet place. Dad and Kyle kept telling me to go see Trent. I'm not sure why, but I'm here, so I guess I'll find out.

As I approach, I say, "Trent?"

I don't yell loud in case someone from the home is out here watching the place. I guess if they are though, they'll see me anyway. I walk directly to the base of the tree and repeat his name.

His head appears in the opening. He's smiling.

"Melinda! I wasn't sure if I would get to see you again before I..."

"Before you what?" I question after he stops short.

"Never mind that right now. Come on up."

I climb and go through the opening. On the table, I see grapes, crackers, cheese, water bottles, and a few other things wrapped in aluminum foil. On the floor sits a picnic basket.

"I see Manuel has been making sure you eat."

"Yeah. Did you tell him about me?"

"I had to. I didn't know when I'd be able to come back to bring food."

"Well, thanks," he smiles and sits down.

Since there is only one chair, I sit on the floor. I'm not hungry so I watch him eat for a few minutes before speaking.

"So, I have to ask you something and I'm not sure how to."

"Why's that?"

"Because I'm not sure what exactly I need to ask. I just know there's something you have to tell me."

After taking a drink from a water bottle, he tells me, "I guess it's time then. I heard about what happened yesterday."

"How did you hear?"

For a minute, he just looks at me. It feels like an eternity waiting for him to say something. Somehow, I know what he's about to say is going to change everything.

"After today, you may want me to leave. I hope not though."

"Why would I want you to leave?"

I won't be happy if he leaves, to state the obvious. I want him in my life.

He walks over to his sleeping bag and grabs a box sitting in the corner. He hands it to me.

"What's this?" I ask.

"Open it. You don't have to worry anymore."

I frown at him in confusion and open the lid. Inside there are a digital recorder and computer CDs. Lots of them. There are so many. He must have recorded it and transferred all of our sessions onto CDs. The bastard.

"What?"

I'm both confused as to how he got them and ecstatic that they're in my possession and not the cop's.

"I didn't listen to them. I was told to give them to you."

"Who? Who said to give them to me?"

He takes my hand and says. "This might explain better than I can with words."

I trust Trent, so I stand up, set the box on the table, and let him take my hand. I think we're leaving the tree house, but he leads me the few paces to the part of the notched out tree trunk. With his free hand, he moves the flashlight that still sits on the little ledge and pushes on the bark. The pieces of wood fall away and I'm looking into an empty, black hole.

"What's in there?"

Before he can answer, the blackness turns to blue. I'm looking at the sky. But how is this possible? I look at him.

He must know how confused and uncertain I am because he says, "Don't be scared. You'll understand everything in a minute."

I have no idea what I'm waiting for, but I stand and stare at the blue hole. I'm transfixed and cannot pull my gaze away.

Trent still has my hand. I can feel my palms getting sweaty. He either senses my nervousness or can feel the clamminess in his palm.

"It's okay," he whispers.

Why is he whispering? What are we waiting for? What's going to happen? My mind will not stop asking all of the questions I'm unable to say aloud.

I see a shadow far out in the blue sky. It's getting

bigger as it approaches. I can feel my eyes widen on their own accord. There are two...no, three...wait. Four shadows?

I involuntarily drop Trent's hand and jump backwards. I hit the small table and fall to the floor. Still, my eyes stay glued to the hole. I see facial features. They're becoming clearer. I can almost make out—

"Mom?"

I quickly jump up from the floor and throw myself toward the hole. All I can think of is being in her arms again. Mom catches me as she comes through the opening and holds me tight. Dad and Kyle follow her through. I close my eyes and bury my face in Mom's shoulder and hair, breathing in the familiar scent of her green apple shampoo. I feel so at home again. It's indescribable, the feelings I'm having.

I hear someone clearing their throat and open my eyes. I pull back from Mom, but stay in her arms. I look and see Beth.

"Beth," I scream out.

I leave Mom and lunge into Beth's waiting arms. I let go of Beth and look around me. I'm starting to cry with joy. Mom, Beth, Dad, and Kyle. My family. I'm back with my family. Nothing else matters.

Yes, there's one other person who also matters. I turn to Trent, who moved away to the other corner and is now sitting on his sleeping bag.

"Mom, Dad, Kyle, Beth, this is..."

"Trent, we know," Mom said.

"But how?"

"Even though we're not physically here, we've been keeping an eye on you. We saw when the two of you became friends," Dad said.

"That's how we knew you were in trouble," Kyle spoke up. "The doctor was using you and I was trying to get through to Trent. He was resistant at first, not quite believing, but I can't blame him for that."

"What are you talking about? Trent?" I kneel down next to him. "Please don't tell me you're dead, too."

He is my only friend, especially now that I find out Alex never was. I need someone who's alive to be here for me…and with me.

"No, not me. Just them," he waves his hand around the tree house.

I close my eyes and exhale the breath I didn't realize I was holding. I'm so relieved. I open my eyes again.

"Then, how? What—" I close my eyes again while I try to formulate my questions. I give up. "I don't understand," I sigh and look at him.

"We needed someone to help look after you. You knew Trent from the home in Idyllwild and we thought once you made the connection, you'd be able to trust and befriend him," Mom explains. "It didn't take a lot of persuasion after he ran away to get him here, even if he didn't realize he was being led to you."

"Yeah, but when I found out and they told me you needed me, I couldn't leave," Trent says.

I know my mouth is hanging open. This is all so surreal. I'm trying to process the fact that my dead family and best friend are talking to me and my new friend Trent in a tree house, feet away from an insane asylum. As the thought hits me, I start laughing. I can't help it. It's like when I laughed when I looked at Alex and Parson in the woods.

I'm laughing so hard, I'm on the floor, rolling around. This is unbelievable. Maybe they shouldn't release me from Skyview. Maybe my mind is making this entire scene up. But I know it's not. This is all real.

It's a few minutes before my laughter subsides. Beth is smiling when I look at her.

"Crazy, huh?" she asks.

That starts me cracking up all over again. Beth and I always got each other. She knows exactly what I'm thinking. After another bout of rolling around, I wipe the tears from my eyes and stand up. The glee is gone, replaced by frustration. I'm somber now.

"Let me get this straight," I say. "Dad is killed by Alex and his cohort because of millions of dollars. Beth is killed because she happened to be there. Mom and Kyle are killed because the same people were trying to find the paper with the account information. Then," my mouth is so dry I grab the water bottle and take a drink before continuing, "they find a way to get to me through Alex and try to get the numbers from me and kill me.

"Dad and Kyle come to the rescue and lead me here to Trent. For what? To find out that Trent, my new friend was deceiving me all along." I'm getting angry; upset that no one deemed it important enough to tell *me* what was going on until after I'm almost killed. I point at Trent. "*You* didn't tell me anything." I swing in a circle, pointing at Mom, Dad, and Kyle. "You guys watch me from somewhere. I don't know where…heaven? It doesn't matter. You watch me and *know* Alex is out to hurt me and don't tell me. And you," I now point at Beth. "What do you have to do with all of this? Wait, don't tell me. You came back to "watch" over me, too." I used my fingers to make air quotes. "What? Did you all expect me to be happy that *no one* can tell me the truth about anything?"

I take another drink of water. Kyle tries to say something, but I rant again.

"No. Don't make excuses. I've been stuck in here for almost nine years now. My life is on hold because Dad decides to what? Hide someone's money? Steal it? What?" I yell at him accusingly.

"First, we were not able to tell you that Alex and Parson were out to hurt you. One of the rules on the Other Side is we can help our loved ones on Earth, but only to a certain extent. Fate needs to play out on Earth. You could not know until *you* remembered it all. I'm sorry, kitten.

"Second, I didn't try and steal anything. I was trying to do the right thing. I found out those men were embezzling money from large companies. They were using the money to fund terrorists and their activities. I had to stop them. I was going to go to the police, but before I could they ran me and Beth off the road and killed us."

I calm down a bit knowing there was a good reason I wasn't told everything and that Dad didn't do anything wrong. I'm actually proud of him for trying to stop it. I am still upset though.

"Still. Mom and Kyle were killed because of it. I would be dead, too if it wasn't for you guys coming to my rescue at the river. I would have been killed back then if I didn't go to the police after Kyle went missing."

Beth touches my shoulder and I turn to her.

"I came back all those times because I missed you.

We were—are—best friends. You were receptive to…uh…ghostly apparitions, I guess you can call it…not even that, since we're in solid form. Oh, never mind that," she waves in the air to signify the definitions don't matter. "I just missed you. That's it."

How can I stay mad after hearing that? I can't. At least not at her. I hug her, happy to be able to.

I break away from her and face my parents and Kyle.

"Nine years. It's been nine long years since I've heard anything from you, Dad. Mom and Kyle, you never came to me until now. Well, Kyle at the river with Dad, but why? Where have you been if you've been watching out for me? If you had been, I wouldn't even be in Skyview. And Uncle L and Aunt Bet, they want nothing to do with me because they think I killed all of you."

I'm feeling sorry for myself again. I need black balloons for the pity party.

"No one was willing to believe that you had actually been talking to your dead father," Dad says. "It was the only way they knew how to deal with you and the situation."

"And honey, we've been here. We were not able to stop them from putting you here, but we were always with you," Mom tries to console me.

"Why reach out to Trent?"

I look around and see Trent is gone. He must have gone down the ladder and I didn't notice.

"Because he is close to your age and he could sort of relate, being brought up in a foster home," Kyle says.

"Well, I'm mad at him, too. He should have told me."

"Don't be, honey. We made him promise and he was trying to protect you, to help you."

"I know, Mom, but geesh. I'm not thirteen anymore." I suddenly realize I still know nothing of this other place and ask, "So you live on the Other Side now?"

"Yes," Mom replies.

"How did you get here from that hole?" I point to where they came in.

"There are a lot of portals if you know where to look. This is only one of many," Dad says. "There's one near the river where I died. That's how Kyle and I got there so quickly yesterday."

"Mom, Kyle? How did the man find us? He took you, Mom, and you too, Kyle. How?"

"You don't need to know the details. He followed us from our house. That night, he got me after I left the room. I went outside to sit in the cool air to think and there he was."

"And Kyle?"

"Fortunately, he didn't know about that burned out camper we found. He saw me in town as I was walking around looking for you. I thought you'd run into the woods, so I went looking. That's when he grabbed me."

"How...how did you die?" I ask this hesitantly, not sure if I want the answer. "No bodies were ever found that I'm aware of."

"You don't need to know that. It's not important," Mom says. "And they won't find our bodies, but you honestly don't need to think about any of that."

"The box," Kyle points to it, "has all the recordings Dr. Leever had in his office. They're all there and there are no duplicates. I made sure of it. Destroy them,

Melinda."

"That was you I heard in his office this morning?"

"Yes. I had to pry open the desk. Not easy when you're dead. That's probably what you heard."

"So that explains why I never saw anyone go in or out of his office."

"I saw you there. I couldn't tell you I had them because the director and the cops showed up. I tried to talk to you in your mind, but you weren't listening."

"Yeah, I think I was way too concerned about what they'd find," I say. "Thanks for getting the digital recorder and all those CDs, Kyle." I look at them all each in turn and ask, "Are you happy?"

"We are," Mom reassures me. "We miss you more than we can say, but we're fine."

"We have to go now," Dad says. "We've been here long enough."

"But wait! I have more questions. I want to know about the Other Side. What's it like?"

"Another time, kitten. Just know we're always watching over you. Right now, it's time you go off and live your life."

"I love you, Dad. I love you all. Beth, will you come back, too?"

"In time."

Mom walked over to me and hugged me.

"Don't be so hard on Trent. He's a good kid, just like you are. We love you."

And that's it. They're gone and I'm left standing alone in the tree house. The blue sky is now back to tree bark. I stand there not quite believing, yet unable to deny all that's happened. Tears trickle down my face. I'm happy that I got to see them and feel sure I will again. My tears this time are part joy and part sadness for everything my family has been through.

I have to find Trent, so I wipe my face with my sleeve. I go down the ladder and as I reach the bottom, I hit something with my foot.

"Watch it! You don't have to step on me."

"Trent! Why are you sitting here under the tree?"

"Letting you have time with them. You okay?"

"Yeah. It's just all weird."

I sit on the ground next to him.

"I'm pissed at you. Why didn't you tell me about that portal in the tree?"

Even as I say this, I know I'm not really mad at him anymore.

"I promised them I wouldn't until it was time for you to know. And I want to explain."

He is looking at the ground when he says this. I've never liked it when someone can't meet your eye when they're speaking to you.

"Explain what?"

He doesn't look up, instead starts plucking grass stems.

"Trent?"

"Okay. I'll tell you, but you can't be mad." He looks up at me, which I am glad about. "It's true; they led me here to you. I didn't know it at first. Then when you found me, it hit me. I still didn't understand a thing, but I knew I was supposed to be with you, here.

"It wasn't long after we became friends that your parents and brother came to me through the portal," he points up at the tree house. "I felt bad deceiving you, not telling you, but I thought you would think I was only your friend because they wanted me to be." He grabs my hand and quickly says, "But that's not why. I was your friend first, or wanted to be before I knew anything. I swear."

"I believe you."

"Good. Anyway, I knew I had to still hide out because I wasn't eighteen yet. By the way, I am today."

"It's your birthday? Happy birthday! Why didn't you tell me?"

"It didn't matter to me. The only thing that did was the knowledge I wouldn't have to worry about them sending me to juvie or some other home once I reached legal age."

"Now you are," I'm smiling.

He smiles back, still holding my hand. "Yes. But now things need to change."

He drops his gaze back to the ground.

"Why?"

"It's time for me to start my life. You, too."

"But I can't lose you, too. You're my friend. My *live* friend."

He looks at me again before moving his gaze to the little cottage. I'm not sure what he's looking at, but I have a feeling he's actually looking beyond it, at something only he can see in his mind's eye.

"I thought you were going to be so mad you'd ask me to leave here. But now that I know that's not true, you won't lose me unless you ask me to leave."

"I won't be asking you to go anywhere. I'm pretty sure I'll get out of Skyview soon and I want you to go wherever I do. Will you?"

He smiles at me, "Sure."

I smile back, knowing for once things are going to be okay.

Epilogue

Somehow, I am able to get Dr. Allcott and another psychiatrist to believe that everything that happened in the past was a product of me being a very scared child, without a family to lean on. I explain that even though Alex was a criminal, he did help me understand that, despite the fact their deaths happened under suspicious circumstances, my family was gone and I have finally accepted that. I can now move on.

When they ask me why Alex and Parson tried to kill me down at the river, I can't have them knowing the truth. They'll keep me at Skyview Haven for the duration of my life if I reveal everything. What I do say is that it was because of the money my parents left me. Parson was greedy and Alex was apparently desperate. At least that's what's Trent told me and I guess he learned that from my family on the Other Side. It doesn't matter how I know. That information gives me a plausible explanation of why he was trying to kill me. How did I get so good at lying? Some of what I say is almost as if someone else is talking through me.

The sad part is that I can't tell all, can't divulge that we are not alone on Earth. Our loved ones are really here for us. Well, for some of us anyway, those who believe.

Funny thing is when the police tracked down the account numbers from that slip of paper they found them to be from a bank in the Cayman Islands. Supposedly, there is a lot of money in the accounts, just like Dad had told me.

After consulting with my attorney Steve Meyer about the trust fund from Mom and Dad and meeting with the other psychiatrist, I arrange a place to live. It will only be a few weeks before they officially and physically release me from a place I called home for nine years. It's the best birthday gift I can hope for.

Once the time comes, Nurse Hamilton—I learn her first name is Felicity—helps me find an apartment not far from hers in Banning. It's a two bedroom with two bathrooms and a small galley kitchen. My intent is for Trent to share it with me. He agrees to.

We have Felicity over now and again for dinner. It's cramped in the apartment, but no one cares. Felicity says she likes being able to come over, to make sure I'm doing okay. She's beginning to feel like another mother, which is not to say she'll ever replace Mom, but it's nice to have someone older around to ask questions like how to cook something. Whites should be separate from colors when washing. That sort of thing.

I finally find out what happened to Trent's parents. He told me were in a terrible train wreck. For some reason, Trent's parents have never come back to see him. We don't know why. There is so much about the Other Side we don't know about. One day, we hope to find out. Then maybe Trent can see his parents again.

There's a whole world out there waiting for us. We want to experience life and see the world. Both worlds.

The thought of the Other Side makes me ask one last question. If good souls like my family can come through the portals, can evil spirits come through openings, too?

Afterword

I asked you in the beginning if you would believe me if I told you what happened. So, do you?

There are those who walk next to us and we don't even know it. Will you believe me if I tell you there are millions of doors that open and close every day? Most people just cannot see them or accept the parallel universe. I couldn't until my father showed me one of the doors. Now, it seems like I can see them all, but I must be careful.

Let me show you another realm. It's right through there…look, that's the parallel universe, the Other Side.

A word about the author...

A paralegal by day, she's an author by night. Apart from being an award-winning author for her short story *Cut*, Gardinier has appeared in a blaze and made her mark on the literary world. Having studied and obtained her Bachelor's Degree in Literature/Creative Writing, she has found her unique style and is known for her works' distinctive voice, making every character stand out.

Gardinier is a former executive editor for *Suspense Magazine*. She has been interviewed in the newspaper and on the radio with relation to her fiction work. She has been a co-host on Suspense Radio.

Gardinier is a member of International Thriller Writers (ITW) and of Sisters in Crime, Los Angeles Chapter and nationally. She has won three Best Speaker awards as well as Best Evaluator at the Voice Ambassadors chapter of Toastmasters. She has always been active in events. As co-chair and main coordinator for the West Coast Author Premiere, she arranged the weekend-long event to help authors from all over network learn and share their work with the public. Gardinier has also been instrumental in compiling authors and planning a local author event at Barnes and Noble in Ventura, California along with the store's event manager.

You can read more about Starr at
www.QueenWriter.com
or visit her blog at
www.qw-blog.blogspot.com.

www.ingramcontent.com/pod-product-compliance
Lightning Source LLC
Chambersburg PA
CBHW051517260626
47170CB00003B/651